TIMEWISE

TIMEWISE

ROBERT LEET

ROBERTLEET.COM

For Marianne.

1

I don't remember the exact date I met Regina Russo, but I do know it was a Saturday afternoon on the Mill Falls Commons in Massachusetts. I would have been thirteen—no, fourteen—competing with the older, but not usually better, patrons of our local weekly chess tournament.

I was an orphan who'd been kicked around so many foster homes that my early memories are a bit disrupted. I recall faces, scenes, names from my grade schools, but I couldn't even tell you in which grade I attended, say, North Fort School. I remember the names of families I lived with—Darston, Greck, Jameson—and some of the kids. Earl and Dick, for instance, were twins, but I'm not sure which family they belonged to. There were two girls named Heather in my childhood, and one of them was also a foster child, but all I remember is that I knew them at different times. I recall meals, living rooms and shared bedrooms, but I have no storyline connecting these memories. I do know a television seemed to be on all the time and the houses were full of both birth and foster kids. I wasn't treated badly, but no one paid much attention to me either.

My first experience with chess was with Mister Froiseth, I think he was my fourth grade teacher, who ran an after-school program once a week to pass on his passion for the game. It seemed like a random event at the time, but learning I was good at chess gave my life its first structure. Meeting Regina Russo gave it clarity.

About a dozen regular players would show up at our weekly chess matches, but we played each other so often that we craved new opponents. Truth be known, my main interest at the time was making side bets—the larger the better. It was the only way I was able to earn pocket money. I never made more than a dollar or two a game, but that could add up to ten or more dollars a week, enough for a candy bar a day and even a soda or two. One of my favorite tactics was to appear to botch a well-known opening, hoping I could make up for a slight disadvantage with superior play later on. This worked best on knowledgeable players who recognized my supposed mistake as it gave them a boost of confidence, perhaps enough to make a bet in the middle of the game. It had no effect on inferior players, but I could usually beat them with half my pieces anyway. Of course the regulars were onto my game, so I particularly welcomed newcomers.

The only regular who never tired of playing me was Mr. Staling, a retired mailman who loved Saturday chess even more than I did. The adult players called him Roger, but I knew him as Mr. Staling. He always wore the same faded blue work uniform with its shoulder insignias and name tag removed. His eyes were small, dark, and so close-set they did not seem to belong on his broad, pale face. I think he lived on soda and pastries. We'd both pretend to bumble through our beginning game to try to catch each other off guard. I recall winning more games than I lost, but Staling's small giggle whenever he won is a fonder memory.

Mill Falls had a small college, and I suppose the town fathers wanted to emulate what they considered to be a scholarly environment to enhance their struggling downtown. The town provided the location, card tables and folding chairs, but we players supplied our own chess sets. Some of the sets were elegant—carved bone or tropical wood—some were cheap molded plastic, like my own. The only town official I remember ever visiting the tournaments was Mr. Farnsworth. I'm not sure what his position was, but weekend chess must have been his personal project. Friendly and insincere, Farnsworth would roam among the tables, occasionally stopping to watch a game. I'm sure he never played as we players wondered if he even knew the rules.

I met Regina on a clear, fresh New England summer day. The Mill Falls Commons, where we set up the tables when the weather was good, was surrounded by colonial buildings that, like old neighbors, had gotten to know each other so well they no longer paid attention. Somehow this creates community in New England.

Mill Falls Commons was inhabited by several magnificent trees. I know one of the largest was a maple because early every spring someone would hammer an old-fashioned spigot into the tree and hang a tin cup on it so passers-by could sample its sweet sap. Another was a hickory. Toward the end of our outdoor season, Mr. Staling would bring a couple of stones to the chess matches. While his opponent made his move, Mr. Staling would crack a handful of hickory nuts—he called them "pignuts"—on the ground between his stones to munch on while he pondered his own move. It was one of the few times I saw him eat something other than convenience store snacks. He often offered to let me use his stones while he made his moves, but I wasn't interested.

On a hot day most of the players placed their tables under one of the trees' cooling branches, but, like cats in a crowded room, we spaced ourselves at comfortable distances from one another. Accordingly, I, as both the youngest and newest player, usually sat in the bright summer sunlight. I actually considered this an advantage against older opponents who played at my table, whom I presumed to have less stamina. Besides, I loved watching the clouds overhead metamorphose.

On the day I met Regina the clouds were mere filaments riding a barely perceptible breeze. Regina, like a cloud, appeared to simply condense at my table without approaching. Her eyes were almost golden, as though she had brought a bit of the sun down to Earth. She was in her late thirties at the time, lithe enough that she appeared taller than she was, graceful enough that she seemed younger. Her blond hair was tied up in a neat bun held together with two burnished-wood hair sticks, one light and one dark. She wore blue jeans and a long-sleeved yellow cotton shirt.

Regina smiled at me as she hovered by my table. I fell in love. Of course, I was a fourteen-year-old boy so that came pretty easy. Her smile was slightly asymmetrical, warm but with a bit left over, as if she were greeting something no one else could fathom. I came to learn that she saw a great deal that no one else could fathom.

"Care for a game?" I asked, as I set the pieces up. I held out my hands with a piece in each hand for her to choose.

""You start," she said, taking a seat.

I put the pieces back and played e4, thinking to try a Ruy Lopez opening.

Regina rotated the board so the black pieces were on my side. "Keep going." She spoke so quietly I wasn't sure I'd heard her.

"Why did you do that?" I asked.

"You're not playing against your opponents—you're just playing yourself. I thought I'd get out of your way."

More than a little intrigued by her comment, I rotated the board again. "I'll play against you."

She smiled at my response. "By the way, I'm Regina," she said, surprising me by only giving me her first name. I was used to addressing adults by the honorifics Mr. and Ms.

"Ron," I stammered back.

She played e5, as I'd expected. I continued with the Ruy Lopez opening. She followed with a well-thought-out Marshall Attack, and we concluded with a draw.

"You're pretty good," I told her.

"I used to play." She took one of my plastic pieces into her hand, and examined it carefully, slowly twirling it around as if she even needed to inspect the seam where the plastic was glued together. She held the piece as if it were delicate crystal.

"Did you have a set like this one?" I asked. "No, mine was wooden, maple and walnut." "That must have cost a bundle."

Regina smiled, almost shyly. "No, I carved the pieces myself."

"Do you still have it?" I wasn't above wagering with her for a nice set.

I think she understood my intent. "Sorry, I think I lost it somewhere." She continued to study my pawn. "I enjoyed making them, but I must admit your pieces may be stronger under your guidance than mine ever were under mine. You could be a very strong player."

I didn't want another adult telling me I should try harder. "Another game?" I asked, trying to change the subject.

That's not necessary. We can just talk."

It would have taken a more mature pubescent boy than I was to be able to just converse with a beautiful woman over twice his age.

Regina must have seen the panic in my eyes, and she changed her tack.

"Okay, another game then."

We played, but at a slower pace. Regina had white this time, and started the same way I had the first game: e4. I won rather easily, but the second game took longer than the first, since we talked while we played.

"What grade are you in?" she started, then asked me whether I liked school, where I lived, what I was interested in, and so on. She asked all the questions a responsible adult should—and all the questions that bore teenagers. I wasn't particularly interested in anything at the time, especially school. It had never occurred to me that I could be a good student or that it would lead anywhere if I were. I began to ask her about herself, mostly so I wouldn't have to mumble answers I didn't have.

"What do you do?" I asked. "I'm a physics professor."

I had no idea what physics was. "Here? At the college? I haven't seen you play chess here before."

"Well, I don't play chess much anymore, and no, not here. I teach at Northern University."

I'd never been to Northern, but I knew it was much larger than our local college, and that it was about an hour away in Foxfield. "What's physics?"

She smiled, again with her shy, slightly crooked smile. "Figuring out how things work."

"Do you like teaching?"

She took a while to respond. "A little, but I like figuring out how things work more."

"What are you doing here?"

"Talking to you," she said, stating the obvious, but making it seem profound. "But what brought you here?"

"I don't know." She paused but I didn't enter the silence. "I didn't have a reason, and now I do."

I felt I'd made her uncomfortable, so I tried to dig deeper. "What do you like about figuring out how things work?"

"I study time."

"Time? What have you learned about time?" "I've learned that awareness creates time."

2

Soon after our first meeting, Regina began to volunteer at my middle school— not in any of my classes, but I often saw her in earnest discussion with the better science students. The school had just received a few "386" computers, but only the top students were allowed to work with them. This generated a lot of competition to gain access for time with the machines, and so many of the students wanted to pick the brains of a 'real scientist' between classes to get an edge on using the computers. This made Regina especially popular.

Regina was an animated talker, gesticulating with the same precision as she spoke, as if she needed her hands to shape her ideas. She seldom was alone, even between classes. Somewhat jealous, I'd wander back and forth down the busy school corridors when she was around, trying to be simultaneously inconspicuous and noticed.

Regina sometimes greeted me and asked how I was doing. In time I realized that when she asked me a question it was because she was interested, not as a pretext to give me advice. And I began to study harder—probably because she was the first adult who had taken an interest in me, and, of course, she was beautiful. (Have I mentioned that?)

When I moved on to high school, Regina began to show up there to teach a few classes. It seemed natural to me, like we were old friends. I even began to excel in certain courses, particularly math.

One day as we passed in the hall I worked up the nerve to ask her something that had been bothering me. "How come you never teach any of my classes?"

"I think you're asking the wrong question, Ron." Her smile vanished, she looked at me as if she was imparting one of the mysteries of the universe.

"What question should I ask?"

"Perhaps you should ask how you can take the classes I teach." She looked at me carefully, as if to see whether I understood her.

"But you teach advanced seniors, and I'm just a sophomore. How could I do that?"

"At least you're asking the right question now. I'm sure you see it's a question you'll have to answer yourself." She paused, then continued, "One of the advantages of asking the right question is not only is the answer meaningful, it's often easy to find."

Regina often incorporated a lesson into her routine conversations, but often I would not grasp her intent until later, as if her words needed to crawl around my skull until they found a place to land. Anyway, by the next semester I managed to show my counselor I was ahead of my class in science and, with Regina's permission, I wormed my way into the advanced senior physics class. Not surprisingly, Regina's style as a teacher was similar to her conversational style—no matter the subject, she'd make her point with unusual imagery, like the way she rotated my chessboard the first time we met. Her voice was always soft, but this just forced her students to listen harder. One of her favorite quotes was from the great physicist Richard Feynman, who claimed that if a subject couldn't be explained clearly to a layman, it wasn't meaningfully understood by the expert either. Regina's explanations were always as clear as they were unorthodox.

Toward the end of my high school days Regina began to encourage me to continue on with school, and I believe she discussed me with my other teachers as well, as several of them also tried to convince me to go to college. I had other ideas.

When I turned eighteen, the state lost interest in me and I had no family to finance me for a few years so I could find myself in college. I'd done well in my math classes, and to an extent in science (at least I learned what physics was), but overall my grades weren't exceptional so I wasn't about to be offered a free ride anywhere either. I needed to support myself, but college just looked like a place for me to get into debt, so I lost interest in school. I knew Regina wanted to talk to me about going to college again, so I missed the last few days of school and skipped graduation so I wouldn't have to lie to her or disappoint her when we said good-bye.

After graduation I moved into a small studio apartment with my high school girlfriend, Keisha Reynolds, for a few months. Keisha had a job as a clerk in a convenience store, and I worked as a construction laborer, mostly lugging sheets of plywood and sheetrock to the upper floors of new houses and apartments. We had seen ourselves as outcasts in school, she being the only black kid in our town, and me being the weird orphan. We thought that was enough for us to be together, but it wasn't really. Once we left school there wasn't anything to be outcast from, and therefore there was nothing we had left in common.

I'd realized there was no serious money in chess, and for me that meant there was no future in it. I also discovered I didn't have the physical talent necessary for pool, so I turned my attention to poker. I became addicted to the then-obscure television show *World Series of Poker,* which was only broadcast for a few hours a year. I recorded the show with a used Betamax machine I bought at a pawn shop and watched it over and over again, trying to find meaning in the slightest expression or gesture. I also spent hours computing the odds of various hands, and how they changed when some of the cards were known. I was convinced there was good money in the game. TV didn't tell the whole story.

At the end of that summer I moved to West Foxfield, across the Connecticut River from Foxfield, one of the oldest cities in the United States and, as I have mentioned, home of Northern University. New England cities are invariably old, at least for this country, and the economic vagaries of the last three centuries have added layers of meaning to many of the original buildings and their neighborhoods. Some old, poor areas have been razed and rebuilt with higher-quality structures; some were allowed to grow worse. There are areas with mansions from the earliest colonial times that are still lovely, and others that are overflowing with decaying tenements. Interestingly, though, most neighborhoods remain neighborhoods, they remain strangely cohesive and evolve together.

Northern University, however, is a jumble of buildings that seem to lack the architectural coherence of most of New England—perhaps because the institution has changed from an agricultural and teacher's college to a full-blown research campus, perhaps because it's been subject to the exaggerated egos of architects enamored with the fashion of their day. Regardless, each building stands apart from its neighbors. Even the few good-looking structures suffer because of the environment. Brick, glass, concrete, synthetic—Northern has all types, but little cohesion.

I rented a room in a Victorian-era working-class house—a building from the late-nineteenth century when families were considerably larger than they are now. This one had been divided into upstairs and downstairs apartments for off-campus student housing. The rooms were stark, but all the windows were in place, the doors closed and could be locked, and the neighborhood seemed safe enough. The first year I roomed in an upstairs apartment with two seniors who barely acknowledged me. The apartment had three bedrooms (though mine barely held a single bed), a bathroom, and a central common room. At one end of the common room was a small kitchen with a stove, refrigerator, toaster, rickety metal table, and four non-matching chairs. At the other end was a big old sofa covered by several blankets, and a small TV which sat on a couple of cinder blocks.

I found a job as a construction laborer for a few months, but I quickly realized I could not carry plywood all day long and expect to stay up late playing poker. Eventually I convinced the local Staples store manager that I was a wiz with personal computers, the latest rage, and landed a job more amenable to my preferred lifestyle.

I wasn't a student, but I figured the university would be a good place to practice my new profession. My plan was to become as proficient at poker as I'd become at chess, and then move to Las Vegas.

It's a cliché to say there's no luck in poker—only an understanding of the odds and an ability to read your opponent's mind while hiding your own intent. This cliché happens to be accurate. In general, I found that there were three basic types of players around campus. First, there were players who had no business at the table and not enough interest in the game to bet big. Uninteresting and unfruitful. Then there were players like myself, who considered themselves competent and worked at it—these I could learn from. And then there were those who were more bold than smart. These would practically hand me their money, if I could beat the other serious players to it.

I quickly learned to be wary of games at fraternity houses—an outsider was always outnumbered. I also avoided the illegal makeshift casinos in the rear rooms of bars—the older men who frequented these venues were not necessarily better players, but they were a rougher crowd than college kids. I began to get invited to money games in dorms and off-campus housing, environments more to my liking. Occasionally I'd head out for a long weekend to Harrah's or The Sands in Atlantic City, where I was as likely to lose a week's pay as earn one. I came to learn that the greatest flaw in my game was in not recognizing the complacency that can arise from a little sustained success. Poker is foremost about odds, and as soon as I felt I was getting lucky, I'd forget about the odds and start to lose.

To support myself I bounced from one unchallenging job to the next, in stores that sold technical gadgets: office supplies, electronics, whatever. My managers always wanted me to apply myself and move up the chain of command, but I did as little as I possibly could to still keep the job. Sometimes less. This allowed me to spend my evenings playing poker. The stakes were often low, but there was always a game.

My landlady, Danielle, was the wife of an English professor at Northern. She had built a small empire of cheap housing by putting as little as possible into her buildings and by knowing her clientele. Perhaps we got along because we understood each other's motives. Danielle was in her forties and her complexion had changed from what had probably been a youthful rosy to a little too red, with a few too many broken veins in her cheeks, to hide her age or drinking habits. She was friendly in an efficient way. When the end of May came, she made me an offer.

"You're not a student, Ron. Do you want to stay on for the summer?"

I liked Danielle, but I knew she wouldn't make me an offer that wasn't also good for her. "By myself? I can't handle the rent for three."

"Maybe we could make a deal. I hate to leave a place empty. Even a few months degrades a vacant apartment. Can you guarantee me the full rent when school starts?"

"You mean find my roommates myself?"

"You'd get to choose who you live with, I'd have a little less work to do. If I see someone promising, I'll send them your way, but the choice will be yours." We agreed I'd pay a quarter of the rent during the summer and resume full payment in September, but it was up to me to find new roommates. This worked for me—it reduced my costs, allowed me some say over my apartment mates, and I figured I got around enough that finding renters wouldn't be too hard. The deal also worked for Danielle—who evidently trusted me—since she got some rent during the off months and wouldn't need to look for anyone in the fall.

The neighborhood consisted of old houses similar to the one I lived in, occupied either by students, older couples who had raised their now-grown children there, or younger couples looking for a place to raise their own kids. You could tell who lived where by the clutter in the yard. The older couples had neat yards that were largely empty except for a table and some outdoor chairs, little flower gardens, and maybe a grill in the summer. The younger couples had yards full of plastic kids' toys. And the students usually had unmown yards and bags of empty beer bottles outside the back door. It was an inauspicious neighborhood, which suited me—I had no desire to do anything except improve my poker.

My first move was to change bedrooms. The largest one was in front and had windows onto the noisy street below, so I took the back room, which was nearly as large and much quieter. I soon filled the empty rooms with two new apartment mates. Tom Jacobs, a civil engineering student, took the large room. Tom was not as tall as I, maybe five foot ten, but was solidly built, with a round face that made him seem softer than he was. He wore his hair in a crew cut, which made him look even rounder. It was still early summer, but he was between his junior and senior years and had an internship with a local engineering company and didn't want to move again when classes began. I was delighted because Danielle hadn't raised my rent yet, so the extra money from his summer rent went directly into my pocket.

Tom seemed perpetually disappointed. I figured he wanted to attend a more prestigious school than Northern, and perhaps live with a more respectable

18

roommate than myself. Like my previous apartment mates, though, he paid his rent and kept to himself. I didn't want more from him, and I didn't get it.

We disliked each other from the day he moved in. We didn't hate each other, not profoundly, we just distrusted each other's modes. Tom apparently believed there was an optimal daily routine, which should be stuck to every day as closely as possible. He rose at the same time every morning, including weekends, ate the same breakfast of Grape-Nuts and orange juice but no coffee, and left the apartment at the same time.

I, on the other hand, regarded each day as I did a poker hand—even with the same cards and the same opponent, I felt one must play each hand on its own merits. I thought Tom was obsessive. I'm sure he saw my life as a waste of time, but I was used to that from my Mill Falls chess days. Fortunately, his rigid pattern made it easy for me to avoid him, so our distrust never interfered with our daily lives. We coexisted quite well.

3

A week or two after Tom moved in, I rented my old room to a woman named Cheryl Liona, who had responded to a flyer I'd hung up at the nearby Laundromat where the neighborhood students did their laundry.

After a quick interview over instant coffee in our sparse kitchen I determined she'd probably pay her rent on time, we agreed to terms, and she started moving her stuff in. I assumed she was an artist as she had several large, flat portfolios of the sort art students lugged around, as well as an exquisite chest I assumed was full of paints, brushes, whatever paraphernalia artists use. She allowed me to help her lug her two duffel bags and chest up the stairs, but she wouldn't let me touch her portfolios.

Cheryl appeared to be a few years older than Tom. She told me she worked as a waitress at Giuseppe's Ristorante, one of the posher restaurants in town, and wasn't a student. She was tall and attractive, athletic looking even, but, unlike many lovely women I've known, she didn't seem that interested in her own looks. Her hair, which was thick and dark brown, was cut in a short bob. Calling her usual attire casual was a stretch—khaki pants with cargo pockets and stains on the knees, thighs, and butt, long-sleeved plaid shirts, almost always a baseball cap. Except when she dressed up for work—then she was stunning. Sophisticated and stunning. Like Tom, Cheryl didn't appear to be interested in me and didn't spend much time at our apartment. That was fine with me—the quieter the apartment, the better I liked it.

One morning I was sitting at the kitchen table studying some poker-hand frequency charts I'd created. I spent most of my time in the kitchen area. My former roommates had taken their blankets and TV, leaving a stained couch with several large tears in the upholstery and the two cinder blocks at the other end of the common room. The three of us hadn't done anything to improve the area, so we avoided it.

As I was working, Cheryl came out of her bedroom in her usual daytime attire, popped a couple a pieces of bread in the toaster, and made herself a cup of our terrible instant coffee. She sat next to me and asked what I was doing.

"Playing around with poker. I don't have to work today."

"You look pretty serious to me." She gave me a sidelong glance, not unlike one a poker player would give another if she smelled a bluff.

"It's just a game," I lied.

"I always thought it got pretty serious when money's involved. You do play for money, don't you?"

"Yeah. I guess it does."

She finished her breakfast, stood up to leave, then turned back to me. "Would you like to go for a little walk?"

"A little walk?"

"Well, it'll take most of the day. We'll probably get back after dark. I'll show you my hobby."

I had nothing better to do that day, so I put my notes away and followed her downstairs. Cheryl owned a small, beat-up gray Datsun pickup with a cheap cap over the bed. She grabbed the pile of tools and bags stacked on the passenger seat and shoved them into the back of the truck to make room for me. The bed was already full of shovels, pruners, machetes, and a chainsaw, along with gas and oil cans, buckets, files, whatnot. I asked her if she was a landscaper.

"No, I'm hoping to avoid doing that for a living. I was studying for my doctorate in botany, but my adviser had a sudden stroke last fall. It left him incapacitated and me without a scholarship. I'm just continuing with my research hoping something will turn up eventually. Anyway, I enjoy searching out plants, and it keeps me from getting too depressed about my current life." "What's wrong with your current life? I'll bet you make more than I do." I knew I couldn't afford to eat at Giuseppe's. I figured her tips alone were more than my entire paycheck.

Cheryl trained her wonderful eyes on me as if she could not comprehend what she was looking at, then softened her face. "And you want to be a retail clerk the rest of your life?"

I'm sure I reddened at the obvious foolishness of my remark. "No, of course not."

"I can fill my stomach on the money I make, though not much more than that, but it's not just the money. In the first place I feel like I'm going brain dead serving the same pseudo gourmet meals every night. But even worse, I need the work, so I can't allow myself to pour hot coffee on the lap of every drunk asshole who pinches my rear end."

Cheryl noticed I was surprised at her outburst. "That's probably nothing you have to deal with," she said. "It's not that I'm so upset that the world is full of jerks, I just want to be able to fight back. Besides, I love plants."

We climbed into her truck. "Today we'll be looking for *Symplocarpus foetidus*—skunk cabbage. It's not flowering now, but it's easier to locate the plants when they're not covered with snow."

"Is this a specialty of yours, skunk cabbage?" I asked.

"Not particularly. I study indigenous wildflowers in general, especially forest flowers." She paused, then continued, "If you enjoy today, you can snowshoe out there with me this winter." Cheryl had a full, bright smile on the few occasions she smiled, which she was doing now. I first thought that meant she was joking, but she wasn't. Her eyes, large and dark, seemed like windows to another world, or doors with an invitation to enter, which I was more than willing to do.

We drove for an hour or so on increasingly smaller and windier roads until Cheryl pulled off onto what appeared to be an abandoned driveway hidden in the trees. She got out and grabbed a couple of small knapsacks, stuffed them with water bottles, snacks, a few tools and other gear, handed me one and we headed into the woods. We walked between two ancient stone walls for half an hour or so without seeing any buildings.

"Just seeing these stone walls out here often makes me want to cry," Cheryl finally said. It was the first time she had spoken since we left her truck.

"Why?" I asked. "They're not the most polished ones I've ever seen, but I think they're beautiful."

"Oh, I love them, that's not the point. I just think of the labor that went into them."

"I've never thought about that," I admitted. "It does look like a lot of work." "It's not just the work that went into the walls themselves. Just imagine coming to these woods with not much more than an axe and a shovel and two kids with one more on the way, and creating a farm. And the stone walls were made mostly just to get all those rocks out of the way."

Cheryl soon turned off the old road. If she was following a trail, I couldn't see it. I wanted to ask her where we were going, but I already felt like a pest, and didn't want to intrude even more into her day. We headed up a slope, through a grove of what I now know to be eastern white pines, large ones. The soft bed of pine needles kept sliding beneath the smooth soles of my cheap sneakers— it was like skating uphill. Then we started downhill, through a dense copse of mountain laurel. This was even harder than sliding up the hill; I quickly learned not to follow too closely, but even so the branches were tough and sharp as they snapped at my face and hands. I certainly lacked the backwoods finesse of my guide, who seemed to flow rather than walk through the woods.

Cheryl finally stopped halfway down the hill when we had reached a sort of plateau with a soggy bog. The odor of sulfur made the heat even more inhospitable. The mosquitoes, however, welcomed us. Cheryl scanned the area while I sat on a log, rubbing my feet and swatting at insects. I heard her exclaim, "Aha!" As we hadn't spoken more than a few words since we'd left the car, I had begun to wonder if she was just playing with me, I couldn't understand why she wanted to come to this place.

"This is skunk cabbage." She pointed to clumps of small plants with large leaves cluttering the swamp. Frankly, they didn't look appetizing. "I've mapped differences in skunk cabbage populations all over the state and figured I might find interesting specimens here. Of course, like I said, they don't flower until late winter or early spring, so I'll have to come back then. Often they're the only new plant poking through the snow." As she spoke, she took a few close- up pictures with an impressive-looking camera, cut a leaf off one of the plants, then jotted some notes in a small journal. When she was done, she sat next to me.

"So, did you enjoy this hike enough to come out again?"

Cheryl adorned her personality specifically for the different tasks in her life. When she headed to her waitressing job, she was sexy enough to be attractive, professional enough to try to create a proper distance from her customers. When she was stalking flowers, she was efficient and no-nonsense in her cargo pants, long-sleeved shirt, and baseball cap. She had advised me to wear a cap too. "The underside of the visor is a better place for insect repellent than your face. It keeps the bugs away and doesn't get in your eyes," she said.

But now, as I looked into her brown eyes again, I thought I saw another side—an invitation to more than a walk in the woods.
I shrugged. "Depends on how busy I am."

"Are you going to be too busy for me?" She pulled a thin foil blanket from her knapsack and spread it over the soft, damp earth. She placed her hands on my cheeks and pulled me near for a kiss. The skin on her fingers was a little rough, but her touch was sure. I became very interested.

As we lay down Cheryl pulled a sheet over us. "It's for the mosquitos," she said. "I don't think anyone will disturb us here."

*

I'd never realized how much of New England is a virtual wilderness. Although I was raised in towns all over Massachusetts, the closest I'd gotten to the woods was two weeks at a summer camp when I was ten or so. Cheryl, on the other hand, knew the rural areas of New England like I wished I knew a deck of cards. Not just the forests but the fields and pastures of working farms, and probably every ranger and farmer in Massachusetts as well.

She tried to teach me the difference between various maples and oaks, where to find jack-in-the-pulpits, how to distinguish between bottle and fringed gentians, magnificent tiny purple-blue trumpet flowers that seemed like they were trying to blast the world with joy. As I continued to hike around the state with Cheryl, the trips seemed to get longer and shorter at the same time. I began to recognize repeated patterns of the different areas we passed through, whether it was dark hemlock woods in damp vales, nearly impenetrable growths of laurel, thickets of small, crowded pines on recently logged land, or the gorgeous stands of massive oaks and beeches of the higher elevations. I often got so lost in my observations that time disappeared, but when we arrived at Cheryl's destination, it seemed as though we'd spent days getting there. Mostly I loved watching her sweet butt roll up and down as I followed her through her world.

When we got back to the apartment Cheryl took several large-scale, transparent maps from her portfolios and fanned them across her bed. She showed me that laying them over a USGS topographical map helped her locate and compare her flowers. I watched as she transferred the information from her field journal to one of the transparencies. She placed whatever leaves she had gathered between two small pieces of cardboard which she carefully labeled and bound together, then stored in one of her wooden chests. Only when she was finished did she explain some of her nomenclature and what she was looking for. She introduced me to a hidden world, which, like one of her overlays, covered a world I'd thought I was familiar with.

Before our next hike I went to an outdoor clothing store and bought a pair of sturdy boots. After slipping up and down the slopes all day I wanted something to keep my feet under me. Cheryl grimaced when she saw my new treads, but didn't say anything; she just asked what size I wore. The next time we went out she stopped me as we unpacked her pickup.

"Put these on instead." She handed me a pair of lightweight shoes with knobby but flexible soles. I have no memory of what plant we were looking for that day, or what types of terrain we traversed to get there, but I do remember the shoes Cheryl gave me felt a lot better than the boots I'd bought, and that Cheryl asked me if they felt better when we took our break. I admitted they did. "I want to explain something to you." Cheryl grasped both of my hands and looked at me intently, as if to force me to stare into her wonderful brown eyes. I complied. "You might think walking through the woods is the same as walking on a sidewalk, but it's very different. Imagine that the entire surface of the Earth, land, air, and water, is a single organism—call it the biosphere, Gaia, Mother Earth, whatever. Think of this...you have a penchant for math, don't you?"

"Somewhat, I guess."

"In a way, the surface of your lungs that touches the air you breathe is still on the outside of your body. Topologically, it's like pushing in on a balloon until you form a sac inside it."

I understood her reference from elementary geometry. Imagine something made of a completely stretchable material: if you can change it from one shape to another without tearing it, the two shapes are considered topologically equivalent. Thus a bowl, a plate, and a spoon are the same topological shape, as are lungs. On the other hand, a cup with a handle isn't (though it is the same as a doughnut). But I didn't get her real point.

"So what?"

Cheryl squeezed and released my hands rhythmically as she spoke. I felt like she was trying to massage her meaning into me with her hands as well as her voice. "So the atmosphere is Earth's lung. It performs all the functions of our lungs and many more. It's just that instead of folding over on itself like our lungs, Earth uses gravity to hold its breath in place. And instead of a rib cage and a diaphragm, it uses weather to move air around. Plants are like the alveoli in our lungs—trees look a little like alveoli for good reason: to increase the surface area in contact with air. So when you go tramping on Mother Earth, tramp lightly, you're tramping through our mother's lung." Cheryl paused, then, as if she felt she needed to reassure me, she added, "The Earth is soft, but she's also tough. Like me." With that she pulled me close and proved her point. Cheryl's comparison of the Earth's atmosphere to a lung did change the way I looked at our walks—or I should say, my observations began to consist of more than just what I saw. I imagined myself as being inside the Earth and part of it, instead of on top and outside. Every instant was full of sounds and smells that didn't exist outside of the deep woods and their bordering fields. I began to tell myself stories about what I smelled or heard. I became entranced by the choir of daily birdsong; the cacophony of the late-afternoon birds— pewees, chickadees, titmice, nuthatches, and more—seemed to create a festive party to which we'd been invited. The mystical warble of the hermit thrush, on the other hand, seemed to create an immense void in the woods with a song that claimed there was only the singer and the listener, and that they could never meet. There was an incessant chirping of insects in the fields, and near swamps often a symphony of bullfrogs, which, en masse, created a din designed to confuse potential predators instead of attract them—all advertising the glorious fact of summer, hot humid summer. And of course, there was always the industrious pounding of woodpeckers, the animal that most reminded me of our own species.

In addition to the sounds, we were immersed in the wonderful, varied smells and feel of the forests. Bogs, pines, oaks—each area had its own ambience that changed with the weather. I came to appreciate it all, but on hot muggy days, when it felt as though we actually were pushing through the Earth's breath, I especially grasped the accuracy of Cheryl's explanation.

I once mentioned to Cheryl that the woods seemed almost magical. "They aren't *almost* magical—they *are* magical," she said. "Magic isn't being able to wave a wand and cast some spell that furthers one's own will. Magic is understanding that we're much vaster than we can know, because we're part of all of this." She slowly waved an arm at the forest as if she were opening a curtain to reveal a spectacle, which was exactly what she was doing for me.

We covered a lot of ground that year, as lightly as we could. I couldn't accompany Cheryl every time she went out, but there was certainly a rhythm to every trip I did make with her, including having sex when her work was done. Sometimes we had sex on ledge cliffs that looked out over the entire state, and further, into other states. Sometimes we just scrambled to the top of one of those immense Ice Age boulders called erratics. Forest, swamp, rock, field, wherever it was, we were never interrupted, and I never grew tired of making love to her.

She had moved into my room, but we never had sex in our apartment, only outdoors. "I can't stand the thought of fucking you with Tom in the next room," she'd told me. I liked to think she enjoyed sleeping next to a warm body as much as I did, but it also meant she could keep her maps spread out on the bed in her tiny room.

One day, when I thought Cheryl had finished her plant work, I took the liberty of taking her little tarp out of her backpack to spread it out for us. She laughed as she put her pencil away.

"Ron, do you just come out with me for sex?" Her laugh disappeared, she tried to look serious, but her eyes were still smiling.

Her question embarrassed me—but just a little. "You should talk—sex is the reason you do this too."

"Me? You know me better than that."

"Your whole life revolves around examining the genitalia of plants." For the first—and I believe only—time I knew Cheryl, she blushed enough to show through her deeply tanned skin.

Then she laughed again. "Touché."

"If you ever write a book, you should call it *The Colors of Sex*," I said.

She took my cheeks between her hands and gave me a long, deep kiss. "I'll try to remember that."

Although Cheryl made extensive use of maps for her research, she didn't use them to navigate during our day trips. It seemed she had effectively memorized the entire state. On one occasion, for instance, after we'd spent the day trudging up particularly steep terrain in a cold fog, she led me to the top of the slope.

"This is Mount Greylock, the highest point in Massachusetts," she explained. A nearby marker confirmed her statement, though there was no view for us to see through the drizzle that afternoon.

Another time we were exploring an area Cheryl said was old growth forest. The trees were large but not enormous. Still, it was nice to know some of them might have been there before the pilgrims landed. This time, when we climbed to the summit a parking lot was waiting for us. "You can see Boston over there," she pointed out. She began exchanging notes on the area with an elderly couple who had come to watch the hawks migrate. We hitched a ride with them down to her vehicle.

On the drive back to our apartment, I asked her if she ever got tired of always watching her feet while she walked.

"Is that how you walk?" she asked. "Of course. Don't you?"

"No, not all the time. Sometimes, when the footing is easy, I even look straight up." She glanced over at me and gave me a quick grin. "One thing I like about you is that you ask the simple questions. There are people who go through their whole lives only looking at their feet, and they never realize it."

"How can you look straight up while walking? Why would you look up?" "Try it in town. Walk slowly and look in different directions, sideways, up, whatever and hold your gaze while you walk, get used to it, train your brain. And don't try it in traffic, obviously, or on a steep slope. But if the path is easy, you can learn to let your feet take care of themselves. You will notice things while moving and looking around that you won't see when you're just standing or sitting, because you see things from continuously changing angles. Birders do it all the time, but I find it useful to spot isolated plants that might be hidden from one spot. And, of course, it will make your walks more interesting." Again, she was right.

It seemed as if she knew every species of native plant in New England. "How did you learn to recognize so many plants?" I once asked her. "A lot of them look the same to me."

"Learning the patterns, remembering the differences and the names is the easy part."
I raised my eyebrows. "What do you mean? It seems impossible to me."

"If you simply learn to recognize what you see, you'll only see what you already know. The trick is to recognize what you don't know, to see what you don't recognize. Then you can begin to learn."

Although Cheryl was extraordinary, she wasn't infallible. One misty day that fall we were caught out late and ended up traversing back to her truck in darkness. Having lost the path, we stumbled through the night with the glow of a small flashlight she had on her keychain. Occasionally she took a picture with her camera, and the flash would momentarily light up the woods. We ended up on the road about five miles from the pickup. She missed her shift at the restaurant, and I missed my poker game that evening.

Once the snow fell Cheryl didn't go out as often, but I did end up snowshoeing out to the skunk cabbage late that winter. Hiking with snowshoes in winter is quite different from hiking in the summer or fall. Although it's a more arduous form of exercise, there are advantages: the underbrush is less troublesome, as it's buried beneath the snow. And the ponds and bogs are often frozen, so there's no need to walk around them. Once one leaves the road, the snow is pristine white and laden with track networks from the local wildlife. And, if there's no wind, there's the silence: snow seems to swallow sound, leaving only a few muffled remnants of noise to float about the deep woods.

I was pretty happy with my life. I felt I was on my way to making a living at poker. I ate well every day, I was warm and dry at night. My greatest ambition was to have Tom leave after the spring semester and not have a roommate again to interfere with Cheryl and myself making love.

One spring night I won a considerable sum at poker from a student on the university lacrosse team named Bill Bishop. The game was at Gunnel Dorm, where I often played, but I didn't know Bishop personally. It turned out to be an unfortunate win. During my assessment of the three types of college poker players, I'd neglected to realize that the third types were often drunk and didn't always differentiate what went on at the card table from the rest of life. A few nights after I fleeced him, he and half a dozen teammates approached me on a dark street as I was leaving another game. At first I didn't recognize my former mark or feel like I was in danger, possibly because he wasn't drunk.

"Haven't we met before?" the man staring at my face asked. He was six feet or six one, not quite my height. It was too dark to make out details clearly, but I noticed a smirk on his face as he spoke.

"I don't think so," I said, annoyed.

"I guess your memory isn't as good as your poker," he said.

At that point I recognized him, but it was too late to matter for me. His teammates, who were all at least as large as Bishop, had already surrounded me. I wish I could say they took turns pummeling me, but in reality they all began hitting, then kicking, me at once. I broke a couple of bones in my right hand punching Bishop as soon as I realized what was going to happen, but that probably just made things worse for me. (It evidently had an effect on Bishop as well: he missed the rest of the lacrosse season with a broken eye socket, though the student newspaper claimed it was an accident sustained in practice.) I should have been thankful they didn't kill me, but they did break one of my ribs and dislocate a hip. To this day I walk with a hitch. Amusingly, they stole my wallet, probably trying to get back Bishop's earnings, but it was one of those nights I had already lost everything. I didn't have a credit card and had left my driver's license at home, so that was the only laugh I got out of the incident.

I never found out who found me or called the ambulance. Evidently I had crawled two or three blocks before I passed out. When I woke up I was at Saints Memorial Hospital and Cheryl was sitting by my bed dressed in her fancy work outfit, a snug, short black dress and high heels. She was gorgeous. "What happened to you?" she asked.

Without answering, I asked, "How did you get here?" It hurt to talk.

"The hospital called me at work. Said you gave them my name and place of work. What happened?" she asked again.

"I was mugged." I was too sore, too tired, too embarrassed to say more. I didn't remember giving anyone Cheryl's name, but that embarrassed me too.

Cheryl scrunched her eyes as if she was trying to see through my words. She didn't press the issue, but even in my semi-delirious state I could tell she knew there was more to the story. "I'll pick you up tomorrow," she said, abruptly standing up. "You're being released at noon."

I'm not sure I stayed conscious long enough to see her reach the door.

Cheryl drove me back to our apartment the next day, and then took care of me for several weeks—bringing me coffee and cereal, helping me walk to the bathroom, taking me back to the hospital for a check-up—but I sensed a difference in her attitude. For one thing, she moved out of my bedroom, but at first I figured that was just to let me rest more peacefully. I soon realized there was more to it; she seemed distracted, preoccupied, disengaged from me. Gradually I was able to get out of bed on my own and eventually sit at the table to eat. One morning she joined me at breakfast wearing a dark business suit I had never seen her in before.

"I'm going to Boston today, Ron. I'll be back this evening, but I'll be leaving next week for good."

I had been expecting something like that. I put my spoon down, picked up my coffee and pretended to sip on it. I was trying not to tear up. I didn't want Cheryl to think I thought she was doing something wrong. When I finally felt I could get the words out I said, "I kind of figured. I guess I've made a real hash of this."

"Well, whether or not you've made a mess of your life, that's not why I'm going. I got a scholarship at Tufts University in Boston and a chance to finish my PhD. Today I need to meet with some of the faculty, to convince them to let me continue with the work I've already started. I should've moved already, but I couldn't leave you so helpless."

"Maybe I could move to Boston with you," I said. Even as I spoke, I felt I sounded pathetic.

Cheryl put her hands on my cheeks, the same way she did when she first kissed me at the skunk cabbage bog. "My dear, sweet Ron. Every gardener knows some flowers are perennials, some are annuals. The annuals may be as beautiful as the perennials, but no matter how you treat them, they only last a year."

I wasn't angry with Cheryl for leaving; in fact, I was glad for her. In a way, I wanted to leave too, but it was myself I wanted to leave behind. And Cheryl wasn't mad at me. She just put it, "We've both got to keep chasing our dreams until we can capture one."

As I watched her dismantle our bedroom, though, I was struck by the fact I had taken for granted much of what she'd brought to my life. The beautiful bed we shared turned into an old mattress with a sleeping bag on it once she removed her paisley bedspread. The walls lost their color when she rolled up her posters of oversized irises. The top of the dresser was transformed back into a desolate plank when she packed her stuffed animals and fake leopard- skin cover into her suitcase. It wasn't that she had many possessions—she fit everything she owned into two duffel bags, which she stowed in her truck with all her maps and tools—but the wild little jungle we shared left in those bags.

Of course, I had lost my job because I could hardly stand up. I couldn't have paid the rent if Cheryl hadn't agreed to pay for her room until summer. I could barely buy food. I had once given an oral report in my high school English class and mentioned "hyacinth days". None of my fellow students knew what I meant, but they didn't react because they didn't care either. On the other hand, my teacher, a small woman with a sharp voice and sharper tongue, had a puzzled look until she realized I meant "halcyon days," at which point she almost choked to death trying to suppress her amusement. In any case, my halcyon days seemed over; my pretty little life had become decidedly grim. When I finally could stand for more than a few minutes at a time, I began to look for another job and a new apartment mate.

One thing that had not changed is that I still seldom saw Tom Jacobs. In my dreams Tom had left and Cheryl and I continued to romp through the forest and could make love whenever we wanted. In my life Cheryl was gone and I had Tom the ghost for a companion.

4

On my way home one evening in late April I found Regina sitting on the front steps of my apartment. She must have spotted me long before I noticed her, but said nothing until I nearly stepped on her.

"Hello, Ron," she said.

"Professor Russo! What are you doing here?" She was dressed, as usual, in blue jeans and a tailored, long-sleeve cotton shirt. Her arms were wrapped around her legs. Her head, cocked to one side, rested on her knees. She was as beautiful as ever.

"I'm here to talk about *you*."

I struggled to sit on the step beside her. My hip still hurt from the fight, and I was sore from having been on my feet for hours. "How did you know where I lived?"

"Lucky guess. You look awful." I had become used to the fact that she seemed to know all about me in school, but since I graduated I'd thought she'd given up on me. Apparently not.

"I'm okay. I just started a new job today." "Selling televisions?"

I could tell she wasn't impressed by a hint of exasperation in her voice. "It pays the bills," I said, then asked again, "How did you know what I was doing?" Regina didn't respond for some time. When she did, she spoke in her usual soft voice. "I care about you, Ron. To be honest, I saw a note about you in the police blotter and decided to look you up. I didn't know you were actually selling TV's though, are you really?"

"More like computers and software, but it's just about the same thing."

Regina looked at me for a while, then said, "You're still playing against yourself, Ron. You need to pay the bills, but you need more than that."

"I'm not so sure."

Again, she said nothing at first, and then even more softly, "I am."

"It's kind of funny," I muttered. "My life seemed so perfect a few weeks ago." Regina smiled, her wry crooked smile, as if she found that possibility amusing. "I've always found the pursuit of perfection shows a profound lack of imagination, as well as a misunderstanding of reality."

"Then what do you pursue? Is there something better than perfect?" "Maybe truth and beauty." Regina laughed softly as she said this. "Truth and beauty?"

"Have you ever read Keats? ' "Beauty is truth, truth beauty," – that is all / Ye know on earth, and all ye need to know.' It might be his most famous line."

"I didn't know you read poetry."

"One line doesn't make me a scholar, but I've always thought it ironic that one of the most romantic lines from the most romantic of poets so perfectly describes the pursuit of science."

The maple leaves had just come out, small and light green, and the earth smelled as fresh as clean sheets. The sun was descending behind the hills. Between two houses across the street we could see the Connecticut River and the city beyond. The shadow of sunset crawled across the river and climbed the tall university buildings on the far side, turning them a red so dark they almost glowed black. Time seemed to pause, so we sat in silence.

Regina finally spoke again. "You need to find more for yourself, Ron. *I* need more from you."

This was the first time she'd explicitly indicated she wanted something from me, but I didn't know how to respond. I hadn't lost my crush on her, and I wasn't sure where this was going. I turned to look at her. Her eyes, which had appeared golden the first time I'd met her, now looked as green as the leaves budding around us. I felt they were growing, as if they might swallow me.

"Why do you care?" I asked.

"I'll make you a deal: I'll pay your way through college. I'll pay you for every class you get an A in. You'll get nothing for B's. You can take any classes you want at any school, any *real* school. I'm not going to pay for you to get a real estate broker license or learn how to be a croupier in Atlantic City."

It was the first time anyone had made me an offer like this, or even showed any interest in my future. "Why do you care about me?" I asked again.

"Maybe because someone helped me once, maybe because I think you could do amazing things if you worked at it, maybe I just feel our lives are entangled. Maybe it's all of those or maybe it's something else. I'm not offering you a free ride, though—you don't get anything until you succeed."

At that moment school seemed better than work, so I accepted without thinking and enrolled in summer courses at Foxfield Community College a few weeks later. Of course, I needed to keep working until my first grades came in.

I didn't care what courses I took at first, I just wanted the payoff. Evidently Regina didn't care either. I spent a year getting my grades up to snuff, then transferred to Northern. Surprisingly, the A's came easily. I never dared take a course from Regina, but we met irregularly to discuss my studies and—once a semester, like clockwork—for her to pay me. The extra meetings were my idea, an excuse to see her. I began to realize that a sexual relationship probably wasn't going to happen between us, but I still fantasized about it.

Regina was true to her word and didn't try to influence which courses I took. I asked her about this once. "I know if you're trying, you'll do the right thing," she'd said.

"What makes you so sure?" I asked. "It doesn't seem I've done anything right yet."

Regina narrowed her variegated eyes. It seemed like she was trying to actually *see* what was behind my words. I didn't want to talk about Cheryl, so I suffered her appraisal in silence. After a while she spoke. "It seems to me you've done a lot of things very well."

She didn't say anything else for a while, then continued, "Anyone who doesn't make mistakes, hasn't tried. I just want you to try."

I wasn't so sure her confidence was well founded, but I had nothing better to do and besides, it was her money.

I spent a semester and a half at Northern looking for a major. The first- year courses were pretty standard, so I looked for anything that seemed easy, figuring that would be the best way to keep my grades up. I quickly found boredom was more odious than work, so I went back to mathematics. I know many people are afraid of math, but for me it was a refuge—a refuge from losing Cheryl, a refuge from my feelings about Regina, a refuge from not knowing what I really wanted to do anymore. When I say I found mathematics to be a refuge I may be understating my feelings. To me, mathematics is a vast array of interconnected mental bridges and tunnels and caverns and castles illuminated by the signposts of mathematical symbols. I suppose most people do not get much beyond simple arithmetic - maybe they just see a long straight path of digits and the only question that exists for them is how far along this path is what they are looking for, perhaps their check book balance or the number of teaspoons of salt in a recipe. They must see mathematicians, endlessly scribbling down their weird meaningless symbols, as a bit deranged. To me, though, the symbols are beacons laying out the forms of a perfect universe. And just when those symbols seem to shine on a dead end, one can create a new path, like convergent series or imaginary numbers, which leads to an even larger universe. But mathematics is also a refuge because it is logical, it is precise, it is unassailable and therefore eternal.

I took some physics classes as well, not so much because I cared about the subject, but because I thought it might give me something to talk to Regina about.

Regina paid me enough to be comfortable in a sparse, student-like way. If I took a full load and got all A's, there was the added advantage that I wouldn't need roommates to help with the rent. This was especially fortunate as I had not replaced my old roommates and needed to pay Danielle full rent once school began again.

After my first full semester I quit my job and augmented my stipend from Regina with earnings from poker—which I approached more cautiously, and, I hoped, professionally, than before. I limited myself to Atlantic City during long weekends and holidays. I had gained enough skill to usually leave with more than I'd brought with me. I shouldn't have had anything to complain about, but I was still frustrated by my feelings for my mentor. It seemed she became more beautiful each time we met, yet her easy trust and friendliness, along with her cool serenity, began to grate on my nerves. We usually met at Diner Ninety-One, an Art Deco style diner at the interstate truck stop on the outskirts of Foxfield. I didn't have a car so I'd bicycle, even during winter. It wasn't that far, and there were no hills. Regina and I both kept late hours, and the diner was open 24/7.

I finally lost my patience during one meeting in the fall of my sophomore year. I challenged Regina in a fit of pique: "I never understood what you meant when you said 'thinking causes time.' It seems so mystical. How can you believe something like that?"

Regina scowled as if she'd eaten a bad peanut, then softened slightly. She spoke in her usual quiet manner, but it was as if she were shouting at me. "I never said that. I said 'awareness creates time,' which I believe is true."

I knew I'd missed something, but I wasn't sure what. "Are we just dealing in semantics?" I asked.

"*Just* semantics?" Her eyes narrowed as she looked at me, as if to see whether or not I was joking. "That's an interesting idea. How about a homework assignment from me in the semantics of physics? I know it's not your field, but this is a simple thought exercise."

She examined my face for a response, and I tried to look straight back into her pale eyes without reacting. I don't think she ever wore makeup. Her skin was so smooth, the expressions on her face so exquisite, that makeup would have looked grotesque. She did, on occasion, wear earrings—small pearls, or gold studs as she had that evening. She continued without waiting for a verbal reply.

"As you know, Ron, physics describes reality as being shaped by forces. The concept of 'force' was the brainchild of Isaac Newton, and it might be the greatest theoretical discovery in all of science, perhaps the very idea that created science as we know it. Newton realized that the attraction between the sun and our planet was the same as the attraction between an apple and the ground— namely, gravity. But you know all this already." Regina smiled reassuringly.

"Yeah, I think we covered that in the first week of freshman physics." I was still irritated with her, and didn't need a simplistic rehashing of Physics 101.

Regina ignored my tone. "Newton then created the mathematics necessary to

describe this attraction. He needed to name the phenomenon of t̶h̶e̶
on one another, so he called it 'force.' Today four forces—gravitation̶
electromagnetic force, strong force, and weak force—are all we need to des̶
the interactions of matter."

"Seems like he got it right."

She pondered my reaction with a serious look on her face, then continued, "Indeed, some consider Newton's very use of the word 'force' to be inspired. After all, he was describing something that wasn't known before, and needed to adopt an existing word to describe a new concept. But instead of 'force,' I want *you* to think of 'command,' a sort of compulsory instruction that has to be followed, for the same concept."

"You mean like instead of a gravitational force between the earth and moon, they're commanding each other?" I was trying to show I thought her idea was absurd.

"Just try it. The next time we meet we can discuss your thoughts."

After this brief sojourn into physics, we discussed my grades. It was mid-semester, so I wasn't due a payment, but we discussed my progress and my courses for a while. As usual, my irritation had been mollified just by talking to her. I was more pleased by the idea of my next meeting with her than I was intrigued by her assignment for me, but I promised to think about what she'd said. Thus began my parallel course in physics according to Regina Russo.

Our next meeting was also at Diner Ninety-One, just after the fall semester grades had come out. We went over my scholastic progress, and I received my stipend. My immediate goal was simply to get as many A's as possible. For me that meant taking as few non-math courses as I could. I was just a sophomore, however, and I needed to take required courses each semester. I complained to Regina, who surprised me by sympathizing.

"I admit I felt the same way when I was in school. I never understood why I needed to take an art course when I always felt science was the true art."

Regina didn't mention the homework she had given me until I brought it up. "I've been thinking about what you said about describing a force as a command," I said. "The first thing that comes to mind is that I need to process a

hings acting
al force,
cribe

't just happen to me."

s right, and to process a command, you must be

to be aware of a force?" I said through a mouthful of
ıg we were talking in circles.

y the case. My argument is that awareness isn't explicitly implied by the word 'force.'"

"But is the inevitability of the result implied by the word 'force' implied by the word 'command'? You can refuse to follow a command."

"First of all, modern physics indicates that results aren't perfectly inevitable. We can explore that later. For now, I just want you to realize that the words you use may affect the way you think about something. It may not seem like a big deal, but perhaps as you explore the ideas behind the words you'll begin to see physics in a different light."

It was two in the morning, a normal hour for both of us. There were only two other occupied booths that night. In one, a trucker in his late fifties sat nursing his coffee, staring ahead as if he were still driving his rig. In the other were two young couples who looked like they never slept and never needed to. I sat sideways in the booth, with my feet stretched out, and stared at the pattern of palm trees embossed on the back of the green vinyl seat, fidgeting with the upturned corner of a piece of tape used to repair a tear in the covering. Truthfully, I wasn't paying much attention to what I was saying.

Regina's eyes, however, gleamed. I thought she was going to leap over the table and grab me. Realizing I hadn't grasped her point, she calmed down enough to continue.

"I believe the word 'force,'" she began, "echoes the dominant political and religious philosophy of the early days of science. Newton, for instance, was very much inculcated in the culture of religion and politics of his time—he probably wrote more tracts on his religious theories than he did on science or math. He also served as England's Master of the Mint for many years, and was instrumental in creating paper money and discovering forgers. The worth and character of a country at that time was seen to emanate from the power of an autocratic leader who ruled his land through force. And God, of course, ruled as absolute master over all of existence. It would have been natural, in that setting, to see the entire interplay of the universe as the result of force. But insightful as Newton was when he coined the word 'force' to describe his discovery, we should consider whether it carries hidden assumptions of his era that continue to shade our thinking. I believe we need to look at the *receiver* of force as well as the generator." Regina had spoken with surprising intensity, but she finally paused, perhaps to see if I was listening. She saw I was and finished, "One of Newton's best-known laws is 'For every action there is an equal and opposite reaction'—but that first action is always a reaction to a previous action. The way I describe it is that every action is the result of *awareness* of a previous action."

"So dark matter would be an example of something evidently not aware of all of the forces around it," I said. Dark matter is a form of matter that's thought to be more abundant in the universe than the matter we're aware of, and it's apparently unaffected by electromagnetic force.

"Ah! You're starting to get it! We should explore the evidence that dark matter actually exists some other time, but if it does, maybe we should call it moronic matter, because it evidently doesn't understand electromagnetic commands." Regina laughed a little at her own joke, which I didn't quite get, and nibbled on a couple of my French fries. She seldom ordered more than a soup or salad for herself, but often indulged herself by freely eating from my plate. I took this as a sign of familiarity, even of intimacy.

Regina began again, "In a way, even Newton used language similar to what I propose when he spoke about the 'laws' of nature. Even today it's common to use the phrase 'Obey the laws of nature,' which implies that the universe must be aware of these laws."

I'd never seen Regina quite so animated. But even though I was beginning to get a glimpse of what she was trying to tell me, I was a long way from understanding why all this was so important to her.

"But Regina, physics is essentially a mathematical description of reality. The very definition of force is the equation 'Force equals mass times acceleration,'" I said. "Why is it so important to you whether we say, 'Force equals mass times acceleration' or 'Command equals mass times acceleration'? The second sentence doesn't even make sense."

"You've proven my point. Mathematics is essential to physics, but the ideas behind the equations are also crucial. Your first sentence, 'Force equals mass times acceleration,' strikes us as a complete idea, but the second statement, 'Command equals mass times acceleration,' raises questions regarding what's commanding, what's being commanded, what's their relationship."

She paused and finished my fries. "Sorry about that, maybe you should get another order."

"How about we split a piece of blueberry pie instead?" I said.

"Sounds good. Anyway, Ron, I can't explain all of physics in one sitting, but if I can get you to look at it from a slightly different angle, I can show you how to reach a new landscape. Imagine I wanted you to climb a mountain you'd already climbed before, but by a new route. I couldn't make you see the whole route in advance, but if I could get you started, eventually you might find vistas you never knew existed." I had been munching on our pie as Regina spoke, but when she was done speaking she pulled the plate back to her side of the table and finished it.

The two hyper couples apparently had thought of something new to do and exited the diner in a whirlwind of excitement. The trucker also had left, presumably to continue his solitary saga behind the wheel of an actual truck. Our waitress, who had to stay until the sun came up no matter what, was scrubbing some booths at the other end of the diner. Regina and I both had our coffee refills in front of us, but we'd pretty much quit drinking.

I thought the lesson was over, but Regina continued. "When you think about force—the word 'force'—it conjures up an image of one entity acting upon another. But there's always a mutual interaction between two entities— it's a bit like a dance, with both bodies issuing commands and obeying them according to their own states of existence. The force they exert depends upon both of their masses—the moon doesn't revolve around the Earth, they both revolve around their mutual center of gravity. Now, none of this changes the mathematical description of the physics of the situation, but using the right words might allow one to explore reality differently, to ask better questions, to understand results more easily, and therefore lead to new equations and solutions previously unimagined. But semantics are just the beginning of the journey."

It was beginning to snow outside, and I was getting antsy about my bike ride back to my apartment. I was also tired. I could follow Regina's train of thought, but I still didn't see why it was so important to her. "But isn't this all a moot point? Hasn't the physics of the last three centuries pretty well validated Newton's ideas and his use of the word 'force'?" I asked her.

Regina's eyes smiled. I'd seen that look in chess and in poker: it meant that the trap had been sprung. "Has it? Haven't you heard of quantum physics?"

"Of course."

"Maybe the next time we meet we can explore these ideas in light of the mysteries of quantum physics."

It was just beginning to snow, just a dusting. The ride home was exhilarating, like being caught in a Christmas card. I imagined I was *command*ing my bicycle pedals to go around, but when it came right down to it, it still seemed like I had to *force* them with my legs. I had no idea where Regina was going with her semantics. It turned out to be a longer journey than I expected.

5

My next meeting with Regina was not planned. It was an unusually warm day in February, a little above freezing. I was heading toward the main library when I heard Regina call my name from behind me.

"Hello, Ron. I hope you are enjoying this beautiful day," she said as she caught up.

In truth, although Cheryl had shown me how beautiful any weather is, I hadn't been paying attention right then. "I guess I hadn't noticed. I've got to go listen to a German opera, *Die Fledermaus*."

"Sounds interesting," she said, and we both laughed at her insincerity.

"I'm sure it is—for someone," I said. "By the way, I've been trying to read a little on quantum physics. Do you really understand that stuff?"

"I guess that depends on who you ask. I'm not exactly a mainstream thinker in those matters." She looked at me carefully, as if she needed to be careful of what she said, then continued, "I'm bringing a manuscript over to the copy center. Why don't you come with me and we can talk."

I accepted immediately. It was only a short walk, and any time I spent with Regina was better than anything else I could think of.

Regina asked, "What have you learned about quantum physics?"

"I'm not sure. You've heard about fuzzy math? This seems like fuzzy science." "I can understand why you feel that way, but actually the field of quantum physics is the most precise field in science. It's that precision that makes it look fuzzy."

"How do you mean?" I asked.

"You must have heard of the so-called 'uncertainty' principle: one can never measure both a particle's location and its momentum beyond a certain precision, described by the Planck Constant. We cannot know both precisely where a particle is and what it's doing. The result is that we can't meaningfully measure a time period shorter than the corresponding Planck Interval of 10^{-44} seconds. Likewise, there's also a corresponding Planck Length, the distance something can travel at the speed of light during a Planck Interval, 10^{-35} meters, which is the smallest unit of space we can measure."

I had heard of the uncertainty principle, but not described in this way. When my face revealed my confusion, she stopped and turned toward me. "Okay, imagine a traffic cop patrolling a school zone that was subject to that kind of principle. The speed limit on the rest of the road is, say, fifty miles an hour, but in front of the school it's only twenty miles an hour. But this cop is a quantum cop, so he can either tell how fast a car is going or where it is, but not both. As you can imagine, he'd be one frustrated cop who wouldn't write many tickets, because he couldn't tell whether a car was actually speeding in the school zone. That's kind of how quantum physicists see the universe."

I was reminded of the day we met, when she turned my chessboard around. She was always able to surprise me with an explanation so simple and clear that even the complexities of quantum physics seemed obvious. "But if awareness is so important, are you also saying the universe is conscious and thinks—like us?"

She shook her head. "Oh, no. Whatever it does, it isn't like us. Sometime we should also discuss how humans think. We can even explore how physicists think!"

We had arrived at *CopyMe,* the copy center. I turned back for the library, but before we parted Regina asked, "Ron, have you heard of the two-slit experiment?"

"Remind me." I knew about the experiment, but I did not want to assume I knew what Regina wanted me to know.

"Why don't you review it? We'll continue this exploration next time we meet."

I agreed, though I wasn't sure our "explorations" were helping. I knew an uncomfortable tension existed between how physicists wanted to describe reality and what reality was itself, but I wasn't yet able to see how Regina's approach made things any clearer.

Before I met with her again, I did review the two-slit experiment. It's a relatively simple experiment that shows some of the differences between quantum physics and the physics of the world we are used to. Thomas Young, a nineteenth-century British physicist, performed the first experiments along this line, first using a single slit. Imagine a seaport surrounded by a breakwater, with only a single opening for ships to enter. As the ocean waves pound on the breakwater, they will pass through the opening and spread out. This spreading is called diffraction. Now imagine there are two openings in the breakwater. As the waves pass through both openings they will diffract and interact with each other as they overlap. In those locations where two wave peaks meet, the waves will become twice as high as the original waves, and in those locations where two wave troughs meet, the new trough will be twice as low. Moreover, in the locations where a peak and a trough meet, the waves will cancel each other and there will be no wave at all. The resulting pattern is called an interference pattern. The picture below on the left shows water waves with just a single source, the one on the right shows two sources with the resulting interference pattern. It's easy to see the places where the waves cancel out.

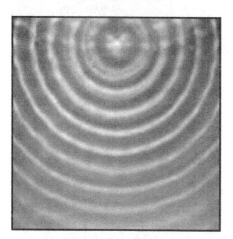 

Light waves behave in a similar wave, up to a point. You cannot actually see the waves like we can with water, but if you project light which has passed through a single slit onto a screen it will diffract and form a fuzzy patch of light centered on the point directly opposite the slit. If you project the light through two slits onto the screen you will observe alternate bright and dark stripes across the screen. Photographic examples are as shown below. On the top is the single slit example showing simple diffraction, on the bottom is the two slit example showing wave interference.

When Young first performed his experiments they became famous because they indicated light does not consist of particles, as Newton had shown, but of waves. Now we accept that light is both particle and wave, which is called "wave-particle duality".

While I was reading about this wave-particle duality I recalled Regina's first lesson in the semantics of physics. We call light "wave-particles" based upon the fact that they behave similarly to the waves and particles we are familiar with in our daily lives, but we do not actually observe phenomena such as wave-particles at our human scale. The words we use help us understand the phenomena, but they can also confuse us. In any case, that's not the most interesting result of this experiment.

Now imagine sending the photons of light through slits again, but only one photon at a time, so that each photon arrives at the screen before the next one is released. If there is only one slit, the result's the same as when the particles were emitted in a steady stream through the single slit: the light shines on the spot directly opposite the opening, but with some fuzziness due to diffraction. But if two slits are present, even though we only have one electron in passage at a time, each photon lights up the screen in a seemingly random location. We cannot predict where any single particle will land, but after enough time they will form the same interference pattern that a steady stream of photons would create. Because there is only a single particle in passage at a time, physicists call this phenomenon "self-interference," as if the photon interfered with itself. The most reasonable assumption is that a photon somehow passes through both slits. However, if we set up detectors at the two slits we will find that a particle only goes through one slit or the other. A curiosity arises, however—as soon as we determine which slit the photon passes through, it will act as if only that slit existed, and the photon lights up our screen showing only the effect of diffraction. The interference pattern disappears.

Physicists say that the photon travels as a "wave function" along all its possible wave paths until it's "observed," at which time its "wave function" collapses to an event. If it's first observed at one of the slits, it collapses there, and only passes through that slit. If it's first observed at the screen, it appears to have passed through both slits and lights up the screen at one of the interference points. Before it's observed it cannot be said to exist at any specific place. The obvious question is "What's a wave function?" The answer is a wave function is a mathematical formula that describes the behavior of a subatomic particle.

Someone unfamiliar with quantum physics might think this seems strange. It seemed strange to Einstein as well, and, though it was his work that first led to quantum physics, he never was comfortable with the apparent randomness of collapsing wave functions. I often wonder if that was what caused his hair to stand on end! Niels Bohr, on the other hand, was adamant that even though we might not be able to visualize the reality behind the wave function, we must accept it because it accurately predicts the results of scientific experiments. There are decades' worth of experimental data confirming his view. As I read about this controversy I wondered what sort of spin Regina would put on this experiment.

Regina and I had agreed to meet at Diner Ninety-One again. She was already seated at a booth doing some paperwork when I arrived. I was always amazed at how easily she could shift her attention from one task to another without losing focus—I personally don't have that gift. As soon as I arrived she put her work aside and cheerfully greeted me.

"I thought I'd grade a few tests while I waited. How have you been?"

I told her things were going well and handed her my latest report card from my second sophomore year semester. She said nothing as she handed me a check, but a small, satisfied smile flicked across her face. Eventually our conversation turned to her theories again, and I recapitulated my understanding of the two- slit experiment.

When I was finished, Regina nodded slowly, then pursed her lips. "In our everyday concept of reality we say an object is somewhere; it's traveling at a definite speed; it has a temperature, et cetera. We refer to this as being in a specific *state*. In quantum physics, however, we consider an object, even the simplest subatomic particle, as a wave function, a system that exists in many states until it's observed. This is called 'superposition.' Once the wave function is observed, we say it collapses into a definite single state. One of the consequences of this theory is that one can't predict exactly which state a particular wave function will collapse into. In other words, quantum physics describes a seemingly nondeterministic reality. I accept the results of this theory—I just feel we should accept the fact of the observation, which I call awareness, whereas the conventional view considers such awareness an inexplicable anomaly."

"It seems odd science accepts something as inexplicable," I said.

"Indeed. Einstein felt there *is* a deeper underlying reality that would re-establish determinism. Niels Bohr believed we simply have to accept the results of the theory of wave functions, without trying to visualize it. I claim that accepting awareness as an actual phenomenon leads to a more complete understanding of time."

To me it seemed as if I was getting further from understanding anything, but I did not say anything as she continued.

"In the parlance of quantum physics, if we observe a particle going through one of the two slits, that's where the wave function collapses and an event occurs. If we wait until we observe the light hitting the screen, that's where the wave function collapses and the event occurs. Of course, the statement 'The wave function collapses' refers to what happens to the mathematical formula describing the event, rather than a description of a real event. In *my* view, time doesn't exist until an observation is made. There's no question of understanding how an unobserved particle can pass through two slits at once and interfere with itself in a logical manner because our 'logic' is based on time and space and sequence. I don't believe time even exists without observation, that is to say, without awareness."

"And you believe your view is more accurate than the standard view?" "I think mine explains more phenomena more simply."

We sat there in the booth, each lost in our own thoughts, either trying to warm our hands with our coffees or warm our coffees with our hands.

Finally Regina flashed me her wry, crooked grin. "The standard view of the universe is like a baseball game where there's a lot of hitting and throwing but no catching. That wouldn't be much of a game."

"I am beginning to understand that awareness—as you call the process of observing—pervades the quantum world, but why do you say time doesn't exist until an observation is made?"

"That's an important question, but I think we should wait until our next meeting to answer it. It's late, and I need to get these papers graded by tomorrow."

That night I rode back to my apartment, frustrated. Regina's ideas seemed so eccentric, yet so compelling that she was drawing me into her world against my will.

6

Poker was no longer as important to me as it had been, but I had achieved enough competence to be confident I would come out ahead in the long run. What I'd once dreamed of as a serious career had become an amusement, but at least it was a lucrative amusement. I didn't have my own transportation, so I had to rely on other students or group bus tours to take me to the casinos.

Foxwoods, a casino resort run by the Mashantucket Pequot tribe on reservation lands in the middle of the Connecticut woods, had just opened a poker room, but they were so busy they kept tight control over who could enter. Group buses had to be full, or nearly full, to be allowed onto the casino grounds, so I signed up as a kind of permanent standby in order to get a free ride whenever they needed an extra body. Usually the buses were full of senior citizens—mostly women, because most seniors are women—who planned to spend all day at the slot machines. The rides were cheerful, and as long as I didn't sit next to someone who wanted to talk religion or winning slot machine strategies, we'd chat the whole way. I saw lots of pictures of grandchildren.

I rode the bus often enough to get to know some of the regulars. A few of the women made the trip several times a week. Slot machines are set up to make you think that you're winning as much as or more than you're losing, and that you're just a lucky break away from winning big. Actually, there are very few, vanishingly few, players who come out ahead in the long run. Of course, it's the possibility of that one big break that creates the thrill of gambling, but it struck me that one would need iron discipline to visit so often and not impoverish oneself. (As I've mentioned, I didn't regard poker as a form of gambling, but as a game of skill like baseball or any other sport.)

Mrs. Isabel Gretchen, one of the ladies I used to sit with, took a liking to me and would hold the seat next to her open just in case I got on board. Mrs. Gretchen was a cheerful, red-cheeked, and lively companion. I was especially impressed by her upbeat personality, because it was clear old age was beginning to wear her body down. She was developing a hunchback, or kyphosis, and walked slowly, with a cane. Every step appeared to be painful. Despite her ailments, when I told her I was an orphan she evidently decided I needed some grandmotherly tenderness—it seemed she had plenty left over from her own six grandchildren. Perhaps it was because her children all lived too far for her to see them regularly that she had a pent-up need to fuss over someone, but mostly she was just a caring person.

"Don't you have any idea at all who your parents were?" she asked me one day.

"Honestly, no," I said. "I was told they both died in a car crash, and I was the only survivor."

Mrs. Gretchen frowned. "But surely your grandparents would have raised you, at least one set of them. I'd never let any of my babies go into foster care." "Yeah, I never believed the whole car-crash story. I suspect my mother didn't want anyone to know about me. Maybe she was too young to raise me or just didn't want me. Maybe no one wanted to tell me that."

She gently patted my knee a few times. "That's dreadful! Everyone needs to be wanted."

I shrugged. "I always told myself it was better than being aborted."

Mrs. Gretchen stared at me as if she couldn't comprehend what I'd just said. "You have an unusual way of looking at things, young Ron Larsen." She spoke as if I really were her grandson. "I suppose you've got a point, but I just can't imagine not having a family."

I couldn't imagine *having* a family, and I wasn't going to make things more difficult by wishing I did. My life was already confusing enough.

One weekend I won several thousand dollars, my largest win ever. I grabbed a taxi from Foxwoods to the nearest town and began to look for a used car. I'd never bought a car before; I'd never even owned one, but I figured it would allow me some freedom to set my own schedule. I had a wad of money in my pocket and tried to look like I knew what I was doing.

It was a hot and steamy August day. I usually dressed in blue jeans and a western shirt for my casino trips—it just felt right for poker. I knew I looked a bit awkward—I had gained some weight at Northern, so my belly kind of rolled over my belt. Western shirts are cut for a trim build, and my shirts also tended to pull apart between the snaps. But looking a little dumb at the poker table can be an asset too.

Being overdressed is also not a bad idea in the casinos, as they are air-conditioned and can be chilly on the hottest days. Walking around outside on a humid summer day is another matter, and it was not long before I was drenched in my own sweat. The first few dealerships I visited were a bit overpriced for me, but I finally found a lot where several of the cars were in my price range. A small one-room office building in a corner of the lot had a sign overhead that proclaimed, DAVEY DICKIE'S HONEST CARS FOR HONEST FOLKS. I decided not to let the sign deter me.

A middle-aged man, with a receding hairline accentuated by a few long strands of hair combed from one side to the other, wearing a rumpled short-sleeved white shirt and dark tie, but no coat, approached me from the back row where a couple of teenagers were detailing and washing cars.
"How can I help you, young man?" he said. "I'd like to buy a car."

He looked at me as though I'd said something unexpected or profound. "What kind of car are you looking for?"

"I'm a student up in Foxfield. I just want something I can afford that will get me back and forth to the casino without a hassle."
"What can you afford?"

"I was hoping for something around a thousand dollars." I had more than that, but I hated to spend it all.
"You're not trying to impress the young ladies? Don't need to carry large loads?"
I shook my head.

"I'm not sure I can help you at that price, son. I have a sedan over here that'll run forever, but I can't let it go for less than twenty-five hundred."

He showed me a faded blue Chrysler sedan with one gray fender and no rear seat. "It's not pretty, but, like I said, this thing will run forever. It's a slant six from down south. A can or two of Krylon spray paint and it's all the car you'll ever need."

I'd gotten pretty good at reading faces from playing poker, but used cars weren't my territory. I had the feeling that he'd sized me up pretty well from the get-go, but also that he wasn't bullshitting me.

"I can't go higher than fifteen hundred, but I have that much in my pocket right now."

We agreed on $1,750 if he'd fix anything that failed the required Massachusetts inspection.

I paid Davey Dickey in cash and he handed me the title. I asked him for the keys.

"I'd rather keep them until you get the car registered—just so I can move it around the lot. I'll even get one of the boys to paint that fender for you."

I had thought I'd just drive out with the car, but I'd forgotten about the registration. Then I found out I needed to get insurance before I could register it. The car eventually passed inspection, but it took me three weeks before I could get it out of his lot. At that point in my life most of what I knew was strictly theoretical, except for poker.

*

I'd become so obsessed with my mathematical studies that I dreamed about Markov chains, eigenvalues, and indefinite integrals. I only visited my apartment to sleep; I ate from vending machines and occasional trips to the student center or, late at night, at the truck-stop diner. I relieved the stress of my nonstop studies by taking several short naps every day, an hour or two in my car at a minute's notice. Soon I found myself sleeping exclusively in my car to save time, returning to my apartment only a couple of times a week to clean up and check my mail.

My next meeting with Regina was at the diner again. We seldom met at her office; she used it like I used my apartment, more a storage closet than an office—even her two chairs were usually stacked with boxes full of equipment for her research.

I needed to pick up my stipend, but I wasn't prepared for a long conversation in Russo physics; as much as I enjoyed seeing her, I was hoping for a quick visit. I'd even tried to think of an excuse for having to leave abruptly at two in the morning.

When I arrived Regina was sitting at the counter talking to a waitress, a blonde in her late twenties or early thirties, so I sat down at a booth by myself. As I watched her, Regina reminded me of one of those grade school teachers who makes each student feel uniquely talented. Everyone seemed to glow a little under her gracefulness; everyone seemed to fall in love with her, as I had. A twinge of jealousy flitted through me, then disappeared as Regina left the counter and took a seat at my booth. Although I sometimes dreaded her lectures because they left me feeling more confused than enlightened, our meetings also thrilled me, as if I were having a secret affair. The problem was the affair was a secret from Regina too.

"Denise was one of my students, though I think she was a history major," Regina said. "She got pregnant and had to drop out."

"Were you trying to talk her into going back to school?"

"No, she and her husband own this place. They're doing fine."

We made a little more small talk, and she gave me my stipend. Denise arrived with our coffees and a cup of soup for Regina. I ordered a hamburger deluxe. For a minute I thought I'd be able to leave without a lesson, but then Regina started up again, as if there'd been no interruption.

"If I remember correctly, during our last discussion, you asked me why I claim time doesn't exist until an observation is made." She looked at me, and I nodded reluctantly. "I've mentioned that the uncertainty principle implies that we can't measure time and/or distance more precisely than their respective Planck units. I feel it follows that no observation can be quicker than the Planck Interval of 10^{-44} seconds, because time as we know it doesn't exist at shorter intervals. Remember when you asked me if the universe was conscious like us?"

"I do. I'm not sure I understand the difference between our awareness, and the awareness you describe in quantum physics, except that we are a lot slower, of course."

Regina nodded, evidently approving of what I said. "That might be the crucial difference," she said. "Consider that we have a nearly uncountable series of Planck Intervals between when an event happens and when it is perceived by human senses, travels through our nervous system where we process it in our brain, and we finally become 'aware' of it ourselves. If you look at it this way, we're only aware of the past—and a sort of distant past at that."

She leaned in toward me. "Think of a batter trying to hit a baseball. By the time he sees the ball, it has already moved. The question becomes 'How can he hope to hit the damn thing?'"

I had learned Regina was a die-hard Red Sox fan, so her analogy didn't surprise me. "He predicts where the ball is going to end up," I said. My explanation was lame and explained nothing. At times I felt like the straight man in a comedy routine, except Regina never made me feel foolish, at least not on purpose.

"But what does that really mean, Ron? The player has to create two simultaneous models of the world in his head: one computing where the ball will be, the other how to move his bat. And then he has to coordinate them to impact the ball with the bat. If we analyze thinking in general, we'll find this common link: the human brain is designed to gather information about events that have already happened and make a prediction about the future, which he or she can then take advantage of—a kind of virtual time travel from the past to the future, during the present."

"Time travel? That sounds like science-fiction, not science." I was wishing I had thought of an excuse to leave.

"I call it *virtual* time travel." She corrected me, giving me a look of admonishment clearly meant to tell me to pay attention. "In physics," she continued, "making predictions is an essential part of a meaningful theory. A theory that does this is considered correct; one that doesn't is considered useless. This might explain why many physicists have felt that the universe must be shown to be deterministic, and any theory, such as quantum physics, that appears to allow for chance is unsatisfactory."

Our waitress brought me my hamburger. As I poured on mustard and ketchup I tried to understand what Regina was getting at. "Would you have it any other way?" I asked.

Regina shook her head. "Not exactly. If the best way to understand the universe is to realize there are limits to what we can know, I accept that. In any case, our conscious awareness is quite different from the type of Planck interval 'awareness' of the immediate preceding instant we were discussing."

"But both humans and the universe are aware?"

"Yes, but we need to recognize the differences as well as the similarities. The entire universe is aware of commands—or forces—that take place in an instant so short that we don't yet properly understand their physics. People often appear to be mostly aware of their own imagination. It's as if we humans live in our own video game. We think of ourselves as moving into the future, but actually we're only aware of the past and we're guessing at the future."

"And where does your theory of time fit in to this?"

"First we need to explore where—or when—time doesn't exist. Maybe we can talk about that next time we meet."

My head was swirling. Every time we met Regina seemed to introduce a new angle or new topic—it seemed to me I'd never catch up. I had walked to the diner because I wanted to be able to catch a ride back with Regina, but I told her I wanted the exercise and headed back alone. I needed a little time to myself.

Regina's ideas were beginning to seem weird. I decided not to see her again until I'd come to grips with the effect she was having on me. Mathematics gave me an escape from the strange world of Regina Russo physics. With math, it's accepted that you're creating your own reality—it just has to be consistent. Physics uses mathematics, of course. In fact, their relationship is as close to magical as most scientists are willing to accept, but physics needs to be more than consistent—it's supposed to describe reality. Mathematics just describes itself.

I'd originally been curious about her ideas, but as I became more inculcated into academic thought and realized her ideas were extremely unorthodox, I was not only confused by her version of physics, but I also became genuinely concerned about her well-being. She spoke with such clarity and calm confidence that, while I listened, I was totally absorbed by her train of thought. But as soon as I left her, my doubts came rushing back.

7

At the same time that I began to resent Regina's lectures and truly immerse myself in mathematics, I also began to lose my touch at the poker table. I'd wanted to play more often, which was why I'd bought my car. I thought if I could earn enough on my own I could forego Regina's stipend, and therefore her personal physics lessons. But there's an old saying: you can't serve two masters, and I found out that was true for me regarding math and poker.

Both poker and mathematics take an immense amount of concentration. One of my math professors, Dr. Cuthbertson, often wore a little button on his lapel that said, "Math Is Not a Spectator Sport." This was certainly true for me—I became totally absorbed in my studies. As a result, and perhaps also because I'd done so well previously, I'd become complacent about poker and began to lose regularly; I'd lost my touch, so to speak. I still understood the odds of all the hands, but evidently I wasn't paying as close attention to the flow of the game, the expressions, the pace, the nuances of the situation.

During a pause after one game, when I was seriously considering selling my car to have another chance of winning, I caught myself. I realized I was hoping to get lucky, the cardinal sin for a poker player, and I knew I had to either quit the game altogether or quit school again.

Nearly broke due to my recent losses, I was forced to schedule my regular meeting with Regina. I decided her unorthodox physics would be a bearable distraction.

We met at Diner Ninety-One as usual. We arrived at the same time and exchanged greetings as we entered the restaurant. When we sat down, Denise didn't bother asking us if we wanted coffees; she just slid them across the Formica table top.

"Anything else?" she asked.

"I'll have a BLT," said Regina. "Wheat toast."

I ordered a cheeseburger with fries. When Denise left, Regina perfunctorily looked at my grades and handed me a check she had already made out.

"What if I didn't get all A's this time?" I asked.

"Didn't consider that. Maybe we should change the agreement to you only get paid if you get all A's," she said with as serious a look as she could muster.

"You can't change the agreement just like that!" I said, feigning indignation. "I can. For one thing it's my money. For another it wouldn't make any difference."

"True on both accounts," I admitted. I was proud of my accomplishments, and occasionally astonished.

Denise brought our meals and Regina asked her about her children, one of whom had just begun preschool. As soon as she left, Regina launched into the physics of time, where we had left off.

"In the past, I've spoken to you about Werner Heisenberg's so-called uncertainty principle. The reason I say 'so-called' is that he actually spoke of indeterminacy, not uncertainty. His emphasis wasn't simply that we can't know with certainty what occurs during those small intervals and lengths, but that, more specifically, that type of precision doesn't exist."

Regina paused and seemed ready to start a new sentence, then stopped. This happened several times; she fidgeted with her coffee cup as she searched for a response. She would tilt her cup on one point of the bottom rim, with her index finger on the highest point of the handle, and twirl it one way, then the other. She seemed to be totally absorbed with making her cup spin, to the point that I wondered if she had forgotten about our conversation.

Eventually, she continued: "The most obvious strength in our ability to understand the universe might also be our greatest limitation. We tend to visualize the new and unknown in terms of what we already know. Think about attempts to explain Einstein's general theory of relativity, which states that gravity is a result of matter warping space. But what does that mean? Physics texts often depict matter creating a depression in space."

She drew this sketch on a paper napkin:

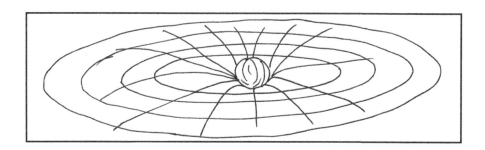

"The idea for this figure borrows from our daily experience, that matter rolls downhill on the Earth due to gravity," she said, showing me the drawing. "With the help of perspective drawing, three-dimensional space is depicted as a two-dimensional plane, and the sphere sinking into the plane shows the effect of gravity. Hence, anything around the sphere would be expected to roll toward it. People are generally comfortable with this explanation, because we always think of things rolling downhill, but 'rolling downhill' is what we're trying to explain! Visualizing the reality indicated by quantum physics is even more difficult. The phenomena it describes are even more removed than is warped space from our common-sense understanding of how things work. In this case I want to describe existence without time, but it's difficult because time is implicit in our act of thinking."

"How do you mean, implicit?" I had taken up trying to twirl my cup, with less success than Regina.

Regina twirled her cup effortlessly in one direction, then another, as if mocking my clumsy efforts. Finally she answered, "There's a nineteenth-century book called *Flatland* that described events in a two-dimensional world," she said. "It was a popular satire of manners that ended with the two-dimensional protagonist realizing he could imagine a three-dimensional world that would allow him to escape some of the social constraints of Flatland. Since then, Einstein has taught us that we live in a four-dimensional universe. And now, I'll ask you to think about looking at our four-dimensional world from a five-dimensional perspective."

"Okay, how do I do that?" I had to quit playing with my coffee cup because Denise had brought us refills. Also I wanted to hear what Regina had to say: I had actually read *Flatland*, so I was interested in her take on its concepts.

"Well, for starters, it means we're looking at time from outside of time." "So we should be able to see all of time—like the future, present, and past all at once?"

Regina nodded. "Let's start there. Now, as you're doing this, you yourself are supposed to be outside time, which means there's no time component to your thinking."

"What does that mean?"

"Frankly, I don't know," she said, chuckling. "That's why thinking about time is so difficult—the very act of thinking is formed by the way thought proceeds with time. Trying to isolate time from our thinking is fundamentally contradictory. All thoughts would need to be simultaneous—one wouldn't follow another, for that would imply time."

She stopped to sip on the burnt diner coffee, then continued, "Let's start with the beginning of our universe—what we call the Big Bang, when the universe evidently started as a single point and began to expand. You know that Einstein revealed that time is a dimension, in some ways no different from the three dimensions of space. However, we know time *is* different from space, at least to us, so we imagine the Big Bang as an asymmetrical event in four dimensions."

Regina paused her lesson while she ate a few bites of her BLT. She poured pepper on my fries and filched some of them, too. When she was ready she began again. "In what we think of as the spatial dimensions, there's a nearly symmetrical expansion, so that one direction appears indistinguishable from another. This is how we normally think of the history of the universe—almost like an explosion, except an explosion is an expansion into already existing space, whereas the universe is expanding space itself. As a result there's a twist, even with this simplified version of imagining the universe: from every point in the universe, one would see stars and galaxies in all directions, as if every point were at the center of the universe. Another twist is that everything we see already has happened—we've spoken about that before—but at cosmic distances, we're dealing with immense time scales. We see things in the night sky as they were millions, even billions, of years ago."

"I understand. Because the universe is expanding, most astronomical objects, especially very distant ones, are moving away from us. Their light appears redder to us because their wavelengths appear longer. That's how we can compute their distance from us."

"Exactly." Regina started drawing on another napkin. "Now imagine the universe in a slightly different way. Instead of it being an expanding ball, think of our three dimensions of space as only two dimensions, so we can use our third dimension to indicate time. As I've said, the universe has expanded immensely, from an infinitesimal point to over forty-three billion light-years across in all directions—but along the time dimension, the expansion is quite different." Regina drew a picture similar to the one below and handed it to me.

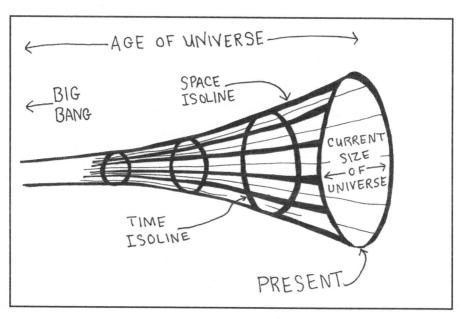

"I've replicated a drawing you might find in an article or textbook about the Big Bang, which shows the universe expanding along its spatial dimensions as it travels along the time dimension. The lines are called *isolines*. The time isolines are circles that indicate the universe at a single instant in time. The space isolines are meant to indicate how a single point in space moves through time. The isolines are assumed not to have any thickness and therefore represent points in space and instances in time. As time goes on, the time isolines become further apart and the circles get larger, indicating the expanding universe. Also, since the entire universe at any point in time exists on the circumference of a circle you can imagine that you could look in either direction from any point and see everything as if you were in the center of the universe."

"That seems pretty clear," I said. I'd seen this basic drawing in my freshman physics textbook.

"This is how I'd draw the picture, though." She made a few changes to her drawing and produced this sketch:

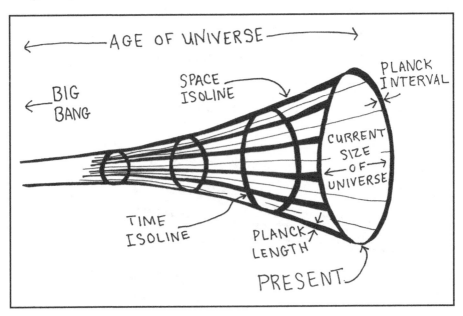

"Here both the space isolines and the time isolines have a minimum dimension, namely their Planck units. The thin circles, for instance, are replaced by a series of thick rings. In my view, we can't speak of infinitely thin isolines of either time or space. It's important to note that although the rings grow in diameter as the universe ages, they don't appear to get thicker. Now think of the intersection of a space isoline and a time isoline as an event—that is to say, a particular place at a particular time is an event. In my drawing we see that an event can't be smaller than its Planck units, so we can call the smallest possible physical event a Planck Event."

"I think I follow you so far." I was finally understanding her version of the uncertainty principle.

"Therefore, though the universe is currently estimated to be some forty-three billion light years across and growing in its three spatial dimensions, it's only 10^{-44} seconds thick along its time dimension, with apparent minimal expansion since the occurrence of the Big Bang."

"I'm not sure I understand," I admitted. We were back in murky territory again.

Regina let out a small sigh. I could see she was putting a great deal of effort in trying to explain her theories to me. "Let's go back to the visual trick of reducing three-dimensional space to two dimensions, and use the third dimension as time."

"Okay. I understand that."

"So, in the picture I just drew, three-dimensional space looks like a ring, which at present has a circumference of forty-three billion light-years."

"Okay."

"And for the other dimension—time—the ring is 10^{-44} seconds thick." "All right. Got it."

"Now consider all the Planck Events that exist at one time—I call this a Planck Moment. It's what appears as a single thick ring in my sketch. From every point in the universe, space extends forty-three billion light years in its spatial dimensions, well beyond our reach. However, we're always at the edge of the universe along the time dimension, constantly moving from one Planck Moment to the next."

I must have shown my surprise at Regina's last statement, because she looked at me as though she wanted an explanation. "It's just that as a kid I used to try to imagine what the edge of the universe was like," I said, "but according to you, we're always at its edge, at least in one dimension."

"Exactly," she said. She sat back in her seat and put her fingers together. The fact that I seemed to have understood this seemed to allow her to relax. "Now imagine that instead of a smooth flow along this time dimension, what occurs is more like a shock wave. To us it appears that space continues unabated through time. Consider instead that each instance of 'now,' each Planck Moment, is created by its awareness of the preceding Planck Moment."

"I'm a little lost, Regina. Is this about using the word 'command' instead of 'force' again?"

She sat up and pursed her lips, then glanced at her wristwatch. Instead of answering my question, she said, "It's getting late, Ron. Think about what I've told you. We can continue next time we get together."

It was early spring, or late winter, depending on your mood. There was a light drizzle of cold rain, but the bicycle trip home was still relaxing. At times I thought I was beginning to understand my mentor's ideas, but at other times it seemed like it might all be nonsense, and the slow ride gave me time to let my conflicting thoughts settle in. I was becoming more and more concerned about Regina's mental health. It was easier to believe she was delusional than to think the greatest minds in physics were wrong. I also wondered why she spent so much effort explaining her ideas to me. It crossed my mind that it was a form of therapy.

On the one hand, it made sense that there might be a smallest unit of time. The Greek philosopher Xeno had great fun with stories like the one about the tortoise and the hare. He described a race in which a hare was trying to catch a much-slower tortoise. In the first unit of time, he'd gain half the gap between himself and his competitor. But then Xeno described a situation in which the next unit of time was only half as long as the previous one, so the hare would only gain half the gap again. Xeno argued that the hare never could catch up, because at each new interval, he only made it halfway to the tortoise. If there *is* a smallest unit of time, however, the argument falls apart because one can't keep dividing time into ever-smaller units.

On the other hand, some of Regina's ideas had been specifically rejected by members of the scientific community. Scientists as astute as Einstein and Bohr, who argued with each other for decades about these matters, both agreed that conceiving of the entire universe as observant was, in their words, "too poetic."

Despite my anxiety, I did enjoy spending time with Regina. My pubescent crush definitely hadn't dissipated: I'd just become an adult. And she was still the only person in my life who'd shown a sustained belief in my talent and a continued interest in my well-being. I realized anguish was largely caused by my fear for her well-being.

Our next conversation took place outside at the end of my junior year, the start of summer vacation. I arrived first and had grabbed a ham sandwich and Dr. Pepper at the student center. I was sitting on the lawn in the center of the campus, which was deserted—typical for the week after finals. The sky was similar to the day I had first met Regina. I began to reminisce about that meeting when she seemed to appear out of nowhere once again. She was just as beautiful and I was just as enthralled as on that first wonderful day.

Regina asked me if I was taking classes over the summer, to which I said I was. (Otherwise I'd need to wait until Christmas for another payment from her.) Then she launched into her physics lesson as though she'd never stopped. It seemed as though she had been thinking about it since our last meeting.

"I've explained that each moment—each Planck Moment—has a finite time dimension—that is to say, duration. This duration is the Planck Interval, which is the smallest meaningful unit of time, so we need to realize that within each Planck Moment time doesn't exist. Think of an analogy to a TV screen. You know that a cathode ray tube consists of an array of individual pixels, right?"

"Sure." I hoped she wouldn't go into detail about something so elementary.

"Good." She, too, seemed relieved that she didn't need to explain a TV screen to me. "For simplicity's sake, imagine this screen has a gradation of white to black from left to right. If you pick a single pixel and look at it closely there would be no gradation within it; the entire pixel is either black or white. The apparent gradation on the screen as a whole is caused by the ratio of white to black pixels at each part of the screen. On the left, all the pixels are white; on the right they're all black, and the ratio of black to white pixels changes across the screen. In the same way, time appears continuous to us, but actually the universe skips from one Planck Moment to the next."

"So are you saying there's nothing smaller than a Planck Length, and nothing shorter than a Planck Interval?" I asked.

"Not quite, but many physicists do believe that. Stephen Hawking, for instance, has commented that the lower limit on the scale of time and space also limits the complexity of the universe. I believe time and space don't exist at smaller units than Planck units, but something else probably does."

"What would that be?" I asked, trying to imagine something other than time and space.

Regina puckered her lips, then looked at her bottle of water. I figured she was going to do some fancy trick with it, like with her coffee cup at the diner, but she started right up again. "I'm not sure. But we can make a few surmises. As you know, Einstein's theory of relativity states that nothing, not even information, can travel through space faster than the speed of light. However, if time doesn't exist within a particular Planck Moment, we can't have a limiting speed of travel within that moment. Speed would have no meaning, because speed is distance divided by time. And if time and speed don't exist, there's nothing to prevent any part of a Planck Moment from interacting with any other part of the same moment."

"Are you saying things can travel faster than light in a Planck Moment?" I asked. It was amazing enough that she was reconstructing quantum physics, but it appeared she was going after relativity as well.

"Pay close attention," she replied, pointing upward with her index finger, as if pointing at her idea. "I'm saying time does not exist in a Planck Moment, so the speed of light does not exist. This conclusion does permit some forms of apparent instantaneous communication, such as the phenomenon known as entanglement, which we can discuss later. For now it's my contention that each Planck Moment must be considered as a unified entity, and no matter how we try to isolate a single event—a Planck Event—in order to analyze how it progresses through time, we can't completely disconnect that event from the rest of its Planck Moment. This is important because one of the most powerful tricks of science is to use analysis, which is to say examining phenomena by breaking them down to their simplest constituents, to see how they behave." Regina paused and took a sip from my Dr. Pepper.

"We do this because we need to simplify our efforts. Once we feel we understand a simple phenomenon, we might try to examine how several such phenomena work together, and gradually try to understand increasingly complex systems. Now imagine two successive events along a single space isoline. We would see this as something happening without motion, because the two events occur at the same place.

"The task of physics is to predict what will happen in the second event, given what we know about the first one. The assumption we must make is that these events are isolated, so nothing else is affecting our experiment. However, because we can't isolate one Planck Event from the rest of its Planck Moment, this assumption isn't true. We don't have simple 'causality,' as we know it, of an isolated event leading to another isolated event from moment to moment. We only have an entire Planck Moment being created by the previous Planck Moment, and each Planck Moment consists of the entire universe during a single Planck Interval."

"So the entire universe at one moment creates the entire universe at the next moment."

"Pretty close. Each moment is aware of the entire command of the preceding moment and creates a new command for the following moment. And for the most part, the transmission is very orderly, which has allowed us to create physics. But each moment has its own internal structure, which we see only indirectly through the measurements that have led to quantum physics. Thus we have a certain amount of what we perceive as randomness—a breakdown of simple causality—which leads to all the collateral strange phenomena of quantum physics. In any case, time is the result of this sequential awareness. That's why I say 'awareness creates time.'"

Now I was confused again, and starting to feel my old resentment well up again. "So why haven't other physicists understood how important awareness is?" I asked her.

"They have, for decades, but it's treated like an enigma rather than a solution."

"There's something about this I don't understand. You said the smallest unit of time is the Planck interval. But in the case of the two-slit experiment, there is a much longer interval than that from when the light leaves the source until it is observed. How can you reconcile this discrepancy?"

"The Planck Interval might be the smallest unit of awareness—and therefore of time as well—but that doesn't mean there can't be longer intervals when we cannot meaningfully speak of time. The important thing to remember is that time never exists without awareness."

Regina finished my Dr. Pepper, then said, "Oops, I've got a class. We can resume our dialogue next time."

It didn't seem like a dialogue to me, but I wished her a nice day and we wandered off in opposite directions. After I had taken a few dozen steps I turned around to watch her leave. She never looked back, but seemed to float away until she disappeared behind the student center.

8

A few weeks later I took a trip back to Mill Falls on a Saturday to visit my old chess friends on the commons. I hadn't been there since the end of my senior year in high school, and I especially wanted to play Mr. Staling again. I didn't see him at his usual location under the hickory tree, so I asked around.

"I think he had a stroke last year," Paul Larrouche told me. Paul was a middle-aged chiropractor who'd been playing at Mill Falls long before my time there. I remembered him as being very fit, and he still seemed trim, but a little white was emerging from his sideburns and a bald spot was creeping onto the top of his head. Even though I seldom had trouble with his game, he was a canny chess player who was able to spot weaknesses in my approach, and would even point them out to me. I appreciated his help and felt we always shared a mutual respect.

"All I know is that he quit coming to Saturday chess, but the rumor is that his kids put him in a nursing home near where they live...somewhere in Ohio, I think. I don't even know if he's still alive. You two used to play each other a lot, if I remember correctly."

"Yeah, he never got tired of my antics."

"Or he didn't mind losing a lot of games," Paul said, smiling to himself. I shrugged. "He won his share."

I played a few games against some of the other regulars and caught up on the lives of the players, their families, and even a few of my former classmates, then returned to Paul's table. He didn't mind talking while playing. He evidently had been on his high school chess team when they'd won the state championship in 1964. He'd seldom beaten me when I played regularly, but my game wasn't what it once was. He seemed to enjoy being able to beat me twice in a row. As we played I remarked on the fact that there were more young players than there used to be.

"That's part of your legacy," Paul told me. "When you left, we realized chess was a dying sport around here. Just us old has-beens were left, so we actively recruited high school students. Some of them are pretty damn good." He gave me a knowing look, as if he were telling me a very personal secret. "I'm not sure any of them would've given you much of a fight in your prime, but I think you might find several of them more than a handful now."

I asked about Mr. Farnsworth, the town official who used to drop by, and found he had become the town administrator in Sandwich, a town on Cape Cod, but Mill Falls continued to support the weekend tournaments in his absence. It was nice to know the show was still going, but I knew that while I pursued my math studies I wouldn't be able to regain my proficiency at chess any more than I could at poker. I'm sure there are those who can do two things at once—walk and chew gum at the same time, so to speak—but I'm not one of them.

I didn't return to Mill Falls again—without Mr. Staling's giggle there was no attraction—but I did occasionally go for long walks in Mill Falls State Forest. I didn't trespass on private property or hike through unmarked woods like I had when I'd followed Cheryl around, but I'd gained enough appreciation of our unbuilt planet to enjoy exploring blazed trails. The long walks helped me reset my wits, and I loved revisiting everything Cheryl had shown me. One day I even called her, and we agreed to have lunch. Maybe my bus conversations with Mrs. Gretchen had made me understand that without a personal life I was missing something.

Cheryl and I met at a Burger King near Fresh Pond in Cambridge, evidently not too far from her apartment. She had changed in the two plus years since we'd last seen each other, but I suppose I had as well. For one thing, she had lost her tan and was working toward her PhD instead of waiting tables. Also, she wore cotton slacks and a printed blouse the day I saw her, instead of her forest trekking gear. Still, she was a beautiful woman, and I was still taken by her big brown eyes.

"I've gathered an immense amount of information over the last few years," she told me, "but now, with the ability to compare the DNA of my samples, I spend most of my time in the lab. I miss the field work, but I've got other work now."

"Is this what you're going to do the rest of your life? I can't imagine you not traipsing all over the woods."

"There's a lot of life left, Ron, I hope. I'm sure I'll regain my balance."

I told her a little about my studies, without talking in depth about Regina. "I told you we each needed to make a dream come true. Maybe we both have," she said.

I wasn't so sure about myself, but I was pleased she was doing something she loved. Before our meeting I wasn't sure how I would feel toward Cheryl, but my feeling of friendship was stronger than any desire to renew an old affair, and it was apparent she felt the same. We wished each other well. When I left, I wasn't certain we'd meet again, but she did remind me how much my life had changed in the couple of years since I'd accompanied her on her research. It seemed a lot longer than that, and I felt a lot older.

My junior year at Northern was kind of a blur—I studied for my classes, and in between I studied more math. I kept my old apartment, but I never brought in new roommates. I met with Regina a few times each semester, and occasionally had lunch with a classmate to discuss a problem. I was not lonely, just engrossed. I discovered I could take two or three extra math courses each semester without sacrificing my grades. Since Regina still paid me for each A, it was worth it.

Some of my math professors were noticing me, which was gratifying. I got advice as to what to do next from several of them, which was confusing at first, as each professor suggested something different. In the long run, however, the confusion was helpful, as each suggestion carried a horizon I hadn't considered. Jack Cuthbertson, the professor with the spectator-sport math pin, helped me research various graduate programs and remarked that a change in scenery might help my creativity. The idea appealed to me.

Regina knew I was looking into several grad schools. "Have you made a decision about next year yet?" she asked the next time we met.

I shrugged. "I don't think it'll be up to me. I'm applying to Princeton, Berkeley, Texas and the University of Washington. I'll just have to see who accepts me. Maybe I should have studied engineering, then I could just get a job."

"Perhaps, but going with what you like to do is usually best. Just make sure you know what that is before deciding on anything."

71

It was typical of Regina not to advise me regarding which course of action to take—just how to decide on that action.

I decided to ask her the question that had been bothering me about her physics explanations. "If it's so obvious that something needs to be observed to collapse the wave function and create an actual event, why are physicists so reluctant to admit it?"

"That's a very important question. It might not be one I can give a convincing answer to, but I will give you my opinion. Do you remember during one of our first conversations on the semantics of physics I said that the word 'force' might carry connotations from Newton's time that continue to shade our current attitudes?"

"I do. You mentioned that it carried with it assumptions from political and religious views about the nature of the universe."

"That's right. Even before Newton there were major controversies between the scientific and religious worldviews. You must remember that Galileo himself was put under house arrest by the Church for years because the pope felt his observations contradicted religious dogma."

"Of course."

"Long before Galileo, philosophers like Roger Bacon had proposed that we should investigate nature through empirical methods. There arose a school of thought that by investigating the 'book of nature' we could discover the nature of God through his works. Of course when those discoveries, such as Galileo's, contradicted the church's interpretation of the 'book of scripture,' the church often reacted vehemently. Science has pretty much abandoned the idea that understanding reality would lead to an understanding of God, although there are individual scientists who do try to use science to prove religious theories."

"Are you trying prove some sort of religious idea?" I asked.

"Not at all. But I do feel mainstream science wants to avoid anything like postulating a conscious universe that could be construed as supporting the existence of God. In fact, one of your first questions was whether I thought the universe was conscious."

"And you said you do not."

"My theory that awareness exists is supported by the evidence. I have never seen evidence that consciousness exists in the universe at large. If I did, I would not hesitate to say so."

"So you think scientists are trying to avoid anything that looks like religion?" "I do. I don't really know much about religion—I was not brought up in a religious household, my family simply never spoke about it. This seems to be a difficult subject for scientists to approach. My own feeling is that it's as if there's this huge, hidden edifice of religion that most scientists try to avoid at all costs, except for the few who are actively trying to prove it exists. This edifice does not exist for me, so I go where the evidence leads." Regina shrugged a little as she tried to gauge my reaction. "Like I said, this might not be a satisfactory answer. I'm a scientist, not a philosopher or theologian."

That night I drove back to my apartment with a new understanding of Regina's point of view. She was correct in remembering that I had wondered if she herself was inserting mysticism into her physics. Still, I remained unconvinced that she might be right and everyone else wrong. Regina's ideas seemed so eccentric, yet so compelling, that she was still drawing me into her world against my will.

9

My senior year at Northern was when I consolidated the base of my mathematical knowledge. Up until then, I'd taken as many courses as I could schedule, but this year I was past that. If I had wanted to, and had been more organized as a sophomore, I could have graduated at the end of my junior year. As it was, I took enough course hours to remain a full-time student and get paid by Regina, but it was pretty much a year of independent study and investigation for me.

By this time I was mostly living in the old Chrysler I'd bought with my poker gains. And though I'd purchased it so I could commute more freely to Foxwoods, I ended up staying closer to the university—I usually didn't get further than the parking lot more than twice a week. I only drove down to the casino two or three times that whole year. I pretty much slept whenever I wanted, seldom for more than two or three hours at a time, and there were several places on campus where I could study through the night. The main library kept the reference room open all the time, and the student center had a lounge that never closed, but my favorite place was the hall just outside the student center cafeteria, where several tables were available twenty-four hours a day. Few students used the area except at lunch and during finals, so a table was usually available. The tables were large, allowing me to spread out my books and notes to work on several lines of thought at once. I kept a separate notebook for each textbook and would hover over the table, moving from one to another then back again. I had come to realize that not all thinking is done consciously—sometimes one needs to let a situation percolate, let the neurons work out the connections on their own.

There were several vending machines nearby, so I could get everything from hot chocolate or coffee to nuts and sandwiches anytime. One night, I'm sure it was past midnight, as I was scribbling out some formulae a young man approached my table. He had the requisite student knapsack over his shoulder and was dressed entirely in black, the same as much of the student body. He was thinner than most though, almost gaunt, with thick long black hair, olive skin, and brilliant light-blue eyes that looked like they were backlit.

"Are you done with that?" he asked, indicating my unfinished sandwich.

His voice was slightly reedy and a little high.

The baloney sandwich he was pointing to hadn't been that appetizing in the first place, and in its unfinished state it looked worse, but I was still gnawing on it and said so. His eyes feigned disappointment, and he began to move on, slowly. I figured he was messing with me, so I decided to play along.

"What the hell...if you want it, take it. I'll get another one." I stood up to walk over to the vending machines. My new friend didn't hesitate; he grabbed the sandwich and practically swallowed it whole. He thanked me and turned away.

"Hey, you want another one? The machines are full of them," I offered. "Sure, I'll take two."

I laughed, and so did he. Then he pulled a couple of sandwiches of his own from his knapsack. "Actually, the ones the cafeteria throws away every day taste better than those. Want one of these?"

"Nah, I'm done." I sat back down to resume my work. The guy sat down opposite me and watched. I finished my last train of thought while he stared at me. We both knew he was testing me, trying to unnerve me by staring at me as I worked, and we both knew the other knew.

"Are you a student?" I finally asked.

"No, I just pretend to be one to keep security from hassling me." "So where do you live?"

"Here," he replied, waving vaguely around. "On campus. "Just 'on campus?'"

"Sure. Where do you live?"

"Hmm, good question. I have an apartment, but I mostly live in my car. About the only time I go to my apartment is to take a shower."

He twisted up his face to show he was incredulous. I thought he was surprised I lived in a car, but he had an entirely different tack. "You go all the way to your apartment just to take a shower? Why not take one here?"

"Where?" I asked.

"Follow me." He got up and waited for me to gather my papers. He was medium height, at least six inches shorter than me, slight, with an energetic, somewhat nervous presence. He took off past the vending machines to an underground pedestrian walkway that led to a parking garage. He stopped at a door I'd passed hundreds of times without noticing. It was a gray steel door with a small sign that read authorized personnel only. My guide opened the door, and I followed him through.

"So, what's your name?" I asked. "Louis. Yours?"

"Ron."

The door led to a stairway that doubled back on itself and ended in a room directly below the walkway we'd just left. To the right and left were swinging double doors opening into long, wide hallways that extended without any apparent end in both directions. Louis opened a single-passage door directly in front of us, and entered a narrower hall. We walked past a couple of unmarked doors to two that were labeled men and women.

"These are university staff bathrooms, but no one seems to use them," Louis said.

We entered the men's door. There was a front room containing a few rows of lockers and wooden benches. The next room had the requisite urinals, stalls, and sinks, along with three showers.

"The far locker is mine." He pointed to one of only three or four lockers with locks.

"How did you get a locker here?"

Louis gave me a puzzled look. "I put a lock on it. It's very handy. You should take one too if you use the showers. You can keep a lot of stuff in there. Hell, take two lockers if you want."

The next time I saw Louis was a few weeks later, in the men's room, just after I'd taken a shower. As I got dressed he said, "You could sleep here too, you know."

"Here?"

"Sure." He stepped up on a bench, placed his hands on the top of the lockers, and using a locker handle as a step, scrambled to the top of the lockers and disappeared. I stood on the bench myself, and although I was tall enough to get a good look across the lockers, I couldn't see him anywhere.

Louis's head popped up from an array of galvanized ducts. "I keep blankets in my locker, but I leave this pad up here." He showed me a corner of a foam pad he was evidently lying on.

"I don't think I could squeeze in there, Louis."

"Probably not, but there are lots of spots around, if you know how to look." "I think I'll stick to my car."

"That works, too."

In the weeks that followed Louis gave me a tour of the university's underground tunnel system.

"Don't go poking around alone. If you get caught in a locked building with sensitive labs or something, it might not go so good," he warned me.

Louis was also an unofficial campus historian. He seemed to know pretty much everything that went on—and had gone on—in the school's buildings. I did not share his interest in spelunking around the campus, but I spent a few interesting evenings seeing the university from a new point of view.

The tunnels Louis chaperoned me through were wide and high enough to easily walk through. Usually there were racks of large and small pipes on one or both sides, and room for workers in the rest of the tunnel.

"These are the lifelines of the campus," he said. "The largest ones are probably steam pipes for the heating system. The others are water lines, electrical conduits, communication lines—practically everything the university needs to function."

"You must know the university underground as well as anyone." He grinned. "I'm sure I know it a great deal better."

"Better than the people who work down here?"

Louis rolled his eyes. "Of course! The staff only know the systems they work on. There are several systems under the university that don't connect with one another. I've shown you parts of this system, which contains all the modern utilities. There's a separate sewer system, and now a separate storm-water system."

"Why did you say 'modern' utilities?"

"I've also found parts of historical tunnels, some of which are abandoned, some of which are still functioning but strangely forgotten. Even the engineers don't have plans for everything under here. Every time they build, they need to explore for forgotten or undocumented infrastructure. And when they find something, they're only interested in what affects their ongoing project. I explore it all."

"Why are you so interested in what's underground?" I asked.

Louis looked thoughtful for a moment. "Well, I'm not, not exactly. I'm not interested in caves, for example. I'm fascinated with things people have built and forgotten. As a mathematician, you're interested in creating new equations and formulas no one has thought of before. I'd be interested in ancient math that could be profound but has been forgotten."

"You seem to have a knack for it. How did you come to explore tunnels?" I'd assumed he would tell me he was homeless and had needed shelter.

Louis was usually quick with a response, but he took a while to formulate an answer. "I'm not sure. I think everyone should enjoy what they do, but often we go beyond that—we act like we've created ourselves, but we haven't. We're born; we have abilities; we learn to use them. This is what I do and what I want to do."

I never became completely familiar with Louis's underground world, but I did find some of the tunnels useful for avoiding winter weather, and they were often a faster way to class than the sidewalks above. Louis had given me an official-looking tag to hang around my neck. "Act like a technician, no one will bother you," he said.

I didn't spend a lot of time with Louis, but he'd occasionally stop by while I explored the hidden recesses of my mathematical world. I don't think he understood or cared about what I was doing, but we shared a respect for each other's passion. I came to understand his seemingly vague statement that he lived on campus; he had several lockers and a myriad of places to sleep, night or day. I pretty much stuck to my car and the student center lounge sofas, but I did confiscate a locker, rent a PO Box on campus, and give up my apartment.

About three months before graduation, Regina and I met at the diner. She seemed a little subdued at first, and then she congratulated me on my acceptance into the PhD program at the University of Washington in Seattle.

She flashed me a smile. "I'm so happy for you...and proud too. But I'm going to miss our conversations."

I hadn't expressed my reservations about her physics, but a
could read my mind, Regina began to apologize. "I never taug
ramifications of my theories, Ron. I need to go over son
phenomena conventional physics never has explained. Standard physics does
postulate the possibility of multiverses—that is, separate universes that coexist and
may or may not interact with one another. But the standard concept of time seems to
assume time travels in a parallel direction for all these multiverses."

Denise must have had the night off, for our waitress was a large, middle-
aged woman who clearly knew her way around a coffee pot. "What are we
having tonight, dears?" she asked.

"Two coffees, please," Regina said.

"Sure you don't want a piece of pie with that? We've got a great homemade
Boston cream pie tonight."

The woman was a pro. Regina and I looked at each other. "Okay, two pieces of
pie."

As soon as our waitress left, Regina started back up without missing a beat. "I
think it should be apparent that I consider time to be a local phenomenon,
specifically the result of one Planck Moment being aware of the previous Planck
Moment, and therefore there can't be an external clock keeping time for all
universes. You might recall that conventional physics says that soon after our
universe came into being it expanded rapidly, much more rapidly than it does now.
Physicists use this concept to explain why matter is so evenly distributed in the
universe, but no explanation has been given for why it happened, or how this
rapid expansion ended. Imagine that at a very early stage of our universe's
existence, less than a second after the Big Bang, another universe crossed its
path on a different time axis from our own. Assuming this other universe is
more massive than ours, it would exert an outward gravitational tug—or a
gravitational command, if you will—on ours that would cause our universe to
inflate rapidly. Then, almost as quickly as it appeared, it would leave along its
own time axis, separating from our universe and ending the accelerated
inflation. This would not only explain how the famous postulated rapid inflation

_d but also solve the even more mysterious puzzle of how it stopped."

knew Alan Guth, a contemporary American physicist, had proposed that our universe underwent what's called *rapid inflation,* which he attributed to negative gravity. Regina was correct in pointing out that the theory had fallen out of favor in some circles because no one had devised a convincing reason why the inflation wouldn't continue indefinitely. In a way her theory was a mirror image of Guth's. Instead of negative gravity acting on matter in the universe, there was normal, positive gravity acting from beyond our universe. Regina barely paused to let me digest her rapid-inflation postulate before launching into another theory. "There's another possible result of this interaction of two universes that may be even more interesting. Consider Einstein's description of how matter affects space, essentially warping it to create gravity, so that bodies of matter attract each other."

At this point our waitress returned with the pies and we took a momentary break from physics as we dove in. The pie was as good as advertised, but after a few bites Regina began again. "One might think of warped space as being like a trampoline, stretching where a body sits on it, then bouncing back when the matter is gone. But matter in our universe doesn't just disappear, it moves around, dragging the distortions it creates in space with it. The matter of the second universe, however, was only momentarily here, and then it disappeared entirely as that universe pulled away from ours. Recalling my theory that awareness creates time, you can understand that awareness of this matter disappears because its entire universe moves away along a separate time dimension. But why would we think the space it distorted in our universe would suddenly snap back to its previous condition? That would take as much work as it took to distort the space in the first place. Because this second universe has a timeline that moves obliquely to our own, it leaves no residual effect except distorted space."

Regina stopped to take another bite of her dessert, and I did too. It didn't seem right to eat while she was trying to explain her views, but it was delicious pie, much easier to digest than Regina Russo physics. As soon as we polished off our pieces she began once more, "I want you to think about this distorted space, Ron. I claim the distortion remains, as if there were still matter distorting it, and those distortions still affect the matter of our universe. This is why it seems there's dark matter throughout our universe, matter that is only affected by gravity. In reality, there's no dark matter at all, only gravitational distortions of space caused by a departed universe many times as dense as our own."

I was dumbstruck—not only because of the enormous implications of Regina's latest theories but also because I was again intrigued with the possibility that she might be right, even though I'd been determined not to get caught in the web of her thoughts.

That night I returned to my usual study table outside the cafeteria. I worked into the early morning on some mathematical ideas I had concerning work I thought I'd be doing in Seattle. I was trying to escape the tug of Regina's theories. Just as I'd decided to go back to my car for the night, a young woman stopped as she was walking by my table. She had long, straight black hair, which draped over her black shawl, which draped over her black dress, which draped over her body.

"Would you like a stale sandwich?" she asked.

"No, not now..." I began, and then I recognized the reedy voice, which didn't seem so high for a woman. "Louis? Is that you?"

She smiled. "Louise."

"You're a woman now?" As I spoke, I realized how stupid I sounded, but the words were already out.

"I am."

"But what are you really?"

"Really? Hmm, really? Are you really into really? Is that what you call what you do, really?" She pointed to my math notebook.

I paused to think about what she was asking. "I like to think it can represent reality."

"Well, maybe I represent reality too." "But..."

"But why do you care if I've got a target or a gun between my legs? Do you want to sleep with me?" She laughed, and so did I. We understood we inhabited different worlds, but we always had been able to connect with each other through humor.

"No, of course not." I paused rather awkwardly. Then I added, "You're pretty convincing either way."

"Thank you." She gave a slight curtsey.

"Is this just part of your 'I am who I am' existence?" "It's part of my explorations, if that's what you mean." "Are you exploring your inner self or something?"

Louise laughed. "Not at all. I don't need clothes to explore my inner self. I like to explore other people's inner worlds. Almost everyone treats men different from women—you are one of the few who even recognized me. It's as if I live on two different campuses, depending on how I present myself."

"Hey," I said, "I've been accepted to grad school in Seattle. I wonder if they have an underground network of tunnels too."

Louise laughed again, "Of course they do. You can't run a campus without one. But like I already told you, I don't think you should go poking around alone."

10

As a future doctoral student, I was invited to a farewell party hosted by the School of Arts & Sciences faculty for those seniors going on to get their PhD's. It was a sort of initiation into the upper ranks of academia.

The party took place in one of the large upstairs rooms of the student center. Along one wall stood a long row of folding tables with paper tablecloths filled with lackluster hors d'oeuvres—buffalo wings, vegetables and ranch dip, stale pastries. Along the opposite wall was a cash bar, and scattered throughout the room were an assortment of unused couches and armchairs. Most of the faculty clearly wanted to get home as early as possible, and the students didn't seem to know what they wanted. There were two other math students I recognized, so we hung around with our professors, and conversation waned quickly. I'd gladly have talked about Hamiltonians and Hermitians (mathematical concepts used in linear algebra and quantum physics), but no one else seemed in the mood.

Half an hour into the party, I found myself standing alone, bored, but not wanting to insult anyone by leaving early. Then I noticed Regina sitting by herself in a wing chair. She had a glass of wine in her hand, but it was full—she didn't seem to be drinking, she just seemed to be absently watching the room. I walked over and sat down next to her. She was in her typical casual attire, but seemed somehow more graceful than usual, and more petite, in this setting.

"Hi, Ron. I hope you're enjoying yourself." Her face lit up a little when she saw me.

"Not really." I explained to her my reluctance to leave.

"You're right," she said. "Even I would be making life that much more difficult for myself if I didn't attend, but as you see I have very little company." She read the look on my face and quickly continued. "I don't have any grad students, and even though the physics faculty would love to get rid of me, I'm still required to attend." This was the first time she had spoken to me about her relationship with the university, and I was somewhat taken aback. Between being secretly in love with her, and being intimidated and puzzled by her physics, I had never been able to penetrate her private life. Her apparently unstable situation unnerved me a little.

We spoke for about fifteen minutes before she stood and told me she thought it was safe for her to leave. I rotated back to a group of my math professors. Professor Randle, a tall, slightly stooped man with a slight Southern drawl, asked me, "Do you know Dr. Russo?"

"Oh, yes—she's responsible for my academic career." I briefly explained our history, leaving out my attraction to her. My professors exchanged glances.

"Well, I'm glad she did something decent," said Randle.

"That's very interesting, Mr. Larsen," said Professor George, a man as tall as Randle but as solid as Randle was slight. He held his hands in front of his chest with his fingertips touching and rhythmically separated one pair of fingertips at a time, as if in a sort of thoughtful prayer. "I wouldn't venture to interfere in a friendship, but a little inquiry into her research might save you some professional embarrassment."

There was evidently a side to Regina I didn't know. I searched the group's eyes for an explanation.

Randle spoke up again. "I dare say none of us knows her, but she does have a past with issues. You should find out more about her."

After the reception, which ended around ten, I had nowhere to go besides my car, so I walked through the student center hoping I'd see Louis/Louise. I wanted to say good-bye and also give her my car. It had served me well, but I wasn't sure it would make it across the continent, and I didn't really need it anyway.

I didn't see her anywhere, so I checked a few halls in the tunnels below, but struck out again. I gave up and started toward the tunnel's exit, and as luck would have it—or maybe not just luck—I ran into Louise on my way out.

"Do you have a minute?" I asked. "I have something for you."

"Ron, I always have time for you," she said with a sly smile. Louise was definitely more flirtatious toward me than Louis ever had been.

"I told you I'm leaving tomorrow, didn't I?"

Louise nodded. "You did. I'm going to miss you. Did I tell you that?" "Yes."

"You're not looking too good, Ron. Is everything okay?"

I told her about my experience at the reception. She listened carefully. "Did you say Dr. Russo?"

"Yes, she's the reason I'm at Northern in the first place. Do you know her?" "I've never met her, but I know something about her. I'll show you."

Louise led me through her tunnel world. I'd often thought of the tunnel system as a maze, but it was just the opposite—it made going from any point on the campus to any other much more efficient, as there were no buildings or roads in the way. Nevertheless, I was quickly lost. Louise moved quickly and confidently until we reached a nondescript door that read MASS 302.

"This is the third basement of the physical science labs, Masson Hall. We'll go up one floor to the second basement. Be careful, be quiet, and don't touch anything."

I followed her down a wide hall overfilled with carts filled with unrecognizable equipment in apparent disuse. It looked like a long warehouse. "We need to be especially careful on these floors, since many of the rooms contain highly classified experiments," my guide warned me. I could see through the windows on some of the doors, but many were covered with paint, foil, or cardboard on the opposite side of the glass. We climbed up a flight of stairs to a floor that looked just like the one below, cluttered and secretive. Finally we approached a door with a clear window. Rather than just look in,

Louise proceeded to unlock it.

"Most of these doors have pretty good alarms, so I don't want to open any of them now, but this room is different." She said this as if opening an alarmed door would simply be an inconvenience. She swung the door open, and I followed her in. What I saw underwhelmed me.

It looked like a basic conference room. No exotic equipment, no charts or computers or other electronic meters—just a table, chairs, and a blackboard. I turned to Louise. Evidently my face revealed my confusion, and she launched into an explanation.

"This room used to be a lab like the rest of the rooms on this floor. Five or six years ago there was an explosion. The lab was destroyed, and a young grad student was killed. Apparently two professors shared the lab. Dr. Russo was one of them, and the student who died worked for the other. It's not clear who was responsible for the explosion, but suspicion fell on your mentor. This room was never used as a lab again. It was turned into a meeting room and named in honor of the student who died, Manisha Kapoor." She paused for a moment, worry flitting across her eyes. "We'd better get out of here."

Louise quickly led me back to the student center. She was used to being on her own, and I think I was beginning to make her nervous. She seemed to enjoy my company when we were bantering above ground, but she didn't always trust me in her underground world. She offered me her hand. "I'm going to miss you, Ron."

"I want to give you something before I go." I handed her the keys to my car, along with the title and registration. "You can't drive it underground, but maybe you can spend a little more time up here."

Louise stared at the keys as if she didn't recognize what they were. Then she smiled. "How do you know I can drive?"

"I don't. You can keep it or sell it. At the least you can sleep under the stars sometimes."

"Is that where you're sleeping tonight?"

"Yes. I don't have places all over campus like some people." She seemed a little puzzled, but I thought I knew what she was thinking. "Don't worry. I've got an extra key." I pulled the spare out of my pocket.

She gave me a coy look. "Is there room for two?"

Now I was surprised. "Of course. Driver's side or passenger?" "Driver's. It's my car," she said, smiling.

"Of course. Anyway, the steering wheel gets in my way."

"Well, sir, you know, it's a dangerous world up here. Would you mind escorting a lady to her new abode?" Louise offered her arm to me as if we were entering a ballroom. I took it, and we walked arm in arm through the array of parked cars to my old sedan. With a bow, I opened her door, then walked around to my side.

My car was stuffed with everything I owned, which I felt bad about unloading on Louise. I'd moved enough junk from behind the front passenger seat so I could lean it all the way back. I settled in, then realized my friend couldn't do the same on her side because of the stuff behind her seat. But she just curled up in her seat, laid her head on my lap, and fell asleep. She reminded me of a cat one of my foster families had owned.

I woke when the sun pushed its rays through the front window. Louise was gone, and I was more irritated than ever with Regina. She'd been hiding her past from me. I supposed she wasn't obligated to tell me anything about herself, but she'd inserted herself deeply into my life, and I was frustrated that I couldn't push through her defenses. Now she was going to drive me to Bradley Airport, and I needed whatever money she was going to give me, so I braced myself for more of her fantastical physics.

Regina drove a thirty-year-old MGB English sports car. It was cuter than practical, but it was a beautiful day and she had the convertible top down, so cute was nice. I mused that it was a good thing I wasn't taking more than a backpack to Seattle with me, but of course Regina knew me well enough to know I would travel light.

She seemed unusually subdued, even withdrawn, when she picked me up. Although I'd become somewhat surly toward her lately, she usually remained calm, gracious, even sweet. I assumed I was finally beginning to irritate her as much as she irritated me. After a silent few minutes, she pulled onto the freeway.

"Ron, I'm going to miss more than our conversations," she finally said, or rather shouted over the noise of the wind. "I'm going to miss *you*. As you must have noticed last night, I don't have a lot of friends around here." I thought she might finally explain her situation, but instead she immediately went back to her explanations of the universe.

"Perhaps you recall that I theorized that one could envision the world as expanding in its spatial dimensions, but evidently not in time. I used the image of a ring expanding radially—but not growing along its time dimension, the direction the successive rings appear to move. And I mentioned that the depth of the universe along the time dimension is equal to the Planck Interval," she yelled. Regina usually spoke in such a soft voice, it was strange to hear her explaining her views so loudly.

"I remember," I replied, in a curt shout. Regina ignored my attitude. I was beginning to realize she was intentionally overlooking my bad manners.

"Of course, reality is a little more complicated. The sketch I drew for you showing the relation between the Planck Interval and the Planck Length seemed to indicate the universe traveling in a straight line. But nothing is so perfect. I believe the universe travels in a spiral, a tight four-dimensional spiral that creates some interesting effects."

I was looking around at the Connecticut suburbs we were passing. I'd never been outside of New England and was wondering about my new home. I wasn't in the mood for one of Regina's lectures, so her words didn't completely register the first time through. "A spiral?" I said, as I imagined the universe as a football pass.

"In my earlier depiction, I claimed that not only does time have a minimum dimension, but space does as well. I drew both the time and space isolines with the thickness of their relative Planck dimensions."

"I remember that, too," I said, the image of the universe as a football fading. "Well, my explanation probably was a little too simple." I wasn't ready for more complications from Regina, but I couldn't jump out of a car doing seventy. "There's a sketch in the glove compartment I want you to look at," she continued.

I pulled out the drawing below:

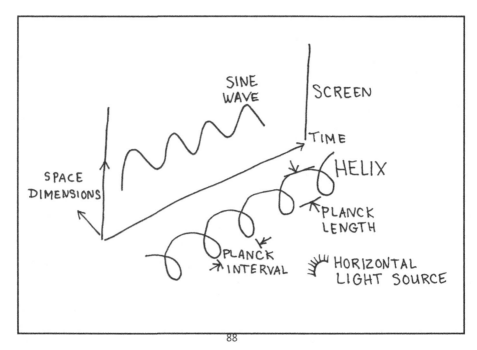

"That drawing is meant to be a close-up of the space isolines, but instead of just fat lines, imagine they are actually spirals. Think of a normal helix, like a spring. There are two important parameters: there's the radius of the spring and the pitch, or the distance from one revolution of the spring to the next. In my theory, the time traveled during one revolution of the spiral, the pitch, is the Planck Interval, and the radius of the spiral is the Planck Length." She glanced over at me to see if I was paying attention.

"In other words, instead of a space isoline having the thickness of the Planck Length, there's a space 'iso-spiral' that has the diameter of the Planck Length," I said.

"That's right."

I interrupted her before she could continue. "I thought one obtained the Planck Length by multiplying the Planck Interval by the 'c' constant, the speed of light. That is to say, the Planck Length is how far light travels during a Planck Interval."

"We need to rewrite the equation. The Planck length and Planck interval are physical phenomena, and the speed of light is their ratio. It's this interaction between time and space that creates the limits described in relativity." She had taken a long, swooping exit off the freeway. I had never been to Bradley Airport before, though I had passed this exit many times on my way to the Foxwoods casino. The excitement caused by the anticipation of my new adventure had started to take over my thoughts, but this new twist on Regina's theories brought me back to the car.

"But I thought you described time as a shock wave, with each Planck Moment being created by the previous moment."

"Each Planck Moment is created by its awareness of the previous moment," she said, correcting me. "But think about projecting a spiral onto a plane parallel to the axis of the spiral—as if you took a stretched-out Slinky and shone a light through it from one side, as shown in that sketch."

We'd reached the departure area for my flight. Regina stopped next to the curb and, ignoring the general hubbub of the airport, she continued to explain her theory while pointing at her drawing.

"You'd see a sine wave," she said, now in her usual soft tone, "and if you were to shine the light from above, you'd get another sine wave out of phase with the first by half the length of the wave, half a Planck Interval. If you can imagine expanding this to three spatial dimensions, each projection would be out of phase with the other two. If you were able to look in only one direction, it might appear as though the Planck Intervals were shock waves, but because of the spiraling effect of the four-dimensional helix—and because space in each direction is out of phase with every other direction—there isn't a sharp disconnect between one Planck Moment and the next. In fact, if you think about it, the fact that each direction in space is out of phase with every other direction means space as we know it cannot exist below the Planck Length."

"Why not?"

"Because space as we know it is identical in all directions, but that can't be true below the Planck Length if every direction is out of phase with every other. If the nature of space depends on the direction in which we are looking, then the assumption of modern science that space is isotropic cannot be true."

As she was speaking an airport traffic cop told us to get moving, so I began to get out of the car while still talking. "So the speed of light is a constant determined by the spiral geometry of space-time?"

"Not quite constant. Again, imagine a spiral, but one that starts at a point. Now imagine each spiral revolution has a slightly larger diameter than the previous one, but the pitch remains constant. As the speed of light is the ratio between the two dimensions of the spiral, and the numerator of that ratio grows, the speed of light increases as well."

I retrieved my pack from her trunk. "How do you know all this?" I asked her bluntly. Her physics was getting wackier each time I saw her.

"Stephen Hawking gave me my first inspiration. He developed the concept of imaginary time."

"That sounds about right to me," I muttered. Her whole world seemed imaginary. I was losing interest fast, anxious to move on to my new horizons. "Hawking used the word 'imaginary' as in 'imaginary numbers,' which we graph as perpendicular to real numbers, but they're very real and very useful. His idea was to imagine time has a perpendicular dimension in order to explain certain periodic quantum/relativistic phenomena. I realized that if space-time progressed in a spiral, the spatial dimensions could be seen as giving time a second—albeit virtual—dimension that would still satisfy Hawking's requirements. Anyway, one thing to remember is that the speed of light is involved with another, even more famous ratio. Rewrite $E = Mc^2$ as $E/M = c^2$. As the speed of light increases, the ratio of energy to mass increases. Assuming there's a constant amount of mass, the amount of energy in the universe must increase. This is the so-called dark energy of the universe."

"So in your theories, you've rewritten Newton's laws, explained time and imaginary time, the rapid inflation of the early universe, dark matter, dark energy, quantum strangeness, and the speed of light." I was trying to sound sarcastic, but Regina blithely ignored it.

"Yes, I have. Like I said, Ron, I'm going to miss you. If you ever come back, I'll give you the evidence."

11

My PhD adviser, Dr. Preston Thayer, had invited me to come to Seattle at the beginning of the summer. I assumed this meant he wanted me to start my work early, so I headed to his office the day after I arrived in town—where I found him closing up his office for two months.

"I spend summer vacation on Lopez Island, up in the Juan de Fuca straits. If you get tired of Seattle in the summer, which you shouldn't, you might like to hike around some of the islands." Dr. Thayer locked his office door, then stopped. "Oh, wait. I want to give you something."

My new mentor was a little rumpled, which was typical for a mathematics professor. He had one of those stubble beards that had become popular among young men, but in his case I think it was because he'd quit shaving for the summer. He was a little younger than I'd expected, but not young enough to still have all his hair, which, being originally blond, didn't yet expose whatever gray there was.

He unlocked his door, and I followed him into his office. It was everything you'd imagine from a distracted mathematician: papers everywhere, a single chair, barely enough room at his desk to put his elbows on. And as Dr. Thayer was a pioneer in using personal computers to work with statistics, more than half a dozen personal computers were scattered around: two at his desk, a couple on the floor, others on a shelf without monitors, all wired together. I'd never seen an arrangement like this before.

Thayer fumbled around for a while, then handed me a shabby-looking booklet. "This is Dr. Gerald Smythe's doctoral thesis. He was one of my students a few years ago. I think he's teaching at a community college in Texas now. I suspect you'll have more luck than he did in developing this line of thought." With that, my adviser and future mentor left for his summer vacation.

The thesis he handed me attempted to use Bayesian statistics to predict stock markets. A few minutes into it, I realized why Smythe was teaching at a two-year college instead of a major research university. He might have been a great teacher, but his use of mathematics was unimaginative.

I don't believe I've looked at his thesis once since that first time. At the time it was more imperative that I find a summer job. I was a little unsettled—I had thought Dr. Thayer would have put me to work right away, but he just assumed I would want to be in Seattle all summer. Although I was on a full scholarship, no funds would be coming from the university until I started working in the fall. I had to find a place to live and employment.

My first job was to stand in a tiny stall making a strange drink called an Orange Julius, which consisted of sugar, orange juice, and a raw egg. It was a great drink for college students, but serving them all day was mind-numbing, and standing there for hours during the slow summer session made it even more so. I was beginning to wonder whether I'd made a mistake. After a week or so I found a different job, at a used bookstore across the street named A Musing Bookstore, and quit selling Orange Juliuses. I wasn't much of a reader, but the owner, Eugene Wallace, didn't care.

"Most of my staff have been literature majors. It'll be good to have a math guy around," he mused.

Though the store wasn't busy during the summer, Eugene made his real money writing papers for students. There was nothing he couldn't write, including fiction. He told me he'd even written a few math papers. For a second I wanted to ask him if he'd written Smythe's doctoral thesis, but I was sure he would've done a more professional job.

Eugene was an elderly African-American, in the Southern sense of elderly. He had impeccable manners, the kind that put you at ease instead of making you feel self-conscious. He was somewhere between small and tiny, yet had a confidence I'd never seen elsewhere, except perhaps in Regina Russo. He never seemed to rush, never seemed to stop. He was attentive when he spoke—in the present, so to speak—but his face revealed ancient epics of remote lands.

Of course, this was just before the Internet made plagiarism so easy that anyone could fake their own papers. Summer was profitable for Eugene because many of the kids were taking remedial courses and needed help. As I mentioned, the bookstore was pretty quiet so I found myself spending big chunks of the day browsing through his books, some of which were truly beautiful. My favorites were nineteenth-century natural histories, particularly a few written in German. Maybe they reminded me of Cheryl and our forest escapades, but they were mesmerizing in their own right. I couldn't understand the text, but the magnificent illustrations allowed me to more clearly understand some of the patterns Cheryl had tried to teach me. I also became fascinated with some of the newer books featuring computer-generated mathematical graphics, especially a gorgeous tome depicting the shapes of various fractals.

One afternoon I read through some papers Eugene had left on his desk, including a few short stories. The word 'polymath' came to mind. When he returned, I asked him, "Do you ever consider that you could have been successful in any number of professions?"

He shrugged nonchalantly and began sorting a pile of books he had bought earlier in the day. "I consider my bookstore a success."

"It's nice, but you're an extraordinary writer. I don't even read much, and I'm impressed. Wouldn't you rather write your own ideas, under your own name, than produce papers for underachievers?"

"Why do you work hard, Ron? Are you trying to be famous? Rich? Powerful?" "None of those. I started working hard because I met someone who expected me to. Now I guess it's because I enjoy what I do."

"I enjoy this." Eugene waved a hand around the store. At first I felt he was talking around my question, but he continued, "I work for my freedom. I read what I want, I write what I want, I go where I want. If I were part of an institution, or famous, I wouldn't have the same personal freedom. Besides, as an underachiever, I enjoy helping other underachievers. You yourself admit you started because someone helped you." As he said this, his smile was like a warm cloak on a cold day.

*

A week or two before classes started, Dr. Thayer called me into his office. "Did you read Smythe's thesis?" he asked.

"Some of it."

He took his glasses off, folded them carefully, put them in his shirt pocket, and looked at me. "How much is some?"

"About two lines."

I didn't know if Thayer was going to tell me to go back to New England, and I'm not sure I cared. I did know I wasn't going to waste several years in Seattle so I could teach at a junior college. He examined me for a minute, then grinned. "Good. I hope you can do better."

"I doubt it."

This time his scrutiny didn't end with a smile. "Don't you think you have more talent than Dr. Smythe?"

"I have a lot more talent than him. I also have enough sense not to try something that's not worth doing. The goal itself is great, everyone from Claude Shannon on has tried to figure out how to predict the stock market."

Thayer leaned back in his seat. I had been standing, but I realized this conversation might take a while, so I sat down on the corner of his desk. He asked, "Then you don't believe in Bayesian statistics?"

"Sure, it's a great tool for the right task. This isn't the right task." "And why not?"

As I tried to formulate an answer, I was reminded of Regina's ideas about predicting the future. Her premise was that we create a fantasy world of the future based on phenomena that already has passed. And it often works, but it isn't an easy thing to do.

"Smythe tried to start by building a simple model that predicts stock prices based on a limited database," I explained, "with the hope of adapting the model to more comprehensive data as the model became successful. Even though I'm certain I'm a better mathematician, I don't think I can make that approach work. More than half the exercise is obtaining meaningful data. Creating a model based on scant or faulty data won't necessarily have relevance for extensive data. With the stock market, we're trying to use the past to predict a future that's going to be very different, for instance when a stable rising market is about to change to an unstable, falling market."

"Do you think you have a better approach?"

"Maybe. I'd like to explore fractals." I had no idea if fractals would be of any value, but I knew I didn't want to follow Smythe's lead. I guess I was enamored by those beautiful graphics I'd been studying all summer.

"Fractals? How the hell could that work?" Dr. Thayer was usually pretty calm and unruffled, but my proposal caught him off guard. I believe he thought I was just trying to bullshit him.

"Well, fractals are self-similar objects, meaning they're nonscalable. You can't tell what scale you're observing, because a fractal has the same patterns at all scales. So as soon as a fractal system—such as I suspect stock prices are— changes, the change should be noticeable at very small scales. In this case, that means incredibly small fluctuations very early in the process will predict larger fluctuations somewhat later."

"So you want me to pay you to fool around with fractals?"

I shook my head. "No, first we need to find meaningful, comprehensive data. Then I can fool around."

It didn't take an expert psychologist to see that Thayer was surprised by my approach, but he surprised me as well. "Let me think about it. We'll talk tomorrow."

I won't claim I spent the next day in great anticipation of my new mentor's decision. If I was worried, I don't remember it now. I do remember being curious—both as to whether Thayer would accept my proposal and as to whether my proposal would work.

Perhaps I was more worried than I recall. I waited in front of Thayer's office for more than an hour before he showed up. "Oh, Mr. Larsen, I'm glad you're here. I've been thinking about your proposal." He led me into his office and we sat down. "On the one hand, I'm highly doubtful that your line of attack will bear fruit. On the other, I agree with your assessment of Smythe's work, and I still need you to grade homework and run my tutorials. Looking at the situation using classical risk analysis, I see a low probability of success but a very high payoff if you do succeed. Fortunately, the marginal cost to the school at this point is relatively low, so I'm going to approve it, on one condition."

"That condition being...?" I asked.

"As you pointed out, you'll need access to high-quality data. I have a colleague in the economics department, Dr. Rastowski, who could help. If you can put together a formal proposal to convince him to help you, I'll give you a year to show me something valuable."

I had no idea how to write the proposal, partly because I'd never done one before, but most of all because I didn't know exactly what I was proposing. So I didn't even try. Thayer made a call and told me when to report to Rastowski's office the following day. I spent a little time clarifying my ideas to myself, but I didn't even make notes. I was beginning to get tired of school, and while walking down another long corridor of featureless doors, I thought about leaving. I wasn't interested in returning to New England, but California beckoned— warm winters would be nice. I had heard some of the defense contractors like Lockheed hired mathematicians.

Though there was nothing distinctive about the door to Rastowski's office, the interior was like the boardroom of a large corporation. For one thing, the office was about three times the size usually allocated to professors. For another, it was completely free of clutter. One wall did consist of a floor-to-ceiling bookcase, but the books were expensive looking and neatly arranged, many of them were leather-bound sets that no one ever reads. In the middle of the room sat a large oval table so polished that it reflected the faces of the seven or eight people sitting around—Dr. Rastowski and his doctoral students.

They were all dressed in business suits, including the two women. Dr. Rastowski stood out because he was the only one over thirty, but he was still at least twenty years younger than Dr. Thayer. And although most professors wore suits, or at least ties, Rastowski's three-piece, tailored Italian suit was several cuts above the normal off-the-shelf wear most of his colleagues sported. "Ah, we have a guest. Ron Larsen, I believe?" he said as I entered the room.

"Yes, sir."

"Please sit down. We need to finish a little business, but we'll be right with you."

They went back to their discussion on some technical point I didn't understand. Rather than attempt to follow their lines of thought, I tried to get comfortable with the idea of making my presentation to a group of highly educated strangers. Since I hadn't even prepared a case for my proposal, and I had expected to talk to Rastowski privately, I was a little unnerved. I took some solace by telling myself I didn't really care what they thought of me or my ideas.

After the group finished its discussion, Dr. Rastowski turned to me. "Our guest evidently has a proposal for us from the math department. My good friend Preston Thayer asked us to listen without prejudice and use our best judgment. We're ready to hear you out, Mr. Larsen."

I'd decided to present my idea using the most technical language I could muster, rather than simplify my explanation. When I finished, the room was silent—silent for just long enough for me to think I'd fallen flat—and then the questions came. Most of them had to do with the purpose of my effort, what I hoped to achieve. A few of the students asked about fractals. Dr. Rastowski didn't ask anything until the questions petered out. After a second silence, he spoke up.

"Do any of you want to spend the next six months helping Mr. Larsen with his project?" He looked around the room.

No one said anything for a while, and then someone asked, "What do we get out of it?"

Dr. Rastowski smiled. "Well, if Mr. Larsen succeeds, you can help him become rich and famous." Silence again. Then one of the women said, "I'll give it a shot."

"Ah, Dr. Park. I thought you might be interested." I'd noticed Dr. Park as soon as I'd entered the room: she was a stunning woman, tall and sleek with red hair tied back in a neat bun and green eyes that practically lit up the room. She was one of the most beautiful women I'd ever seen, but she certainly didn't look like a 'Doctor'. If I was the youngest person in the room—and I was—then she was next. "I'll let you two work out your own arrangements. Everyone's dismissed."

As the students stood up to leave, Dr. Park slipped me a business card. "Give me a call," she said. Her card simply had her name, Sheila Park, and a phone number.

I admit I was staring at her as she walked away, until Dr. Rastowski's words dragged me back to him. "Mr. Larsen, we need to speak before you go."

I was relieved to have a word with him. "Mr. Larsen," he began again. "Just call me Ron."

"Fair enough, Ron. I have no idea whether your project has any hope of succeeding, though I hope it does. But I do want to talk to you about Sheila Park."

"Good. She's very young."

We were standing face to face. He took half a step toward me and lightly placed both hands on my shoulders. "Are you being funny? She's not as young as you."

"True, but I was wondering how she'll find the time to help me." "You're what? Twenty-three?"

"Next week."

"And you've managed to get into our mathematics doctoral program, which is commendable, since it's a very competitive program. When Sheila was your age, which was nine months ago, she was defending her doctoral thesis— exceptionally well, I might add. Currently she's a postdoctoral fellow and can do what she wants with her time. Her father, Jake Park, is a successful and influential broker on Wall Street. She aims to follow in his footsteps. In any case, he's provided enough of an endowment to this department that Sheila can spend as much time here as she wishes, doing whatever she wants."

I'm sure I showed my surprise at the name of Jake Park. Mr. Park was well known as a maker and breaker of major corporations, as well as a confidant of politicians and presidents from both sides of the aisle. I had not associated Sheila with her father. "Good to know. Thank you." I turned to leave, wanting to track down my new partner.

He put a hand out to stop me. "That's only a small part of what I want you to know. To put it bluntly, if you're as successful as you hope to be, you might be able to keep up with her. If not, she won't even notice her wheels squealing over you as she leaves you in her dust."

I wasn't sure whether he was advising me to stay away from her or not, but she seemed like the most promising partner I could ask for, as well as being gorgeous. "Thanks for the warning," I said, anxious to find my new associate.

"Again, that's only the preface. As competent as Sheila is, her mother died a few years ago, and she's the darling princess of her family. If her father decided he needed to protect her, he'd churn over you until there was nothing left. And her two older brothers—both lawyers—could and would do anything he demanded."

I looked at Rastowski to see if I could find hidden meanings in his countenance. "Should I be worried?"

He shook his head. "I don't think so. Sheila's not unkind, just ambitious. As long as you're as straightforward as you seem, the only thing you risk is failure. Anyway, you should call her soon. She's pretty impatient, and you two have a lot of work to do."

12

I lived just north of the campus. The houses in that neighborhood, though quite elaborate, were smaller and newer than those in my old Foxfield neighborhood. They were a combination of the Craftsman school from the early twentieth century, with a few touches from the Swedish immigrants who moved to the northwest then. Seattle is a newer city, and the histories of its neighborhoods are less complex than Foxfield's. There was some ongoing gentrification occurring at the time I was there, but the boom and bust cycles of Seattle have been more rapid than those in the older Eastern cities, and their effect on housing less pronounced.

The University of Washington seemed like a more integrated campus than Northern's, perhaps because it had started as a public research university instead of an agricultural school, and had been built up over a shorter period. The university, however, had changed the neighborhood around it quite profoundly. Unlike the buildings in Foxfield, most of these structures weren't large enough to divide into separate apartments, so it was common for a family to occupy the house and rent out the extra rooms. I had rented such a room about three blocks from campus. As I didn't have a private phone, I called Sheila from a pay phone on campus.

"Hello," she answered.

"Sheila, this is Ron Larsen. I'd like to get started with you as quickly as possible," I said. "I don't think my mathematics adviser has much faith in me."

She gave me an address. "Why don't you come over now? We can begin right away."

I was thrilled she was ready to get started and headed directly to the address she had given me. It was only a few blocks from my own room, one street east but right next to the university campus. I was surprised she would rent a room like me. It turned out she owned the house herself and was the sole occupant. Sheila met me at the door. She was wearing a black ankle-length silk dress, quilted and embroidered with what appeared to be gold thread. Her red hair was thick and undone, surrounding her head like a halo of flames. "Would you like a coffee or anything?" she asked as she led me inside.

"No, I'm good." I was a bit hesitant. I was still thinking of Rastowski's warning and was wondering why she wanted to meet at her place.

"Your presentation was impressive, Ron, but do you think you can back it up?" She got right to the point.

"I have no idea. That's why I want to try." There was no use in overselling my idea, but I wanted her to understand I was serious.

"I like it. Let me show you something." I followed her through the large parlor to the rear of the house. I felt like I was following a Druid priestess to a sacred copse.

The most remarkable thing about Sheila's home was that it didn't look anything like a student's lodging, at least not any student I knew. There were no shelves of cinder blocks and boards, no mattresses strewn on the floor, no unmatched chairs. Her rooms were remarkable in how normal they were—not quite ostentatious, but everything worked together. Though the furnishings were used, all were of obvious quality. In short, it looked like a real home.

I supposed this was how comfortable wealth must work: useful, with no need to impress. The rear entrance she led me to was locked, and as she reached for her keys I noticed it was protected by a steel door. Inside were two large computers. Louise had once shown me the room that housed the mainframe computers at Northern—these looked like the same type. As I examined the room, Sheila examined me.

"Impressive. Rastowski told me you had resources," I said. I didn't want to cover up the fact that we had discussed her. I decided from the start to err on the side of too much honesty with Sheila.

She nodded. "I *do*, but what's important is how they are used. These machines are castoffs from Park & Goldfarb, my dad's company; they're switching to smaller, more flexible units. But when we set up the economics department with a state-of-the-art system, we decided to piggyback these onto it so we could use the same software and access the same files. I bought this house so I could set up a line directly from campus. Anyway, I can obtain any type of market information, historical or real-time, that you want. Where do we start?"

We stayed up most of the night discussing my project and spent nearly every night from then on working until morning. I have a distinct proclivity for late nights, as did Sheila. But though I was used to working long and odd hours, I'd always worked alone before. Sheila was beautiful enough that I wouldn't have needed any other reason to spend time with her, but to have a companion who not only grasped my ideas, but could respond with her own creative augmentations made the project that much more interesting.

We settled on a conventional choice of studying the S&P 500 stocks for the four decades from the mid-'50s to the mid-'90s. We felt there was plenty of data, many different kinds of market trends, and it was recent enough to be relevant.

Sheila and I hit it off from the beginning. We had different backgrounds and different strengths, but she was incredibly bright and had no trouble following my mathematical lead. She also had a profound knowledge of markets, and made sure I stayed on track with my theorems. Almost as important, we shared a dry sense of humor, which allowed us to work closely for long hours without much irritation. I understood Dr. Rastowski's warning would be relevant for anyone of lesser talent or energy, but our personalities and ambitions were in synch.

I had other duties besides my research project and felt enough gratitude toward Dr. Thayer to try to discharge them properly, but Sheila and I spent every spare minute we had trying to understand the data. Just two months into our research, we felt we understood enough of the fractal nature of the market to move from historical simulations to real-time predictions.

It was then that I first understood why Regina had emphasized the importance of prediction for scientific studies. There was an excitement in foretelling the future that was different from simply understanding a phenomenon. By the end of my first semester we felt we had proven to ourselves that my initial impulse had been correct and that we were on our way to creating a useful model.

It hadn't taken long for me to move out of my room into Sheila's house, and not much longer to move from the extra couch to her bed. We spent nearly all our time together, so in some ways it wasn't that different from my senior year, when I spent nearly all my time in my mathematical world, except now there were two of us. I have said mathematics was a refuge for me. I now felt I had a partner to help me create a whole new world.

Sheila often said she lived by the motto 'Work hard and play hard'. "What good is it to amass a fortune if you don't enjoy it?" she asked me one morning. We were eating at our usual breakfast spot, Simon's Simples, a café about four blocks from her house on University Drive. Neither of us could cook, and we found the routine of a short walk and a quick meal to begin the day served us well. Some days we would split up for our separate tasks, other days we would simply go back to her computers together.

I replied that I hadn't amassed a fortune and wasn't sure she had either. "Then let's enjoy the fortune my dad has amassed."

I had considered myself wealthy when I could afford my own apartment, so I'd never considered how to enjoy a fortune. Sheila had.

One of her regular entertainments was to throw a party once a month for faculty and grad students of the economics and business schools at the university. She'd also invite various influential members of the Seattle business community. These weren't perfunctory get-togethers like the one Northern had for its soon-to-be doctoral alumni, but well-planned, enjoyable affairs. They were catered by Dimitri's, a local Greek restaurant that made some of the finest desserts I'd ever tasted—baklava, loukoumades, galaktoboureko, pastafrola, and more—as well as incredibly rich, thick coffee that seemed to come from another planet, one more richly endowed with flavor than our own. And of course there always was a free, amply stocked bar with a professional bartender. Sheila said she'd bought the house primarily for her computers, but it was equally well set up for her soirees.

At first I felt out of place at these functions. No one discussed their research, or anyone else's, unless it had to do with some profitable market share. But there was always a pleasant camaraderie, with the emphasis on ambitious networking all around.

"Your parties are fun," I told Sheila one evening after her company had left, "but it seems everyone's using everyone else." We were in her living room enjoying a bottle of Retsina together. Sheila saw her soirees as an extension of work, so she herself never drank during a party, and I soon followed suit just to act responsible. The caterers were cleaning up, but we knew better than to get in their way by trying to help.

Sheila showed no irritation with my naïveté. "These are people who either control the world now or will in the future—movers and shakers, if you will— and they all know it. Their purpose in life, and mine, is to use one another. The only ethical question is whether they're using each other properly."

I was trying to digest this frank and, to me, novel way of looking at people when she added, "Humans are, after all, primarily social animals. That's our great advantage, the wellspring of our intelligence. And what does it mean to be social other than to be able to use one another?"

I took a sip of the wine while I pondered her statement. "Perhaps to help each other?"

"And isn't the person being helped using his helper? As I said, the question is whether you're doing it properly. My guests know who I am. They come here to meet people who'll be useful to them, and they'll remember me long after I leave Seattle. They'll probably be useful to you one day as well."

Sheila's "work hard, play hard" motto also extended to our routines. She once told me, "My father used to claim he needed at least three months a year to himself and his family, away from work. He'd say, 'If I couldn't get twelve months work done in nine months, I'd just quit.'" Though she and I worked ungodly hours for weeks at a time, she could quite spontaneously announce that we needed a break. This was a new concept to me.

"Let's go skiing," she announced one day. It was January, and the weather was typical Seattle January weather: cool, drizzly, gray.

"Where?"

"Fernie, in the British Columbia Rockies, would be nice." I agreed, having never skied and not knowing where Fernie was.

The next day we headed out just after midnight to Canada. It was a nine- hour drive to the lift; we got there about midmorning. Sheila's car was a twelve- year-old bright yellow Cadillac, which I had found to be unwieldy around the city. On the highway, however, it came into its own. The ride was easy, and the front seat was one of those old-fashioned bench seats. It was like traveling in your living room, with plenty of space to move around.

Sheila outfitted me and introduced me to an instructor at the pro shop before going off on her own. I was awkward at first, but before the day was over I'd glimpsed some of the exhilaration of free-falling down a slippery slope on planks.

Toward the end of the day I watched Sheila for a while. My legs were shot. She'd spent her childhood flying around the world to ski the best resorts, and her technique and grace were inspiring. She glided like a bird through her turns. I wondered at the freedom great wealth could bring. Her athleticism also startled me. She was young and healthy, of course, but she wasn't one to exercise for exercise's sake. She did something because she enjoyed it.

The ride back felt anticlimactic. We had nine hours of pavement to look forward to, with only the lights of the other vehicles to relieve the darkness. During the daylight, the drive had showcased outrageous sequences of dense forests, northern deserts, and hair-raising mountain passes, but now it was night, and all we saw was the road in front of us. We stopped at the border and for gas a couple of times, when we also switched drivers.

I was driving the final stretch when Sheila announced, "I'm bored." When I turned toward her to agree, I saw that she was taking off her clothes. Next she unzipped my pants and began to fondle me. I relaxed into the prospect of her playing with me when she nimbly scooted onto my lap and gently settled herself onto my very solid member.

"What are you doing?" I asked rather stupidly, straining to peer over her shoulder to see the road.

"You know what I'm doing, just keep driving."

Screwing at seventy miles an hour, hurtling down a mountain, might not have been the safest thing I've ever done, but I didn't ask her to stop, and I did get us home.

*

"Do you realize the kind of money we're going to make?" she asked me one lovely spring day. We were on the ferry to Victoria. The trip took three hours each way, and we made a full day of it by visiting Victoria's famous gardens. Even though Victoria is in Canada, north of Seattle and on an island, it is often warmer and drier than Seattle.

At first I thought this was just another of her spontaneous breaks, an escape from the gray. Only later did I realize she'd planned a day away from our work to bring up this subject.

"I'm a little overwhelmed. I understand the mathematics well enough, but the world of finance is yours, not mine."

"Oh, but I think it *is* yours now as well." She gave me a sympathetic smile.

I recalled Dr. Rastowski telling me Sheila would treat me fairly but would leave me in the dirt if I couldn't keep up. For the first time, I began to grasp his meaning.

"This could be big—huge—but timing is everything. If you stay in Seattle to complete your PhD, we might miss the opportunity to be the ones to get it going. If we move to New York we can get the financing to start something right now."

Up to that point I was more concerned with the mathematical viability of my work than its real world implications, especially as it might affect my personal lifestyle. It wasn't that I objected to moving on, I just hadn't thought about it. "There's more than the PhD. I also have some responsibility to Dr. Thayer."

"Well, there's old promises and there's new promises. You'll be able to offer Thayer a lot more than graded papers."

I'd never had much to offer anyone before except friendship, but I was beginning to see that life looked different to the rich and powerful. It wasn't that I needed to be ruthless; it was just that the "lot more" I could offer Thayer could only happen if I succeeded, which meant leaving Seattle.

I looked over the railing at the waters of Puget Sound. We were passing a few islands, including the one where Dr. Thayer spent his summers. I felt I was about to embark on a project that could revolutionize the human understanding of the universe, but I was mesmerized by the same white-capped spume that had been blowing on our planet for billions of years, long before life even existed.

I turned back to Sheila. "I'll talk to him. There are only three more weeks left in the semester. I'll leave then."

*

A few days later, I went to Thayer's office and told him about my plan to leave.

He didn't seem surprised. "Frankly, I don't think you're cut out for academic life anyway. You may or may not be the most brilliant student I've ever had, but I'm sure you're the first doctoral student I've told to leave because you're too good for school."

Sheila left for New York a few days after our conversation. She had arranged for her house to be put up for sale as soon as I vacated it. I followed her about three weeks later. The Pacific Northwest was stunning, but the truth is I barely saw it. My grad-school experience, which I felt I'd worked so hard to attain, was over before I could enjoy it. But if I thought my Seattle tour was a whirlwind, it was nothing compared to my new life in New York City.

13

Sheila had a small apartment on the Upper West Side overlooking Central Park—a gift from her father when she was an undergrad at NYU. Evidently, once you had a place in Manhattan, you kept it for life, even generations. Sheila had rented it out while she was in Seattle and was now returning to her true home.

The building was more than three-quarters of a century old. Neither the bathroom nor the kitchen had been renovated for at least forty years, and we had to walk up three flights of stairs because there was no elevator. However, the apartment was surely one of the most sought-after pieces of real estate in the world. It was even more comfortable than Sheila's Seattle house, it had the feeling of permanence and home.

At first I felt like a foreigner in the Big Apple, but before long I realized it's true that New York never sleeps, that you can get anything there, and that you can be anyone you want to be if you can afford it. It helped that I could now afford whatever I wanted, with Sheila's (and her dad's) help. I was getting used to the idea of having money at my disposal and, again with Sheila's help, becoming confident that I would soon be earning it through my own efforts. It turned out that one of the most valuable commodities the city had to offer was free—namely the crowded, frenetic streets. I'd never found a better place to be alone with my thoughts.

As Sheila had promised, financing our venture was never going to be a problem, but there were important questions regarding the administrative shape it would take. It was a given we would go into business with her father, Jake Park. Mr. Park, as I always called him, was offering us start-up financing, as well as his reputation, to help us recruit clients. He proposed that Sheila and I would each own 24.5 percent of the firm, while he would keep 51 percent. "It's my money, so it's my company," he said.

Jake Park had always treated me cordially, but I wasn't happy with this proposal. I knew I couldn't fight both Parks, though, and I wasn't going anywhere without them. "Your dad will accelerate our launch, but we're bringing something unique to the table. I want an even split," I told her one evening as we dined at Jean-Georges, certainly one of the finest, and most expensive, restaurants in the world. I think she took me there to remind herself that she was home again.

"Dad's bringing more than money to the table—he's thinking about the long-term success of the project. He's not about making money off us. We'll talk to him."

"Can you stand up to him?" I asked her.

"I can, but you'll have to convince him. I won't undercut you, Ron, but I know how he thinks."

We scheduled a meeting for later that week and kept busy in the meantime. I wasn't about to bluff Mr. Park, and I wanted him to know that ahead of time, so I didn't attempt to look elsewhere for funding and support. In poker there are always winners and losers, but in business sometimes the point is for everyone at the table to win. I won't pretend I wasn't intimidated—it's one thing to stand up to an aging academic but quite another to face one of the most canny and truly powerful businessmen in the world. Especially when you're sleeping with his daughter.

Jake Park's office was set up to give him an advantage from the start. His brokerage firm occupied the top three floors of a thirty-five-story building near Wall Street. To reach his office, one had to take the private elevator to the thirty-third floor, get by the receptionist in the firm's main lobby, then take another elevator up two floors to his private secretary, who inevitably made everyone wait a few minutes more.

After entering his office, there was an inordinately long walk to Jake's broad, ornate mahogany desk, behind which lay an expansive view of the richest city human civilization has ever created. The effect, of course, was to create the impression that it belonged to the man sitting at the desk—which had some truth to it.

Jake's building was an exquisite postmodern structure, stately and imposing inside and out, but there was nothing modern about Jake's own office. From the African fertility goddess he used as a paperweight to the enclosed Chinese bookcases to the tapestries and paintings hanging from his walls and lovely Persian rugs on the floor, the space was full of ancient artifacts from all over the world, from every period of history. The result was not gaudy, but rather timeless. And breathtaking. If I had had any doubts about the breadth of his intellect, his office would have disabused me of my error.

For our meeting, Mr. Park was sitting in his chair and had another single chair next to him, which he offered to his daughter. He clearly wanted to impress upon me that it was him and his daughter against me.

"I'm okay, Dad," she said, and remained standing. These were probably the most important words spoken during the formation of our company, as it showed Sheila was aware of what her father was doing and was strong enough not to play along.

"Well, then, let's begin. Ron, I gather you're not satisfied with my proposal." "No, sir, I'm not." I had no intention of being either rude or disrespectful, and I thought I could best convey this by being simple and direct. "And yet you are already spending my money."

"I'm not dissatisfied with that, sir," I joked. A very slight smile flashed across Jake's face, but it was so fleeting I couldn't tell whether to be afraid.

"Indeed, that doesn't surprise me. You realize, I'm sure, that I'm giving you an opportunity that anyone else would grab at twice the price?"

"I do."

My candor took Jake by surprise. I was sure he was looking for me to question the fairness of the arrangement. "So what do you object to?"

Sheila interrupted us. "Dad, can we all sit down?"

"Of course. Pardon me," Mr. Park agreed, as if he hadn't choreographed the entire scene in advance. He led us across the office to a small rattan couch and coffee table with a simple wooden chair on the other side. He sat on the couch and patted the seat next to him for his daughter. She gave me a quick glance. We both understood the dance, but it would have been an affront for her to refuse to comply this time, so she sat down. I took the chair.

"What do you want me to do?" he asked. I almost laughed when he predictably put his arm around his daughter's shoulder.

"We need to set up the organization so that it leads to effective decision-making. I'm sure you agree that Sheila and I will be running the company, but the structure you propose will leave us vulnerable to an override at any time. This will inevitably undermine our confidence. That isn't the kind of mind-set we'll need to be successful."

He nodded once, then stroked his chin. "I see. What do you think would be more 'effective'?"

"Each of the three of us will get the same 25.5 percent share. That will leave 23.5 percent for us to sell or give as incentive to staff."

"And why would this 'lead to effective decision-making'?" Mr. Park said, using air quotes and mimicking my tone. He wasn't convinced yet, but at least he was still talking.

"For different reasons, you and I both have natural alliances with your daughter. As long as she and I are working well together, we control the company, and you'll also be satisfied. If, for any reason, I fall out of favor with her, all she has to do is turn to you and take over with your assistance."

Jake sat back on his couch and gave me a long, considered look, as if he were seeing me for the first time. He looked genuinely interested now. "And you'll be okay with that?'

I glanced at Sheila. "We're pretty solid. I think it'll work out just fine."

"I can see why you're a good mathematician," Mr. Park said. He turned to Sheila. "And what do you think, dear?"

Sheila looked at both of us as she considered the question. As quick as she was, she knew when to compose her words carefully. Her serious look gave way to a smile. "Given the way Ron has laid this out, I'll always be in charge. I think it makes a lot of sense. If we're all confident regarding our places, we'll make one hell of a team."

"I'll let you know tomorrow," Mr. Park said a bit curtly. He returned to his desk, indicating the meeting was over.

Sheila and I left the office complex together, in silence. We knew anything we said in the building would probably be reported back to Mr. Park. The subway stop was half a block from Park's building, but we didn't speak until we got onto a train. As the doors closed and the subway started moving, Sheila gave me a high-five and beamed. "Damn, you knocked that one out of the park!"

I'm sure my look didn't exude the same confidence. "Are you sure that wasn't more like a foul ball?"

She laughed. "No way. The hardest word for my dad to say is 'yes,' and the easiest is 'no.' If he wasn't going to agree, he would've let us know immediately."

*

She was right, of course, and we soon had a company of our own, Victoria Sound Investments. We rented offices in mid-Manhattan and went to work. We didn't have a salable product yet, so the next several months were the busiest of my life as she and I completed the initial work and expanded it to other markets, such as the Fortune 500, Futures Commodities, and Dow Jones. It's one thing to explore unknown territory in the mathematical universe, quite another to be immersed in a human rush with multiple deadlines and an endless succession of crucial snap decisions. Sheila was the CEO, and we hired an experienced manager from outside her father's firm, as well as a CFO from within. My title was vice president, but everyone understood that the company revolved around my brainchild, so I was expected to be everywhere at all times.

We started by handling somewhat less than twenty million dollars put up by Jake Park and a few close friends. At the time, the market was rising quickly and steadily—too quickly, it turned out, as it was the era of "irrational exuberance." But Sheila and I were able to anticipate even fairly small dips in the market, and using my models along with conventional best management practices, we outperformed the market by nearly 20 percent and expanded into exchanges in Germany, Britain, and Japan.

Life was both hectic and smooth. Sheila and I went from living together to getting married without a hitch. After our successful negotiation with Mr. Park, I knew I could trust Sheila through most anything, and I believe Sheila gained a new confidence in me as well. We didn't lose our passion, we just gained a deeper affection to add to it. Her dad wasn't particularly happy about our marriage, but only because he thought married couples should have enough time alone to be able to stand each other. That was never an issue for us.

During the first two years of our company, Sheila gave up her dad's dictum of doing twelve months' work in nine months. There were no ski trips, no ferries, no soirees. We put all of our combined energies into Victoria Sound.

Then came what was known as the dot-com crash. At the time, Victoria Sound was approaching a quarter of a billion dollars in managed assets, and although I warned Sheila that a substantial change was coming to the markets, we were both a little unnerved at the thought of pulling the plug on those investments. The first indications that the market was unsettled took place in December of 1999, but by the next February my numbers were screaming, and we switched everything to bonds.

For the next months we wondered if we were going to be the laughingstocks of Manhattan as the stock market clattered along, but then the markets crashed precipitously, and we were vindicated. Even though we warned clients that we wouldn't be re-entering a profitable market in the foreseeable future, investors started flocking to our doors. Victoria Sound was ready for the flood.

Although I liked to think my work was the centerpiece of our enterprise, the fact is, between Jake Park and his associates we probably could have stayed in business until the dot-com crash using Dr. Smythe's simplistic Bayesian approach. After the crash came and my model proved accurate, we realized we were exhausted.

"It's time for a break," Sheila said one day as we rode the subway back to our apartment.

"Skiing in the Andes?" I asked, only half joking.

"No, I was thinking of something more remote, and more intimate." She could have suggested hitching a ride on the space shuttle and I wouldn't have been surprised. "My family owns a little fishing camp up in Quebec," she continued. "I think you'll enjoy it. We have a good team here, and your fractals tell us the markets will be stable for a while."

The camp was on the north shore of Lac Perroche in Quebec, and was only accessible by air. We flew to Montreal the next week, and then took a two-hour, half-full commercial prop flight to Wabush, Labrador. As we entered the small terminal in Wabush several men were waiting to greet my wife.

"Mademoiselle Park, *bien*, it' so good to see you," said one, a burly man with a thick black mustache and thicker Québécois accent.

"Ah, it's good to see you, too, Laurent. And Gilles, and Richard," she said to the other two men. "But it's Madam Larsen, now. This is my husband, Ron. Ron, this is Laurent Castonquay, his son, Gilles Castonquay, and Richard Stokes. Laurent and Gilles operate the iron mine here, and Richard is the mayor of Labrador City, Wabush's big brother."

Richard Stokes spoke next. "Brys mentioned you were coming. Are you staying in Labrador West long?"

"No, I think Brys is ready to take us up to Lac Perroche now. On our way back we can all sit down and have dinner. Have a nice wine ready."

We had a short conversation about the weather for the next week, and when we would pass through again, when another man joined us.

"Brys, I see you're punctual as usual," Sheila said, offering her hand.

"But, of course, Mademoiselle—Madam Larsen." He gave a small bow as he accepted her hand. Brys was a small, quick man with a thick, curly mop of black hair and a penetrating look that he now directed at me.

"Brys, this is my husband, Ron. Ron, meet Brys Chouquette. He's going to take us the rest of the way." We said our good-byes to the greeting party and followed Brys out to his plane, a single-prop four-seater Cessna with amphibious floats. Brys opened the front door for Sheila, but she insisted I get in front.

"I've seen the view before. It's much better from the front."

Brys had us up and away in no time, and to say the view was breathtaking would be to sell it short. At times it was difficult to tell whether we were flying over thousands and thousands of lakes, or a massive lake with as many thousands of islands. In fact, it was a bit of both. I think the flight took less than two hours, but I was so mesmerized I did not notice the passage of time. Our pilot pointed out a few items below, but mostly he was attentive to what he did. I thought that an admirable trait in a bush pilot.

He landed us on the lake, then taxied to a floating dock in front of a simple, but modern-looking, log cabin. We unloaded our gear in a few minutes, and Brys took off after assuring us he would return in three weeks.

As I watched him fly away I heard Sheila behind me yell, "Last one in's a monkey's ass!" I turned to see she had already left her clothes on the dock and was diving into the lake. Without thinking, I did the same, but when I hit the frigid water I thought my heart was going to stop. I popped up, gasping for breath, only to be met by a huge splash in my face that Sheila had timed perfectly. Thus began one of the most amazing three weeks I have ever had— three weeks of frolic.

I did not last as long in the water as Sheila did. I clambered onto the dock and found a blanket in one of our bags. I wrapped it around my shoulders and shivered as I watched her calmly swim toward me and slither onto the dock herself. As she stood there, nude and iridescent, I felt I was looking at a red- haired Aphrodite arising from the sea foam. I decided she might need a little warmth. I wrapped the blanket and my arms around her, then picked her up as she wrapped her legs around my hips. As we made love I heard the far-off cry of a solitary loon. It was as if the boreal forest was joining in our joy.

"You seem to be well liked in Wabush," I said to Sheila that evening over our dinner of popcorn and wine.

"I've known those men since I was a child. The iron mine nearly went broke in the seventies. Dad secured the financing to get it back on its feet, and recruited Laurent to run it. He probably saved the town, and it has paid him back. He fell in love with the boreal forest, and built this place to come to— sometimes to be alone, sometimes to entertain important clients, and often to be with his family. I feel I grew up here almost as much as New York City."

"It's wonderful. Even the Riesling is chilled. Does this place have some sort of refrigerator?"

"Did you happen to notice how cold the lake is?" Sheila said, her green eyes sparkling with amusement. "There's a stream under the house that keeps the cooler as cold as a modern refrigerator. There's a gas stove and kerosene lamps. All the conveniences of home. Brys flew in a couple of days ago to stock food and fuel for us and make sure everything is in good order. And yes, he knows I can't cook."

Once again I was amazed at the apparent simplicity great wealth could create. The camp had a modest yacht named the *Louisa May* where we spent most of our time—mosquitos avoid open water, and there were plenty of mosquitos around the shores of Lac Perroche. The yacht was named after Sheila's mother, who died of lymphoma during Sheila's senior year in high school.

"My mom was named after her mother's great aunt, Louisa May Alcott. She loved this place as much as my father, that's why we spent so much time here. It was her idea to have a yacht on the lake."

Even more fun than the yacht was a canoe we towed around with us. It was fitted with a small outboard motor, so we could quietly paddle through the bogs, then move a little quicker when we wanted to explore the shallow waters of the myriad inlets.

As we watched a moose wade in a small bay one afternoon, Sheila said, "Moose are ancient animals. As a kid I always imagined these woods were made just for them."

"I can see why. I've never seen one before, just cartoons."

"I never got the cartoon thing. They're...they're regal." I agreed.

We often heard, but seldom saw, the same pileated woodpeckers I had listened to with Cheryl. We saw eagles and osprey, loons, cranes, ravens in abundance. It seemed strange to me that a place that must have been completely frozen in winter could be so rich with life in the summer.

And then there were the Northern Lights. The dazzling display of shimmering purple, blue, and green celestial curtains put to shame all the fireworks I had ever seen, and their ghostly silence made the show all the more impressive. I wondered, if we saw the ocean, the sky, or a forest only rarely, would it hold the same wonder? After the lights disappeared, Sheila and I would be alone with the stars. They felt much closer than the nearest human.

Late one night after we had settled into bed on our yacht, which was moored not far from shore, I was startled by a bloodcurdling screech. "What the hell was that?" I said. I jumped to my feet, ready for a fight.

"It's a lynx, dear," she said as she turned on the light. She examined my nude fighting stance with evident amusement. "Come back to bed, my big pussy cat, you'll be safe with me."

Occasionally we would land during our daytime forays in our canoe and wander a short way into the spruce forest for lunch or lovemaking, but Sheila cautioned that we needed to respect the danger as much as we appreciated the beauty of the north. "If we were to get lost, there's no one to find us."

We even fished a little; trout were abundant. We threw everything we caught back in the lake, though, as neither one of us wanted to try our hand at cleaning and cooking.

I had been amazed by the wonders Cheryl had shown me in Massachusetts, but the vastness of northern Canada was unimaginable. Sheila and I spent three weeks without seeing another human being, and not missing anyone. We always got along, but having so much time to ourselves with nothing more important to do than enjoy each other, laugh, and make love reinvigorated our souls and our marriage. We returned to Victoria Sound feeling ready to get back to work.

What we weren't ready for was for our neighbors, the World Trade Center Towers, to come tumbling down.

Jake Park's building was slightly damaged, as it was only blocks from the collapse, but our company's offices weren't touched. Several of Sheila's friends were killed, though, and all of Manhattan went into shock. The stock market business, of course, came to a standstill. They say the whole world became New Yorkers for a while. I had considered myself a foreigner in the city until that day, but certainly not since.

I know every New Yorker was changed by the collapse of the Twin Towers, but I also saw that people were changed in different ways. Sheila and I—and nearly everyone in our firm—reacted with defiance. We were determined to be even more potent and more successful in the aftermath of the attack. I'm not sure we worked harder than before, but we were more resolute. It took months, a few years really, before we could call the situation "normal." Normal but scarred.

14

If I'd received Regina's letter a year earlier, I don't know if I would have responded. I hope I would have, as it was a plaintive note, but we don't always do what we know we should. It came at a time when the market was calm and our company did not require my constant input.

The note was a single line written on an otherwise blank scrap of paper, with no date or salutation: "I could use your assistance with a sensitive matter." It wasn't signed, but her name and address were on the envelope, and I recognized her handwriting in any case. I showed the note to Sheila.

Sheila handed the note back to me and smiled softly. "Of course you need to go. This woman gave you your life. Do what you can to help her. We're in good shape here. I think a little time away from the grind will do you good."

I slipped the note back into the envelope and made preparations to return to Northern University for the first time since I'd left for Seattle.

*

Foxfield hadn't changed much in the four years I'd been away. If anything, it looked a little cleaner—but only a little. Although a few new buildings had popped up on campus, I easily found my way to the physics department. What was new was that Dr. Russo's name was no longer on her door, which was locked.

I realized it must no longer be Regina's office, and returned downstairs to the department directory near the front door, but I didn't see her name there either. I headed to the department office. The receptionist gave me a blank stare when I asked where Regina Russo's office was. She got up from her desk and spoke to someone in another room. An older woman, whom I recognized from when I'd roamed Northern's halls, came out.

"Who are you looking for?" she asked, which I thought was strange as she obviously had just been given the name.

"Regina Russo," I repeated. "Doesn't she still work here?" "Oh, heavens, no!" was the reply.

"Do you know where I can find her?"

She shook her head vigorously. "No, but a good guess would be jail."

I realized I wasn't going to get any more information there. I remembered the tale

Louise had recounted, as well as the attitudes of my math professors. I figured Regina's past had finally driven her away. In her note, she hadn't mentioned leaving Northern, but then again she hadn't mentioned anything. I took the envelope out of my backpack and looked at the return address: 58 Race Street, #6, which was where I went next.

Race Street lay parallel to one of Foxfield's historic canals. These canals were relics of the late-nineteenth century, when New England was the center of the industrialized world and water power ran it. The building at 58 Race Street was a large former factory between the street and the canal. It was shaped like a wide U, with the bottom of the U two blocks long along Race Street between Fifth and Seventh Avenues. Sixth Avenue dead-ended in the center of the long wall before it reached the canal, but the building had a gated archway passing through what appeared to be a continuation of the street. Through the archway I saw a sort of courtyard, basically a dirt lot, next to the canal. The sides of the U were each a block long, and both Fifth and Seventh Avenues continued past the building across the canal. Wide alleys separated the canal and the building at the upper ends of both legs. Along the canal was a short stone wall, maybe two feet high on the land side. The water level in the canal was about ten feet below the top of the wall. Even to my untrained eye, the building appeared to have been built in several sections. It also looked like it was being renovated in sections. Along Seventh Avenue and the west end along Race Street were several new storefronts with recessed doorways and large picture windows. The windows in the upper floors also appeared to be new. East of the archway along Race Street the structure began to look shabbier, and there were no more new storefronts.

In the middle of this older section of the building was an old double door with a bulletin board next to it. This entrance led to a room that was used for various large classes—tai chi, tae kwon do, and ballet lessons were advertised on the board. At the far end of the block was a single, worn-looking door that could have been the main entrance to the factory in another age. This door wasn't recessed and the wood had cracked and softened with age. Patches of green paint remained, but much of the wood was bare. The door sported an old-fashioned frosted window with hansel bros. tools barely legible in black paint across the glass. Above the door, the number 6 was chiseled into the granite header. I assumed this was Regina's door. I knocked several times, but there was no answer and no sound. I turned the doorknob. It was unlocked, so I went in.

The door led to what once had been a reception area. The room looked much like it must have when the factory was functioning, except for the extra dust. There were two enclosed glass shelves opposite each other on the side walls. One appeared to hold samples of the items once manufactured here— an assemblage of hand tools I didn't recognize. The other was full of ancient citations and awards. Two long tables filled the middle of the room, modern folding tables like those used in church banquet rooms. They were covered with what appeared to be architectural drawings. Behind the tables, two doors led farther into the building. I tried the door on the right, but it was locked.

The other door led to an office, which could be seen through the window. It was one of the most cluttered offices I'd ever seen; I knew immediately it was Regina's. A large note pinned to the far wall was addressed to me: "Ron, thanks for coming. I'll be back at two."

It was only noon, so I decided to grab some lunch and look around the neighborhood. I continued around the corner and followed Fifth Avenue over a low stone bridge across the canal. This side of the building was a solid brick wall at street level. There were windows in the two stories above, old and shabby, unlike the new replacements on Seventh Avenue. I paused on the bridge to look at the canal.

Even though the factories that once had relied on water power had either switched to electric power or gone out of business, the canal was still used to run the electric turbines that powered much of the city, so it carried a swift current of water. The sides of the canal were vertical walls of massive stonework. I marveled at the craftsmanship and industry of the workers who had built these edifices.

As I looked down the canal I noticed that the old factories had what looked like tunnel entrances in the canal wall. I realized these were the entrances and exits of the sluices that had run under the factories and powered the turbines housed in their lower levels. I noticed a few of them had been walled up, and that this more recent work done to plug the arches was much less impressive than the original. They were built of either smaller concrete blocks or just solid concrete, and many of the newer sections were in poorer condition than the original stone walls.

The far side of the canal was much busier than the Race Street side. It wasn't a wealthy area, but all the buildings were occupied. Fifth Avenue continued up the hill into a residential district. The houses weren't ornate, but they were lived in and well kept. The first street parallel to the canal, Front Street, was lined with two- and three-story buildings: stores downstairs, offices and apartments above. The storefronts were all occupied. These buildings had been built for their present purpose, unlike the old factories across the canal, and the street appeared to be what 58 Race Street now aspired to be part of, a bustling business district.

I turned back onto Seventh Avenue and re-crossed the canal, returning to where I started. Another abandoned factory occupied the west side of Seventh Avenue. Ahead of me, away from the canal, the street was lined with a mixture of houses in various states of repair or disrepair, along with a few empty lots. Farther on lay more factories and another canal. Clearly, this was the wrong side of the canal, to paraphrase an old saying.

I paid closer attention to the stores at 58 Race the second time around. The first one, an upscale vintage clothing boutique, was about half the size of the other stores. The next, a doughnut and bagel shop, was the largest store on the block, and fortuitously located, as I was beginning to get hungry. I grabbed a bagel sandwich to go and headed back to Regina's office, passing a video/record store, a package store, a law office, a hair salon and nail spa, and a Mexican restaurant. I had no idea what a nail spa was. A sketch of the first floor of the building and its surroundings is shown below:

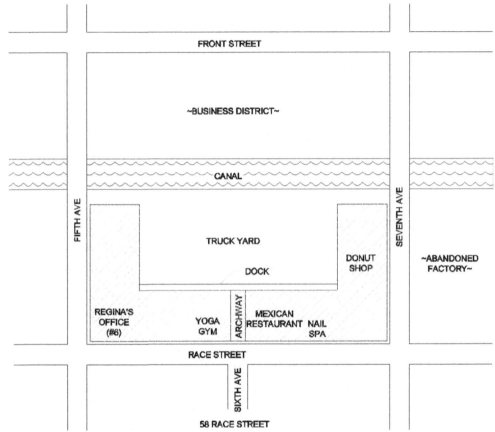

I was back at number 6 early, but Regina was already there. She hadn't changed a bit since I'd last seen her, at least in appearance. She had the same long-sleeve shirt, blue jeans, athletic shoes, and wry smile.

"Ron, I'm so glad you came. As I recall, you couldn't get away fast enough from me when you left for Seattle. And you've done quite well, extremely well. I've dabbled in fractals myself. I'm very impressed."

I wasn't surprised that she knew what I was doing, even though it was a trade secret. It was apparent from the days when she had taught at my high school, and when she visited me after my fight, that she kept tabs on me. I was, however, taken aback at her casual revelation that she was aware of how much I'd wanted to leave. Rather than open old wounds, I gestured at her office. "This is a change."

She took a deep breath. "It's a long story."

I'd accomplished a lot since my undergrad days and had learned to deal with powerful people. I wasn't going to wait weeks for Regina to spill her story. "Does it have anything to do with the explosion in the basement of Masson Hall?"

Regina flashed her wry, sincere smile again. "You've grown up. I shouldn't be surprised. Well, yes and no. That was a terrible incident with Ms. Kapoor... Manisha Kapoor. I had no idea she... There was another incident since then, while you were away. I'll explain everything, Ron, but I'm afraid I'll first need to give you another physics lesson. Do you think you can stand it?"

She seemed a little flustered, or maybe she just had too much to tell me all at once. "I want to hear it all, including why you rented this office."

"Rented? Oh, no, this isn't a rental, this is *my* building. I guess property management is my new profession." She chuckled. "Can I show you around?"

She gave me a tour inside and out. As I'd already surmised, the renovation was less than half done. The finished portion of the second floor was occupied by professional offices, the third by apartments. She explained her plans as we stood at the edge of the canal. "I need to use this courtyard for parking, but I want to fix it up. My landscaper was supposed to have been here last week. I never realized how much patience this stuff requires." A dozen or so cars were parked along the building, but it still looked like the truck loading yard it once was. "I've been told they can bury paving stones that allow grass to grow through."

I had no idea what she was talking about, but clearly she did, which was surprising in itself. Remember, I was able to recognize her office by the mess. I'd never known her to be interested in her surroundings, especially landscaping. Perhaps being a landlady had changed her. Something had.

"Let's go over to the dock," she said.

The courtyard was four feet lower than Race Street, and there was a truck loading dock along the entire building on this side. We climbed onto the dock next to the freight elevator and entered a large room filled with construction materials.

"This is my new playground, Ron. That door over there leads back to my office. And that one over there leads to a multipurpose gym."

I headed toward the first door she'd gestured to, but Regina held me back by the elbow. I think that was the first time she'd ever touched me. "Let's go this way."

She led me through the piles of stuff intended for the building to another door, a new door. It opened onto the gated archway that was now full of tables and diners. It seemed to be part of the Mexican restaurant I'd seen from Race Street. As soon as Regina was through the door, the elderly Latino maître d' saw her. "Ah, *Señorita* Russo! You have a guest today. A table for two?"

"*Por favor.*"

Clearly Regina was a well-liked landlady. She ordered in Spanish: Pollo con Mole, Huachinango a la Veracruzana, Pico de Gallo, Frijoles Negros, and Tortillas de Maize Azul. It was Mexican food unlike any I had ever had, and delicious. I mentioned my observation to Regina.

"This is real food," she said. "I was lucky to find Eduardo, here he comes. Eduardo, you must let me pay when I bring a guest," she addressed a stout, extremely strong-looking man in a cook's outfit who was approaching our table.

"No, Regina. You could have a party of ten, and you still couldn't pay." He sat down at our table. "When you come, I have an excuse to sit down."

Regina grinned. "I didn't think you ever got tired, Eduardo."

"I learn from you." As if to prove her point, Eduardo got up almost immediately. "Do you know when the courtyard will be done?" He nodded toward the rear of the building.

"They told me last week; they told me this week; now they tell me next week." Regina shrugged.

"*Comprendo,*" Eduardo replied.

As our host left, Regina turned back to me. "There's no time off in this business." She took a sip of the delicious coffee. "But we need to talk physics. Where did we leave off last time?"

"If I recall correctly, you'd just explained the early cosmic rapid inflation, dark matter, dark energy, and the cause of the speed of light."

Regina again ignored any possibility of sarcasm in my voice. "Good. But remember these are secondary effects. The basis for any comprehensive description of reality is to understand that everything we know is based on the reception of information, specifically that awareness creates time."

"You've mentioned that before." I was beginning to wish I hadn't come back to Foxfield.

"I've also explained that as the universe expands in its spatial dimensions and moves along its time dimension, it traces a four-dimensional spiral. As I've also told you, the radius of the spiral is equal to the Planck Length, and the length it moves in time with each revolution is equal to the Planck Interval. This rotation mixes the spatial and time dimensions, kind of like shaking a cocktail, creating the resonance that provides the basis for the forms of matter that populate our universe."

"So you think the universe is like an alcoholic drink?" I felt she was getting carried away with her imagery, but evidently she didn't. I thought maybe I should order some alcohol.

She shrugged, as if to agree her imagery was a bit farfetched, then continued, "Maybe a symphony, an incredible symphony with the vibration of the helix providing the musical key and tempo."

I found this analogy as unbelievable as the first. "Amazing, I guess, but when we last spoke, you told me you would give me real evidence."

Eduardo dropped by to ask if everything was okay. We assured him it was and he produced a couple of glasses of sherry. Regina and I paused to sip and look at each other, a little like boxers before a match.

Regina closed her eyes for a moment, then began. "I did promise you results. Imagine a particle traveling along a spiral path inside the universe's spiral, so that its path is shorter than the path traversed by the universe itself."

She pulled a small notepad and a pen out of her back pocket and quickly drew a sketch...

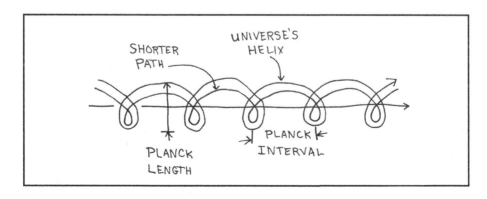

"Now imagine we can send a particle of light," she continued, "a photon, along this shorter path inside the universe's spiral, which, because it's taking a shorter path into the future, but traveling at the same rate, arrives sooner than the instant it started. Because we can plan ahead, we can anticipate the photon's arrival at a specified time and create a target for it when we begin the experiment. Let's call the time we start the experiment 'time zero' and the time the photon reaches the target 'time ten.'"

"Ten what exactly?" I had no idea what she was talking about.

Regina looked at me incredulously but then softened. I knew this all seemed so simple to her, but fortunately she had a lot of patience with me. "We'll get to the actual time scale later. I just want you to understand the sequence. By the way, would you like dessert? Eduardo makes fantastic churros." Regina knew I had a sweet tooth.

She summoned our waiter and ordered churros for both of us. They were crunchy, sweet, and covered with chocolate. Delicious, perfect with the sherry, but I thought I might need a stronger drink if I had to listen to Regina much longer.

"Before we go on," Regina said, "I want to make sure you remember what entangled particles are."

I probably grimaced at first, but tried to cover it with a grin. "Of course I do. That was another phenomenon that drove Einstein nuts. Once two particles are entangled, they can be separated spatially, and yet a change in the state of one will be instantaneously seen in the other, no matter how far apart they are."

Regina's eyes lit up, as if she were proud of me for remembering. "Yes, Einstein couldn't understand how two particles seem to communicate with each other instantaneously. Of course, I've explained to you that at times shorter than the Planck Interval, we must consider time and space, and therefore relativity, inoperable, so you shouldn't have the same difficulty as Einstein. Anyway, we send one of two entangled photons on the shorter path and set up the target at time ten so that some small amount of information about an event, the price of a single stock for instance, is presented in such a way that a particular pattern of changes to this entangled photon can be read at, say, time five, by observing the behavior of the other entangled photon, the one we keep."

"It's my understanding," I interjected, "that even though entangled particles seem to communicate with one another instantaneously they couldn't be used by two outside observers to do so."

"That's true, Ron, but in our case they're separated by time, not space, so communication between them takes time, albeit backward time, over virtually no distance. To be precise, we use entanglement swapping to do the trick."

I shot her a confused look. "What's entanglement swapping?"

Regina gave me another of her sweet, patient looks in return. "It's a way to create time-separated, instead of space-separated, entanglement. I guess you can say we do a reverse entanglement swapping. My point is, this process takes time, but we still don't have to wait for the actual event to occur at time ten to find out what will occur. In this way, we could glean information from the future."

"You can do that?" Regina's lesson was suddenly becoming very interesting. She cocked her head to the side. "Well, it's a little complicated. As you can see, this is tantamount to traveling faster than light. Of course, relativity says you can't accelerate past the speed of light. Even so, imagine what would happen if one traveled from here to Seattle instantaneously."

"Yeah, imagine." I started to remember how fanciful her physics could get. "But that would mean occupying the entire route in a single instant."

"I suppose so."

"Unfortunately, the entire route is also occupied by everything we'd normally see there."

"Sounds messy." I was beginning to imagine the situation.

"Indeed. The most powerful machines the human race has created, particle accelerators such as the Tevatron in Chicago or the RHIC on Long Island, are meant to force minute particles to collide at speeds close to the speed of light. In our hypothetical case, we're talking about an instantaneous collision of a huge amount of mass. Much worse."

It dawned on me that she was finally going to tell me about herself. "Is that what happened in the physics lab?"

"Possibly," she admitted without hesitation. "If the particle one is sending into the future lands where something else already exists, the result is such a collision.

In those early days, I accidentally created several small explosions. My approach wasn't sophisticated, and my equipment was primitive too. I ran my experiments at night, to avoid the possibility of injuring someone. I had no idea Manisha was working late as well. I've never really recovered from thinking it was my fault. I almost quit physics."

She stopped talking and looked at me closely, examined me for a while. "You know, that happened only a few months before I met you. I toyed with the idea of teaching high school for a while, but really, this work is too important." Her eyes had teared up, she looked down into her glass as if to find an answer or some solace there.

I decided to pick up the slack. She had requested I come for a reason, and I thought I might be getting close to finding out what it was. "So, essentially, you can make a single particle outrace the universe, and send us a message from the future?"

"Ideally, I could completely control the motion of one entangled particle at a time to outpace the universe, but it's impossible to know what that means. As I've explained, the radius of the helix is the Planck Length, so we're operating entirely within the domain of Heisenberg's uncertainty. To overcome the uncertainty of the path of any single particle, naturally one must use multiple particles to interact with the targeted future event and then relay the information back to an earlier time. Of course, we're talking about short periods of time, and no spatial movement, so it's possible to enclose the entire event in a vacuum, to minimize interference from stray matter. The whole setup is delicate—any unexpected movement of the equipment can create a catastrophe."

"And you really don't know what actually killed Manisha?"

"No. Despite the rumors you might have heard, the authorities didn't bring any charges against me. They even considered the possibility Ms. Kapoor blew the lab up herself. But of course I assumed it was my mistake, and I moved my work to my house on an old farm about forty-five minutes from here, where there was a much smaller chance of my hurting someone. And I tried to improve my equipment. That's where I had my lab when you were at Northern."

"What happened to it?"

"One of the local FBI agents decided I was a terrorist. They raided my house one night, not long after you left for Seattle. I think they jostled my equipment when they broke into the lab, and the whole place blew up. No one was hurt this time, but it was too much for Northern University, and I was fired. So now I'm in the real estate business."

"So why did you ask me to come here?" I said.

Regina gave me an unassuming smile, then ate the last bites of her desert without answering.

15

Finally, Regina stood up. "Let me show you the rest of the building." She led me back to the freight elevator, and we went up a floor. The room we entered was similar to the one below, though free of clutter.

"I'll divide this area into apartments or offices, depending on how things pan out," she said, waving at the empty area.

I followed her up to a similar third floor, and then to the roof. The entire rooftop was covered with black glass panels, except for a few walkways between them. "This might be one of the most state-of-the-art rooftop solar installations in the country," she said.

"Impressive."

"Oh, this is the lesser half of it."

We trudged down the stairs and got into the elevator again. This time we took it to the basement. The room we entered was bare and clean and smaller than the one above, basically the width of the elevator. A set of double doors were set into each of the side walls. Instead of going left toward the center of the building and under the gated walkway and Mexican restaurant, Regina took me to the right, under her construction "playground."

She turned the lights on as we entered. The room was filled with massive batteries, enormous electrical panels, and a wall of some kind of control equipment.

"This is the electrical control center for the building," Regina said. "Theoretically, the panels and these batteries could power the entire completed building, even if we were completely off the grid."

"Theoretically?" I prodded.

She didn't answer, but said, "I need to show you one thing more."

We went back up to the first floor, to the anteroom of her office, the first room in the building I'd entered. She unlocked the door I couldn't open earlier. It led to a narrow stairway infused with the thick smell of oiled wood. Not the lemon-scented oil of fine furniture, but the odor of oily machines, of sweaty clothes rubbing against the wall paneling, and steel-toed boots trampling through the place for hours, days, years. One set of stairs went up, but the floor above had been built over the opening, so it led nowhere. I followed Regina to the floor below. The stairs were so narrow that we couldn't walk side by side.

As I descended, the treads rocked slightly beneath my feet, telling of generations of workers who had loosened them. A frosted window high in the front wall provided the only light for the shaft. Although it was enough light to see with, Regina still warned me about a board that was missing from the landing where the stairs doubled back.

At the bottom we were in a dark, narrow room, a hallway that seemed to lead nowhere. I gathered we were next to the battery and electrical-control room, but there were no doors in the concrete wall separating it from us. The long wall opposite was a stone wall—an old building foundation, I assumed—which also had no opening. At the far end of the hall was another blank concrete wall. Regina turned back under the stairs to a tired-looking steel door. She unlocked it, revealing a dirty closet nearly filled with a massive cast-iron structure. "Not much to look at, is it?" she asked.

I was intrigued. "What is it?"

"It used to be a furnace for this place. Now it's another door." The door to the furnace snapped open—controlled, I found out later, by an electronic key in Regina's hand. As it opened, the furnace floor slid away, revealing a stainless-steel circular staircase. In and down we went.

At the bottom of the steps was a sort of locker room that reminded me of Louise's shower room at Northern but smaller and much cleaner. Regina handed me some white Tyvek coveralls and put on a pair herself. I knew they were used when preventing contamination of the wearer or of the environment, either of which could be an important issue.

Mine fit perfectly. Regina had planned for my visit.

I'd assumed that because we were in the second basement, we might be entering a hazardous waste area, but instead we walked into a long, immaculate office. Waist-high tables stood along both long walls, crowded with computers and other electronic equipment. One of the long walls was the front foundation wall. The other had a continuous window that faced onto a large sunken room that appeared to be a miniature industrial plant. In the center was a concrete bunker that looked like an Egyptian sarcophagus. It was approximately eight feet wide, maybe seven or eight feet tall, about half of the ceiling height. If Regina said anything I do not remember it, but I knew what I was looking at.

"You haven't quit your work, have you?" I asked her.

"How could I? Let me show you." Next to the large concrete structure was a three foot high bench with about two thirds the footprint of its neighbor. I followed her onto the bench via a built in ladder so we could see over the large bunker. There was another ladder leading to the top of it that we did not climb. "The piece we're standing on contains the refrigeration unit." She pointed to a steel loop sticking out of the slab. "I use the overhead crane to just lift the whole top off to work on it."

I looked up and noticed a crane assembly hanging from a large steel beam. Regina continued, "There's a smaller door in the top of the main unit which

I use for minor repairs." I noticed another loop which was evidently the handle to the smaller door, whose outline I could clearly see. It was about three foot square.

"It seems funny that you can lift this entire top off, but you only have a small entry into that entire bunker," I said.

"There's a large door on the other side, let me show you."

We climbed back down to the floor and walked around to the far side. It looked like half of this wall was on a sliding rail system so it could be moved aside. "This door is much too heavy for hinges, but this mechanism is a pain to work. Every time I open it, it takes nearly an hour to reseal it. That's why I located most of the equipment close to the top door."

"So you have to reach down to make repairs?" I asked.

"Oh, no. I lower myself in with the crane. Of course it's radioactive in there, so I need to wear more than Tyvek coveralls."

Regina then led me through the lab to the only other visible door. It opened onto a machine shop, which was full of lathes, drills, welders, grinders, whatnot. "This is where I spend most of my time."

To the right was an elevator door. I realized the freight elevator must come down an extra floor. "The canal had a diverted sluice that flowed under the building and supplied the power for the original factory," she said. "This second basement is where the turbine was housed. What do you think?"

"More impressive."

"It was supposed to be filled in. You're the only other person who's ever seen this."

"So why do you need my help? I know next to nothing about your work. In fact, I barely understand your elementary explanations."

"I'd like you to help me explain how my stock trades do so well. It seems you've created the perfect cover." She flashed me a crooked smile.

"I have? You mean you want me to cook your books?"

"I've gotten a little ahead of myself financially. As you can imagine, this project is pretty damn expensive."

I laughed. In my other life, the entire world was asking me to take their money and invest it with my expertise. But Regina wanted me to hide how she was making hers.

"Are you doing something illegal?" "I don't think so. Just dangerous." "Because of the explosions?"

"No, I think I have that under control. The concrete walls and lid in that tank are more than two feet thick. I'm more afraid of what people would do if they could know the future."

"Like who?"

"Like a government, for instance. Or certain businesses. Or both, together." Finally her situation was beginning to make sense. I knew from my early days in foster care that though government could be helpful, it was soulless, and could not always be counted on to do the right thing. And I had certainly seen in my last few years as a businessman that some people would do anything for power and wealth. Although I was often irritated with Regina, I did trust her, and she must obviously have trusted me to show me her lab. I decided I would try to help her.

"You know, there's a limit to how fast I can make your money grow. I'd estimate about a 20 to 30 percent faster rate of return than the market average, and most of that comes from avoiding downturns."

"I'll take what I can get. I'm pretty sure I can live with that."

"Back to the time scale. It's almost impossible for me to believe you have invented a time machine—not a virtual one, but a real one. How far into the future do you claim to see?"

"I'm sure you know that milliseconds are enough of an advantage in the world of stock trading to make a fortune."

Stocks were now my world, as Sheila had foretold. "Of course. That's why all the brokerages have found they need to be right next to the stock exchanges. Even at the speed of light, distance matters. So are you talking milliseconds here?"

She shook her head. "It depends on how much information you need. I can read a single stock nearly ten minutes in advance at this point."

"Ten minutes!" I exclaimed. "That's unheard of! Ten minutes!"

"Ron, I understand you predicted the dot-com crash months in advance. I can't do that...yet."

"Yes, but I see very vague, general trends, no real resolution. You're evidently seeing an actual event."

"True. I can see more at a shorter interval. But it's very energy-consuming. Maybe you can help me with that as well. Let me show you an example of how it works." She led me back into the narrow control room and sat down at a computer console. She invited me to sit down next to her as she started typing on her keyboard.

"First of all, let's make this quick—we'll look ten seconds ahead. Secondly, it's simpler to make a profit on a stock that increases in value than on one that does not change or decreases. Therefore, before I start I look for sectors that appear to be volatile. For instance, right now the energy markets are in a bit of turmoil, so we'll start there. BP is very active in the Balkans, so we'll look at BP stock. First I will initiate an exploration, and see if it goes up." She hit a few strokes, then said, "Nope, not that time, let's try again." She tapped the keyboard again and waited a few seconds. "Bingo! Now let me review this for you."

She turned the screen so I could see it. "The first time the BP price listed at 53.85 both times, so the computer didn't initiate a trade. The second time it started at 53.81, then two seconds later we were informed it would trade at 53.84 in another seven seconds, so a buy and sell was initiated for $10,000. We made three cents a share, or $5.60."

I didn't know if the computer was for real, but the actual result didn't seem that impressive. "Not a big gain," I said.

"Not for one trade, but the point is I can make that 100 percent of the time." Regina hit a few more keystrokes, then turned back to me. "The whole thing is automated. Let's say every twenty seconds I make five bucks. That's nearly eight million dollars a year. Of course I make sure I miss about 30 percent of the time, for a net profit of around three million."

"You just have your computer run all the time, automatically buying and selling."

"Yep, pretty slick, huh?"

"Yeah, but not what I expected for a time machine."

"Maybe you were expecting a police booth, or a DeLorean?" She laughed. "And this is why you spent so much time trying to get me to understand your theories?"

Regina quickly became serious. "Ron, if I have ever taught you anything it should be that it is the wonder of existence that drives my pursuit of knowledge. As amazing as you may find this machine, or any other technological invention, they are merely the tools we use to show how much we understand. I taught you what I know because I hoped to share that wonder with you, because I thought you would get it."

"And you need me to make your wins and losses more believable."

Her grin came back. "Mostly that. My other big problem is I use too much power. Those solar arrays should power this building, but the truth is I spend tens of thousands on electricity because this beast uses so much juice. Theoretically I should be able to reduce that significantly. I think you could help me there as well."

I made several trips to Foxfield over the next couple of months, trying to wrap my head around Regina's finances. It was trickier than I'd expected. After all, I was a mathematician, not an accountant, and I had to return to the big city, my real job, and my wife.

Once I was back in Manhattan, however, I felt like a fly in molasses, and the molasses was flowing inexorably to a destination I wanted to avoid. Sheila had bought a modern apartment for us, an eight-room condo on the Upper East Side, on the twenty-third floor of a building overlooking the Queensboro Bridge. I preferred the old, quiet apartment we already had, but Sheila wanted something larger and better equipped for her soirees, which had far more powerful attendees in New York than the ones she had hosted in Seattle. The new place had a utility elevator that opened into the back of the kitchen, as well as a main elevator that opened directly into our living room. This was a great boon for having a party catered, which even I appreciated, as neither of us could cook anything more complicated than cold cereal. My claim to culinary fame was the espresso machine I'd bought Sheila for our one-month anniversary. Hers was that she had learned to use it. It was a significant step above instant coffee.

I suppose buying an eight-million-dollar apartment should have been fun, but I was having trouble concentrating. Of course, part of the problem was that the work I'd done using fractals to predict the market paled in comparison to the possibility of actually knowing the future using a real time machine, such as Regina's, however limited it might be.

The other part of the problem might have been that the World Trade Center disaster had steeled Sheila. The part of her that knew when to relax and have fun had vanished. I had to find her missing half. I also realized that despite her attempts to support me, she'd grown uncomfortable with my trips to Foxfield. It had been about three years since the market had crashed, and our indicators told us it would soon be ready to change again.

"We need you here, Ron," she said. "More important, I need you back. I value loyalty to an old friend as much as anyone, but I'm your wife." She was nearly crying.

I decided to quickly finish my business with Regina and then convince Sheila we couldn't let terrorists take away our love of life any more than we could let them take away our business. I promised her I'd only make one more trip. I had told her I was helping Regina get her books in order, but it was becoming difficult to explain why that was so involved as to necessitate my repeated visits.

In Foxfield my routine resembled my days as an undergraduate. Although the pace wasn't as frenetic as my real job, my New York job, I pursued it with my old nonstop immersion into mathematical theory. I stayed in an unfurnished apartment on the third floor. It had a mattress and a bathroom.

I'd successfully managed to make Regina's earnings appear to have resulted from the fractal analysis I'd developed with Sheila, but this wasn't helping her income, as stocks were still in a bear market.

I also developed some improved algorithms for gleaning information, as it were, from the future, which was an extremely challenging task.

Regina had discovered that the temperature of absolute zero—0 degrees Kelvin or -273 Celsius—is the temperature at which a particle has the same underlying motion as the universe. She concluded that temperatures below that do exist and discovered a way to create particles that could "shoot the tube," meaning they move through the helix and reach the target sooner than time. A particle with a temperature of minus infinity would have no spatial component to its existence but probably wouldn't be controllable. We only needed a few degrees minus K to make our machine work.

The algorithms—the mathematical and computer routines—I refer to were mainly to increase the efficiencies of Regina's experiments. So I spent a great deal of my time either cooking her financial books or reducing her electric bill. There was a further irony to my effort, as I'd decided the best approach to reduce the power usage was to create a self-learning routine using the same Bayesian statistics I'd scorned in Smythe's thesis. It was not particularly exciting, mathematically speaking, but working on a project which could look into the future, a real time machine, was so exciting I did not mind the drudgery.

16

I'd been in Foxfield for about four days on what was to be my last trip. I was using Regina's front office, the reception room with the long tables and construction drawings, as my work area. I'd piled the blueprints in a heap on the floor and spread my computations across the tables. Regina was silently leafing through the blueprints when my wife walked in. She was beautiful, as usual, but she had a stone-cold look on her face.

"Sheila, what are you doing here?" I said.

"I'm not sure, maybe taking you home." She turned to Regina. "You must be Regina Russo."

The two women assessed each other carefully. "I am. And you're obviously Sheila Park. It's good to meet you. Now I can thank you in person for the loan of your husband."

Sheila gave a bitter half smile. She glanced down at my table. "I see he's been busy." I understood this statement to reveal her annoyance, as lately I hadn't been able to concentrate at all on my work with her at our firm.

Regina ignored her tone. "Ron's very talented. You're lucky to have him, but I'm sure you know that."

"Indeed. *When* I have him." There was an awkward silence. Sheila turned to me. "I don't want to waste any of our time by dragging this out. I feel this has gone past helping an old friend. I don't understand what you're doing, but I need to know you're coming home now. For good."

Sheila's lip trembled as she spoke. She glared at Regina first, then at me, then at Regina again. Regina's face remained placid. There was nothing for her to say, so she stayed silent. I hadn't gotten over seeing my wife here and was trying to process her words. I muttered, "I don't know what to say—"

Sheila interrupted me. "You don't have to say anything." She gestured toward my work table. "This is way beyond anything Professor Russo could possibly need to fix her finances or this building." She looked closer at some of the pages. "You know, Ron, this looks like it's beyond anything you've done for *us*."

My face heated up. "It's not anything—"I started, but again I was interrupted. Sheila exhaled with a sigh. "Oh, come on, Ron. You know me better than that. Damn it, if you gave me a few weeks, I might even figure out some of what you are doing. But it's none of my business, and I really don't care." She smiled, a small smile, but without irony or malice. "As far as I'm concerned, there are only two meaningful responses: either you drop everything and say you are coming home now, or you don't."

"Sheila, this will be my last trip, but I need to finish what I'm doing." Sheila turned to leave and I followed her out the door.

"You can't just leave," I nearly shouted.

"I can, I am," she replied, "unless you tell me exactly what you are up to with *her*." She nodded at the building.

"Uhh, it's nothing really." I felt I couldn't reveal Regina's secret without her permission—I had come to agree with Regina that no one should know about her work.

"Then our marriage isn't anything either." She turned to leave again, then turned back and said, almost as an afterthought, "We'll be in touch, to tie up loose ends."

"Wait," I called after her, but she had already stepped into her limousine and was whisked away.

My head was spinning as I trudged back into the office. Regina was still standing there. We just stared at each other for a while. An emotional tornado had just whipped through my life, and I needed to assess the damage.

"Damn it!" was all I could muster.

"Do you want to take a break?" Regina asked. We both laughed, a little nervously.

We cut through the back of the building and crossed to the rear of the donut shop. Regina had set up two parking spaces behind the shop, both marked reserved, for the benefit of the police. As a result, cops often used the back door instead of the front and could walk through the kitchen area to get to the tables. The police liked this arrangement because their cars were less obvious than when they parked on the street. Regina and I liked the informality.

The shop was run by Frank and Ina Shoupe. They both worked long hours to make it work, but it was just named Frank's because he was a bit of a local legend. He had taken North Foxfield High School to the state football championship and then had gone on to a successful college career and even had spent a few years as a tight end for Green Bay and Denver in the pros.

Regina and I both still took our coffee black. As we sat there, my thoughts wandered back to the truck-stop diner where we had spent so many nights. I'd just thrown a marriage and millions of dollars away and couldn't quite grasp the finality of it all. Not so, Regina.

"Are you going back to New York? Are you going to stay here?" "I don't know," I said.

Regina wrapped her fingers around her mug. "In some ways I'm not that different from Sheila."

She caught my surprise and waved her hand vaguely. "I don't mean I want to marry you, Ron. I know how good you are at what you do, but I can only use you, make a place for you, if you're serious. There are a lot of options for you, and working with me won't be the easiest."

"But it would probably be the most interesting."

"That may be," she agreed. "Think about it for a while. I'd love to have you around, if you want to stay."

Regina's words upset and confused me. I didn't know what I wanted to do. Maybe that was what Sheila had sensed. It occurred to me that I didn't know if I was reliable.

I took a couple of days to assess my situation. I thought about going back to New York, but I would have to explain to my wife what I was doing with Regina to have any hope of winning her back. I also realized I didn't really want to return to our expensive condo on the Upper East Side. I recalled Dr. Rastowski's warning about Sheila running over me if I couldn't keep up. Maybe that was what had happened to me; maybe the only way to live with Sheila would be to live the life she wanted.

For the next week I stayed at my unfinished apartment at night but wandered the streets of Foxfield by day. I even returned to the Northern University campus once, perhaps hoping to run into Louise. Not only did I not find her, her locker in the underground men's room was empty, and her bedding was gone. I could only hope my car had taken her to a richer life.

One afternoon I decided I was ready to talk to Regina. She was in her outer office, talking to a couple of contractors, when I walked in. I waited in the inner office until she was finished. She came in with the same shy, crooked smile that I'd first seen nearly twelve years prior.

"So is it roots or no roots? Are you really interested in working with me?" "I guess I want to know I'm considered reliable, that I can be trusted," I replied.

Her voice grew a notch softer. "I never considered that an issue, Ron. Surely you realize I've shared my life and ideas with you in a way I haven't done with anyone else."

I smiled. "I'd like to work with you then."

Regina seemed to ponder my words for a while, as if she hadn't expected them. "Well, then, that's the easy part. We have a lot to discuss." She went to her desk and shuffled through some papers. "I have a few things I need to finish right now. Why don't you come back around five or six?"

When I returned, she lost no time getting right to the point. "I guess there's not a lot more you can do for my finances right now. How about the work you're doing on our pretemporal information collector?"

Calling the machine a "pretemporal information collector" was Regina's idea of a joke, but calling it "ours" was a new twist. I tried not to let it distract me. "You should try what I've done to date before I try to refine my ideas," I said. "Without some real-world results, I'll just be spitting in the wind. I have another approach for preparing the target as well, but it would be premature to even try to work on that now."

"Sounds good. How are your construction-management skills?" "Huh?"

"I'd like to spend more time in the lab. I spent all day today authorizing paints and door handles, trying to finish the second-floor apartments."

"I don't know anything about paint or door handles," I said.

"No need to. Like I said, I did that today. It'll be windows, or something, tomorrow. And the nail spa has a plumbing problem."

"I don't know anything about plumbing. Or windows either," I blurted. "That's why we have plumbers and carpenters, and good ones. And a contractor to run the show. You just need to be able to call them, coordinate them, listen to the architect and the tenants, keep the building inspector happy. In other words, use a phone." She paused, then continued, "You may wonder why I bother with the offices and apartments and stores. I certainly don't make anything off of them and won't for years. And I don't need the long-term investment either. But this building needs to be run like a business anyway, to give me a reason to be here. Who knows, the FBI could still be watching me."

I followed her around for two or three weeks, and then I began to run the place. Also, Regina insisted I rent an apartment away from 58 Race Street. "I might be a little paranoid, but that's probably a realistic attitude for me. It might be good if you could be absent at times."

17

When I finally did take over managing the building I found myself pretty busy. As Regina had explained, she had solid crews in place so it wasn't that difficult. At least it wasn't difficult until the building inspector called and asked me to meet him in his office. Actually, it was Foxfield's assistant building inspector, and he requested Regina.

"This is the first time the inspector didn't just show up for an inspection. I think something's going on; I think you should go. You can always plead ignorance in order to stall him." Regina seldom looked troubled, but she did now.

"Don't you think it's just some forms you need to sign?" I asked, though it was clear she didn't.

"If that's what it is, you can sign anything they give you." It was true; she had made me a principal in her firm, Race Street LLC.

The next day, I headed over to meet with the assistant building inspector. The inspectors' offices were on the third floor of the town offices building, and I took each step with a bit of trepidation. Regina's anxiety and my inexperience were formidable opponents, and I hadn't even met the assistant building inspector yet. I was trying to be prepared for anything, but I still wasn't ready for what I found. The assistant building inspector turned out to be my old apartment mate, Tom Jacobs. He was clearly as astonished as I.

"Ron Larsen! I didn't know you were involved with this project. I thought you were doing big things in New York." Tom stood up to shake my hand, then offered me a seat and sat down again.

I was surprised he'd heard of my exploits, but I decided to try to develop a rapport. "Tom Jacobs. You know, I owe you a huge thank-you. Yeah, I had big ideas in the big city, but people got in the way."

"Why do you owe me any thanks? If I recall, you were a lot closer with Cheryl

Liona than you were with me."

"Ah, yes, Cheryl. I wonder what ever happened to her."

"I heard she's a professor in central Vermont somewhere, one of those liberal arts colleges. And all along I thought she was just a waitress." It seemed Tom had developed an interest in others that he didn't have when I knew him. "So anyway, why do you owe me a thank-you?"

"Well, I was pretty confused in those days, and I realized I needed to steady my life. I was impressed with the way you managed yourself." Nothing could have been further from the truth; I'd thought I'd shrivel up and die from boredom if I had to live Tom's life. "So, what's up?"

He leaned back in his seat. "I was hoping Regina Russo would show up to explain a puzzling development. How long have you been with her?"

"I've known her since I was in middle school," I answered, purposely misunderstanding his question.

"That's interesting, but I meant with this particular project." "Oh, I guess a few months."

"That's probably unfortunate, but let's get to it." He led me to a long table, not unlike Regina's, with what appeared to be blueprints for 58 Race Street. "Do you see the difference between these two drawings?"

I had a feeling I knew where this was going and tried on my best poker face. One of the drawings appeared to be the official, sealed drawings, which showed Regina's lab as non-existent because the second basement was filled in with a "structural" soil. The other plan was nearly identical, except it showed the lab area open, as it had been built, and it didn't have an engineer's seal.

I pointed to the official plan. "That's the one I'm familiar with, which shows how it was built. This one looks like an earlier design that was evidently rejected. Where did you get it?" I was stating the obvious, which was untrue.

"Well, of course, that's what we thought, but evidently one of the workers said it's not so."

"One of the workers?" I asked.

"Some guy—I think his name is Andrew—involved in the foundation construction is saying this area wasn't filled in. He says there's a big room down there." Tom was trying to act nonchalant, but he would have been an easy mark at poker. I had the distinct feeling he'd been instructed not to reveal his informant's name, and that he realized he'd made a mistake.

I was able to hide my own astonishment a bit better. "Who did he say this to?"

"Let's just say we have reliable sources." Tom was trying to slam the barn door after only half the horses were gone.

"I'm not saying you don't." I knew being resistant was necessary but not sufficient. I was also trying to gain a little time to regain my footing. "What are you getting at, anyway?"

"If we cut a hole in one of the walls, or the floor above, we could find out if our source is accurate."

I groaned. "You want us to cut up the building to prove whether one unknown source talking to another unknown source was lying or not?"

"If you don't agree to this, we'll be able to get a court order." The knives were coming out.

I walked over to the plans. "Tom, were you at the ceremony when the city dedicated the solar array?"

He shook his head. "No, that was above my pay grade. My boss takes the photo ops. I understand the event was pretty impressive."

"It was before my time here, but I wouldn't have been invited either. I understand the event was indeed pretty impressive. Your boss's boss—Mayor Ryan—was there, as well as our state and federal representative. Senator Kerry was in attendance too, and the project was funded through the efforts of Senator Kennedy. The building has a brass plaque commemorating the occasion." Tom was listening to me carefully; I could tell he was wondering where I was going with my monologue. I pointed to the plan that showed the underground room.

"This area is completely below grade, so we'd need to excavate to even access the walls. The room above, where the plaque is, contains the electronic controls and the batteries for the solar power system. I'm sure the people whose names are on the plaque are also going to be interested in any attempt to cut up their room."

Tom's face grew a little red as he digested my words. He realized if this went wrong, his job would be at risk. "Wait here." He disappeared around some file cabinets into a back room. I heard him arguing with someone. I made my way to the door and opened it. Tom was there with another man in a room that wasn't much larger than a closet. "I asked you to wait," Tom barked at me.

"Sorry. I was just wondering where the bathroom is," I replied. He told me and I left.

A few minutes later, when we met at the table again (without the other man), Tom had recomposed himself. "We're going to find out what's beneath that floor. If you and Regina have nothing to hide, we'd appreciate your cooperation. We'll be satisfied with a six-inch diameter hole drilled through the floor. You could easily do that without contaminating the room." Tom leafed through the plans. "Does this represent the layout of the mechanical room?"

I examined the blueprint. "I don't know if it's exact, but it's close."

He pointed to a spot in the middle of the room. "You could core the floor right here. And I want to be there when you do."

"I'll have to talk to Regina first."

"I understand. But you both need to know I won't be able to stop this process, and neither will you."

"Okay," I said. I turned to leave, but Tom called after me. "Ron, did your stock analysis system work?"

"It did and does work," I said as I left. I wasn't interested in small talk.

I rushed back to Race Street and recounted my meeting to Regina before I could forget the details. "What did this guy in the back room look like?" she asked.

"Kind of like that guy on that old science fiction t.v. show, *The Twilight Zone,* except his face was a little more rugged." "You mean Rod Serling?

"Yeah, Rod Serling."

"Damn," Regina swore. "Let's go for a walk."

I thought it was an odd time for a walk. It had been sprinkling all day, but just as I had returned to the office a good old summer thunderstorm let loose. It was pouring, and the sky lit up every few seconds, followed quickly by a monstrous thunderclap. When we got outside, Regina shouted into my ear, "It's Paul, Paul DeVries."

"Who's that?" I shouted back.

"The FBI agent who blew up my house and got me fired from Northern. He's convinced I'm a terrorist. Ron, we're going to have to take him very seriously. The building, our phones, our cars might be bugged. You did well, but we've got to stamp this out. I'll take care of the hole in the floor, but I want you to visit Leo."

"Leo? Who's Leo?" Her words had been drowned out by the latest thunderclap.

"Leo Casillo. He's the contractor who did all the work on that room. I presented the official plans to innumerable contractors, and he was the one who told me it would be cheaper not to fill the space in. I explained that my engineer had insisted that the foundation was unstable. Leo assured me he could fix it and make it safe. I didn't care about the savings as much as having that space and not arousing suspicions."

"But I saw an engineer's plan showing that room."

Regina laughed a little. Her face had relaxed a little while we spoke. "I lied to Leo about that; I already had this plan, I knew it could be done, but I didn't want to present it to the city. In fact, Leo improved on my engineer's plan."

"Where do I find him?"

She gave me that wry smile again, then turned serious. "Well, he's an interesting person. Be very careful and respectful. He works out of Pawtucket, down in Rhode Island. I don't think he's in the mob, but he clearly knows people and has a bit of an attitude. We need to explain that this Andrew guy has to be silenced."

"Is he going to, like, knock him off?" I asked. This was getting a little too weird for me.

She shook her head. "Let's not overreact, Ron. Leo can be persuasive without being violent. He just needs to get this Andrew fellow to shut up for a few months." She paused, and then added, "After all, whoever Andrew talked to was probably trying to dig dirt on Leo. We're probably secondary targets. I think Leo will appreciate the heads-up."

"Maybe you should talk to him," I suggested. I had no desire to meet this guy.

Regina considered this, then said, "This is serious for all of us, but I don't want Leo to know how serious it is for us in particular. Also, I'm afraid I might be followed."

147

*

Regina didn't dare call Leo because she was afraid his phone might be tapped, so I had to pay him an unannounced visit at his office. Since he was a contractor, we decided the best time to find him would be early in the morning. Because we thought even my car might be tagged, I had to get up extra early to get a rental.

I was getting paranoid, realizing it was impossible to make sure I'd covered my tracks. The ninety minutes it took me to get to Pawtucket felt like a whole day. I found Leo's office in the industrial section of an industrial city—though it was more of a warehouse than an office, with a large parking lot surrounded by a chain-link fence. Construction workers were loading several vans, and a couple of dump trucks were leaving. Everyone in the yard seemed busy, and they all looked like they knew what they were doing; nevertheless, an older guy was shouting orders to one and all. It wasn't clear anyone was listening, but he was clearly in charge. Assuming he was Leo, I walked up to him. "Mr. Casillo?" "Who's asking?" I had no idea what his accent was, but it was pretty thick. His voice was raw, a smoker's voice. I towered over him, but he probably weighed as much as I did. He had a body built by carrying cement bags and eating rich food. He had a large head with a shock of thick white hair on top, and a face that was once probably movie-star handsome.

"I work for Regina Russo. My name's Ron Larsen," I replied. His countenance changed.

"Ah, Regina! A true beauty! How is she?" He held out his hand, and I shook it. He had a powerful grip, and he knew it. Fortunately, he didn't want to break the bones in my hand.

"She's doing well. I think she prefers real estate to the university." I was telling the truth, somewhat.

"She'll do fine. I told her she was pretty smart for someone with all those degrees." He let out a deep, rumbling laugh. "So why did you come here instead of calling?"

"Regina wanted to be safe. We have a little problem."

He narrowed his eyes. "Problem? What kind of problem? Is the building okay?"

148

"No, no, the building is fine. It's your help we've got to worry about." I told him the story.

"Andrew? I don't have anyone named Andrew on my crews." He spat his words out. "Are you sure about this?"

"I roomed with the assistant inspector for a year. He's a lousy liar. He let the name slip and practically had a heart attack. Someone named Andrew is talking."

"Oh, shit!" Leo obviously had figured something out. "It's Drew! My dumb nephew. I love my sister, but she married an idiot, and her son's no smarter than his father."

Leo stared at the pavement for a minute then pulled out his cell phone. "Hey, Tony, I need a favor. I want you to gut an apartment today.... No, the owner doesn't know. Just gut it. Get rid of everything—the wallboard, plumbing, wiring, everything—then admit you made a mistake and offer to fix it for nothing.... Today—it has to be today, now, subatomic. I'll pay for everything, but I can't be involved." He gave an address and put the phone back in his pocket before grabbing my arm hard.

"So was Regina playing me?" I didn't answer, and he continued. "Well, whatever. Drew's got a new live-in girlfriend who I knew was too good for him, I'm sure she's the one. The FBI might be spying on me, and Regina got caught up in my world, or vice versa. Anyway, Drew's gonna be crushed. It's a good time for him to take a vacation, and I just made sure he doesn't have a place to stay here now anyway, just to make it easier for him to leave. Say hi to Regina, tell her there will be no more tales from this end. I hope you can take care of yours."

*

Regina laughed when I returned to 58 Race Street and told her the story. "I like Leo." She was on top of some scaffolding she'd assembled in the middle of her lab. She was working on a fifty-five-gallon steel barrel she had fastened to the concrete ceiling. "When we drill through the floor we'll find the gravel in this thing." She knocked on the steel with her wrench and it returned a dull thud. She appeared to be very pleased with herself, but I thought she looked a little incongruous. She climbed down from her perch. "I want you to call this company,

Concrete Wizards. Order a four-inch-diameter corer and explain that it needs to be a clean bore, no dust allowed in the room."

"But Tom wanted a six-inch core."

"That's what DeVries wants, and he'll be pissed." She laughed. "Are you good at acting stupid?"

I grinned. "The best."

18

I made a date with Concrete Wizards for later that week, then called Tom. "We're all set for you to come by at ten on Friday morning to observe us cutting a hole in our floor." I didn't ask if he was bringing DeVries, and I didn't tell him a reporter and an aide from Senator Kennedy's office would be there.

I had scheduled Concrete Wizards for 9 a.m., so the drill was already bolted to the floor, and the dust collector was in place and our other guests had already arrived when Paul DeVries and Tom showed up. Regina had decided to stay away.

I met them at the front door, but Tom didn't introduce DeVries. "Hi, Tom," I said as casually as I could, "We're already underway." I led them downstairs to the control room, where a tech from Concrete Wizards already had begun to drill the hole.

"Who are all these people?" snapped DeVries, gesturing to the other man and woman in the room. Both were young professionals dressed far too formally for the occasion.

"This is Janice Korbell," I said. "A reporter from the *Foxfield Gazette*. And this is Henry Ridge, an aide from Senator Kennedy's office."

"Who invited them?" DeVries snapped again.

"Well, we thought Tom invited Ms. Korbell." I turned to the woman. "Didn't you say the call came from the town offices?"

"That's what I was told," she said. Of course, I knew Regina had arranged the call.

"And I contacted Senator Kennedy's office."

Henry Ridge stepped forward and offered his hand. "And you are?" he asked.

Tom stepped up to shake his hand. "Tom Jacobs, Foxfield's assistant building inspector."

Henry turned to DeVries, who clearly was very uncomfortable with the situation but didn't dare insult a US senator's aide. "Special Agent Paul DeVries, FBI."

Henry's eyebrows shot up. "What interest does the FBI have with a building inspection in Foxfield?"

"We received intelligence that indicated there might be an anomaly with this building, and the owner, Regina Russo, has a history of possible terrorist activity."

Henry Ridge did not seem impressed. The entire conversation took place above the screeching of the concrete corer, which finally shut off. The tech vacuumed under his plastic tent for a few minutes, then carefully unfurled his shelter to let us see. There was dirt at the bottom of the hole.

"I specifically requested a six-inch hole," DeVries said, his face turning red. It was my turn to stick the needles in a little farther. "Agent DeVries, Tom did say six, but the technician here only brought along a four-inch bit, and I thought we'd better get this over with."

Tom was visibly embarrassed by his companion's reaction. "I wanted six, but it's pretty obvious this building was done as approved."

DeVries knelt and stuck his hand into the hole. As Regina had planned, there wasn't much room to dig around, and she had made sure the soil in the barrel below the floor was compacted, making it even harder to dig through.

Janice Korbell crouched next to him and said, "What did you expect to find?" He glared at her but didn't say anything. When he pulled his hand out, she put hers into the soil, felt around, then took a picture down the hole.

Henry turned to Tom and DeVries. "Is everything okay here then?" "Yes, sir. Sorry for the inconvenience," Tom said.

DeVries seemed to mutter an assent and turned to leave. As he walked away, Henry turned back to me. "Thanks for inviting me, Ron. Please don't hesitate to call the senator's office anytime you have a problem. He's very proud of this project." He said this loud enough to make sure DeVries heard him.

After the small crowd left I walked around the corner to the donut shop, where I thought I'd find Regina. She was sitting at the booth with two of the city's finest. As we returned to the office, I gave her a rundown on our little spectacle.

152

"We did what we had to, but it sounds like DeVries threw a fit. He'll be back," she said.

*

A few days after the coring incident, Sheila's lawyers (her older brothers, Greg and Mark) contacted me. It had only been a few months, but my New York experiences seemed far behind me, and I was so busy with my new life that I sort of had forgotten that we did have some ends to tidy up, namely a divorce and buyout.

Sheila offered me ten million dollars if I promised to renounce all rights to my fractal methods and never engage in trading stocks for a living. I refused. I didn't care about the money or the trading, but I wasn't in a mood to give up anything. After her brothers and I had several curt phone discussions, I told them that if she wanted to negotiate directly with me, we could work things out.

She finally did call, against her brothers' advice I'm sure. I'd come to realize how much I'd hurt her and was on my best behavior. We had an amicable, though not warm, conversation.

"Sheila, I'll sign the divorce papers today, but I won't forfeit the rights to my creations."

She was silent for an interminable few moments. "Okay. But I don't want you involved in Victoria Sound."

"Fair enough. Buy me out."

"Or competing with me," she said.

I recalled Dr. Rastowski's warning about Sheila running over me and leaving me in her dust; I knew he was right. The last thing I wanted was to go up against her. "Let's take a breath," I said. "I know—and you know—that you'd crush me if I did anything like that. Forget about your lawyers, Sheila. I hurt you— I know that, and I'm sorry—but I didn't lie to you and won't lie to you. I've given up your world and have no interest in returning."

When she realized I wasn't going to compete against her she relaxed. We agreed on five million for my share of the company, which was only a fraction of its worth. I gave up no rights to our work, and neither did she. We were to simply go our separate ways.

153

A couple of weeks after our coring party Tom Jacobs came back to Race Street, without Paul DeVries, ostensibly for a regular inspection. I assumed he wanted to mend fences. I'd finished the last units on the second and third floors above the donut shop, so Tom needed to go through his inspection checklist. Afterward, he asked if I wanted to have lunch with him. I offered to treat him at Eduardo's.

"I don't know why I keep showing up at Regina's building," he said, just as our tacos and tostadas arrived. "You two never leave much for me to complain about. She taught you well."

I didn't want to mention why Regina and I were paranoid about inspections, so I made light of it. "You're not going to make me drill holes in any walls, are you?"

Tom blushed. "I hope you realize I was forced into that situation." "Yeah, DeVries wasn't very subtle."

"He seriously believes Regina is up to something bad. He never told me what exactly. I'm not sure even he knows."

"Regina has made mistakes, but she can't figure out what DeVries is about either." I lowered my voice. "He evidently blew her house up and destroyed her academic career several years ago, 1997 if I recall correctly."

"DeVries tells a different tale. Anyway, you and Regina both appear to be refugees from more illustrious careers."

This was the second time Tom had referred to my work in the stock-trading business. I decided not to cut him short this time. "Well, I had a great product but the wrong partners. Now I have a lesser product"—I waved a hand at the building around us—"but a more reliable partner."

"Rumor has it you must have had a time machine to do what you did in New York," Tom said, chuckling.

I almost choked on my tostada, but covered it with a laugh of my own. "Nothing that exotic, but the method does work."

Tom leaned in over the table and addressed me in a whisper, "I have a brother-in-law in the trade business who got laid off during the dot-com crash. He swears you were the only person in the world who foretold its timing. So when's the crash going to end?"

If he wanted to be reeled in, it seemed like the time for me to do it. "I've just jumped back in with both feet," I said, leaning back in my chair for effect.

"You're kidding." He sat up with a look of wonder.

I wasn't kidding; my metrics indicated the market had bottomed out and was ready to rise. "Not at all. I think we're about to see another boom, in the short run at least."

Tom went back to his meal but quickly put his fork down. "So, does your method only work for large sums?"

I shook my head. "That has nothing to do with it. It's just that traders make more money off large investors."

"And you're still in the business?"

"Not really, but I take care of myself and my friends." "Meaning Regina?"

"Including Regina." "Anyone else?" he prodded.

"Listen, Tom, what's even more important than the method is confidentiality." He took my point. "Would you be interested in investing for me?"

"I could, but I can't promise a miracle."

"I'm in it for the long run. It's not like I make a fortune with this job, and the more I have when I retire, the better."

"The thing is, I'm not set up with a proper prospectus or contracts or anything. Let's keep this simple. How about this? Once a year, you give me a sum you want invested. A year later, I'll give you your entire investment and earnings back, and you decide how much you want to reinvest."

He agreed to give me fifteen grand the first year, and reinvested everything plus a little more every year after that.

As we parted I said, "You can't go wrong, you're using a time machine." "Sounds good to me," Tom said with a laugh.

It sounded good to me as well.

19

Our lives, Regina's and mine, calmed down somewhat after we neutralized DeVries's attempt to use Tom Jacobs against us. Regina continued to insist I have an apartment away from Race Street, a possible refuge from whatever, but in reality I spent very little time there, though I didn't start sleeping in a car again either. Maybe I was growing up.

The drama of our encounter with DeVries had helped me get over losing Sheila a little, but only a little. She had been the first person in my life who was truly a partner and a friend. My marriage hadn't just been a business convenience to me; I'd intended to stay with her, for better or worse, and was shocked when she left me. Still, I began to understand her jealousy toward Regina as well.

I no longer feared for Regina's sanity or avoided her physics discussions, so to that extent my feelings toward her had changed. I knew her so well that I often could predict her movements and thoughts, and yet I'd accepted that she'd also remain ethereal, lovely but somehow beyond me. I know of no other word than *love* to describe how I felt toward both Sheila and Regina, but those emotions deserve a richer vocabulary. I came to realize Sheila might have understood the situation better than I did—I know I hadn't sorted my feelings out at the time. I'm not sure I have done so yet. I spent some of my time overseeing the work on the units above Regina's office, but she was in no hurry to fill her half of the building with strangers yet. I also reinitiated Regina's struggle to make the old truck yard both useful and appealing. We needed the parking spaces for tenants, but Regina also wanted to provide a place where the people who used Race Street could appreciate and adore the canal. She had become a businesswoman, and a damn good one, so naturally she wanted a profitable venture, but I believe she wanted something more—she wanted a community. Her isolation at Northern University had affected her, and she wanted to create a place that people enjoyed—perhaps more than anything, a place that she enjoyed. This made my job more interesting but also more difficult.

My old roommate and new friend Tom Jacobs recommended a landscape architect, so I began a new education in that field, trying to fit what he told me was possible with what Regina wanted. At times that seemed more difficult than creating a comprehensive theory of the universe.

I also continued to manage our financial records, so we could reasonably explain what we earned scanning the future as though we were still using my fractal methods. Regina had her computer making small trades continuously, and if she wanted she could have made a few bucks on every trade. I had developed algorithms to help determine how far in the future to look at a stock price. By that time I had enabled her machine to look as far as thirty minutes ahead, but it took much more energy than, say, ten seconds, so we could make far fewer trades in a day. Furthermore, looking that far ahead didn't necessarily result in a larger profit per trade, because the price of the stocks usually fluctuated in the short term. We discovered that between five and fifteen seconds was the most profitable, but we needed to vary the times in order to understand and develop our protocols better.

Before I arrived Regina had randomly set her machine to lose nearly one-third of the time. I set up a program to observe the fractal behavior of the stocks in an identical manner to the way I had done for Victoria Sound, and then triggered the time machine to mimic those results. In truth, we didn't need to generate a profit greater than what I could have managed with my fractal theories, especially after my settlement with Sheila and her father, but we did need to continue to make actual future purchases, to prove our method worked and to gauge its efficiency and time range—that is, how far in the future we could read.

I spent a great deal of time refining the theory of launching and targeting Regina's time machine—or as she called it, her "pretemporal information collector"—and could no longer single-mindedly pursue my mathematical inventions. This was the life of scientists: disciplined, even boring in our daily routines, but exploring the most fantastical phenomena in our intellectual lives. Regina and I were enthused about our work and progress.

There were, of course, days when one, or both, of us got on each other's nerves, but we seldom let that interfere with our work—we just went our separate ways for a while. There were also times when we disagreed about how to proceed, but we learned that if we listened to each other, our disagreements usually led to fruitful results neither of us had foreseen. Regina had a calmer disposition than Sheila, and we did not feel the pressure of having to get a product to market before the competition, but our project was even more complex than understanding how to predict market trends.

It was fortunate that we had Eduardo's wonderful Mexican restaurant next door. If I ever were able to live my life over, I think I'd try to be a chef. As it is, I've never learned to cook, nor have many of my close companions. Of course, when I was with Sheila, it didn't matter, as Sheila, a true New Yorker, was a master at having gourmet meals delivered if we were too busy to get to a restaurant. Neither Regina nor I had ever taken the time to even order Chinese takeout, but having a place next door made it easy for us to eat well. Between Eduardo's burritos and Frank's bagels and donuts, we seldom traveled far for a meal.

My day typically began with a shower and a quick trip to Frank's for a large coffee and a bagel sandwich. Ina and I would say hi and discuss the weather or whatever. Then I'd head through the kitchen, where Frank would already be halfway through his day, and out to the truck yard to talk to the contractors. Some days the lot would be full of large pickups and guys with cell phones stuck to their ears; other days I'd see only one or two men. Sometimes I could wrap up my business in half an hour, while other times I'd get stuck working on the building all day.

My next step would be to find Regina. I'd first check her office, and if she wasn't there, I'd head downstairs to the lab or shop. When I found her, we'd talk about how to implement my latest ideas into her experiment. Sometimes she'd ask me to work on something specific. Afterward, I'd check my e-mail and hope I could have the rest of the day to myself. If I did, I'd usually go for a long walk. I missed the anonymity of the Manhattan crowds, but a long solitary walk would often reset my mind so I could tackle my theoretical problems.

Occasionally I'd even leave town and hike in the Massachusetts wilderness for a few hours. Though I couldn't match Cheryl's knowledge of the New England woods, she had taught me about their serenity. I no longer had the time to work on mathematics eighteen hours a day, and I missed the simplicity of those earlier days. Getting away from Race Street helped me recall them.

Often I'd end up at a fast-food joint at night, working on an idea, but since I usually had to meet with workers early the next day, I'd try to get home at a reasonable hour. If there was time, I'd head back to Race Street and drag Regina over to Eduardo's for dinner. It might be her only meal of the day, and I worried she might not eat if I didn't insist. Sharing a meal with her gave me the opportunity to discuss some aspect of her physics. Besides, I was still in love with her.

One night, toward closing time, we were finishing off our Sopa Azteca, tostadas, and a bottle of California Malbec when I asked Regina something I had been wondering about. "I know you've explained the impossibility of measuring the speed of light, or the speed of anything for that matter, at intervals smaller than a Planck Moment, and have concluded that the Planck Interval limits the applicability of relativity at units of time shorter than that," I said. "Yet our whole theory is based on the reality of four dimensions, as Einstein first claimed. Is there some deeper relationship between your ideas and Einstein's?"

Regina nodded enthusiastically, though she hadn't finished her soup. "Very much so," she replied when she had swallowed her mouthful. "Much of my explanation shows how the apparent absurdities of quantum physics can be explained by understanding the relationship between awareness and time. But at a deeper level, the physics you and I work on are directly descended from relativity. Think about it—the entire logic of Einstein's structure is based on the manner in which information is transmitted and received. We all know how Einstein proved how matter and energy are transmutations of each other, which certainly is an amazing result. His work was based on thought experiments of people riding in rockets or trains or elevators, usually near the speed of light. For instance, to explain gravity he conjured the image of a person riding in a closed elevator, far away from any other objects and without the ability to see anything on the outside."

She paused and took a sip of wine before continuing. "Einstein imagined this elevator to be continually accelerating, and he showed that, to the person inside, the effect would be exactly the same as if the elevator were standing still, relative to a nearby large gravitational body. From this he constructed his general theory of relativity to show how matter deforms space.

"Think about this for a second—he used the way information is received, relative to how it's transmitted, to show not only that time and space must be considered equally as dimensions of the universe, but also that space-time is warped. If you go back to classic Newtonian physics, the emphasis was always on the actual characteristics of the objects of our universe, as they're analyzed under various experiments. In Einstein's relativity, the emphasis changes to how information is conveyed.

"Now, Newton's work doesn't apply when one is describing objects in the universe approaching or at the speed of light, though the approaches he created are still of paramount importance. In the same way, Einstein's theory can't describe a universe where time and/or space don't exist, but his methods remain important. Although Einstein was convinced that the outcome of events couldn't be due to an observant universe, I think our theory of how awareness creates time is actually a direct descendent of his method of describing how we use information to plumb the secrets of the shape of reality."

During one of our conversations, Regina told me she wanted to expand the target we would use. Up until that point, we used an electronic counter, a simple switch that told us whether a predetermined stock had just gone up or down in the future. We held the switch steady for a fraction of a second— many lifetimes for an electronic message—so we could smear our transmission signal, in order to reduce the number and severity of the inevitable explosions. "I want to photograph a future event," she explained. "We could start with a camera held steady on a still scene, but eventually I'd like to capture a sequence of events, maybe even make a movie of sorts."

"Do you know what would happen if you took a future picture of an event, then tried to change it before it happened?" I asked. I had also thought about expanding the scope of our machine, but was troubled by some of the possibilities.

Regina gave me what appeared to be an unusually rueful smile. "Not exactly, but I think it would be bad...." Her voice trailed off. I knew she'd eventually finish her thought, and she did. "Again, it has to do with awareness. With our current experiment, we aren't aware of how our action of reading a stock price in the future affects the event we're exploring. There's only one event, the price of a single stock at a specific time, and we aren't explicitly trying to change its outcome—we only want to profit from knowing what the price is ahead of time. Any single purchase we make is too small for us to calculate its effect on its price. Even so, we must tread carefully, for this question is at the very core of why I'm afraid of what would happen if our discovery fell into careless or unscrupulous hands."

We'd just developed methods for seeing hours ahead, but only for simple signals. Regina's new proposal wasn't dissimilar to early daguerreotypes, which require a lengthy exposure to obtain an image. She and I had reduced the amount of energy needed for our operation by many hundredfold, which was why she felt we could expand our investigations.

We planned to create our first complex target by placing a camera in the old staircase next to the anteroom, facing toward the dead-end hall. We set up a digital clock that only indicated the hour. Regina suggested that we could take pictures at two successive hours and capture the difference in the clock reading. We knew nothing else happened in that room, so we could proceed without fear of interference.

We quickly and easily were able to generate the pictures of the hourly change, so we changed the duration to minutes. Unfortunately, the new setup created a great deal more heat than the old one. As I was looking at some blueprints one afternoon, I noticed smoke crawling from under the door into my anteroom office. I dashed over and opened the door, only to be overwhelmed by the onrush of acrid smoke. I managed to douse the smoldering camera with a small fire extinguisher, ruining some very rare and expensive equipment in the process.

We moved the entire experiment back to the lab for further refinement. Within six months, Regina was able to take a "future" picture of a clock in her lab at night, when no other visible activity took place. I continued to work on improving the efficiency of all aspects of the process. Soon we were able to take recognizable photographs in the lab fifteen minutes into the future, at thirty-second intervals. At first each image took about two hours to process, so we didn't actually see the results until the events were over. Eventually we were able to reduce the processing time by adding more computers, to the point where we could see a photo of something happen before it happened.

Regina and I worked side by side, as near equals. Although I don't think I could have achieved anything on my own that resembled her results, I believe my work was instrumental in pushing the envelope, so to speak, and realizing our extraordinary results. But more than the results of the experiments, I felt I had not only her trust, which for some reason she'd always accorded me, but also her respect.

20

One spring evening, while I was fooling around with something in the front office, Regina asked me to come into her office. She sat at her computer and motioned for me to take a seat next to her. I moved some boxes onto the floor and sat next to her.

Regina was easy to work with. She was engaging and almost never angry (except at DeVries), but she was also invariably focused and serious in the lab. That night, though, she was grinning—not her ironic grin, but a full, lovely smile, as if she were going to show me her favorite film for the first time. On her computer screen was a very grainy picture, a street scene.

"Do you recognize it?" she asked. "It looks like the street out front."

"It is. I'm just getting the news from Race Street!" She laughed. "I don't expect it to be terribly exciting news."

I stared at the screen in an attempt to pick up more clues, but the resolution was poor. It looked like the security camera attached to the front of the building was malfunctioning. A series of four pictures appeared, much like very early animations, not quite depicting movement but intimating it. In the second frame, the front of a large, dark SUV was poking around the corner, and in the third it had stopped in front of the archway. In the final picture, four vague figures were outside the van, and two of them were half-disappeared through the iron gates. I was trying to figure out how they had opened the gate so quickly, but Regina gasped, "What the fuck? That's DeVries!"

I could hardly make out the people, but the one who had just exited the front seat did remind me of Agent DeVries. No sooner had she spoken than the lights flickered, the room shook slightly, and the computer screen went blank.

Regina grabbed me, then dragged me through the rear of the office, instead of onto the street, where the action was. We ran down the stairs and to the rear windows. I could barely keep up with her. By the time I reached the rear wall, she had shoved a window open. Because we were in the basement, the windowsill was four feet up, but nearly even with the grade outside, underneath the truck dock.

"Hurry, Ron. Climb out and run to the wall over there." She pointed to a point on the canal wall close to Seventh Avenue. "Then walk back along the wall to the point directly opposite us and then walk—don't run—back here."

I did as she told me. By the time I got back to the window, she had closed it. "Okay, now break in," she shouted through the pane, then backed up a few feet. She had left a short stick of lumber outside the window for me to use as a club. The glass splintered when I smashed it, and the building's alarm went off. I wondered what the hell was going on, but as soon I climbed back inside Regina dragged me back to her office, where, thankfully, the alarm wasn't as piercing. From a drawer she pulled out a small clay stick with a plastic button attached to one end. She placed it in a small, crumpled paper bag, which she carefully re-crumpled.

"You saw where the SUV is going to park?"

"*Is* going to?"

"Of course. Oh, Ron, you didn't realize! That little flick we saw was courtesy of your self-learning energy-efficiency routines—and it still took over six hours of recording to get those four fuzzy pictures. The first frame should occur in three or four minutes, so you need to hurry. Put this in the gutter where their rear wheel ends up—I think about a foot past the storm drain. Then go home. Don't come back here."

Regina had told me what to expect, but I was still a little rattled when I went out front and the SUV wasn't there. I placed the bag in the gutter as she'd instructed. It looked like an inconspicuous piece of trash. I was about to cross the street and head up Sixth Avenue to my apartment when I heard a vehicle approach the corner. I quickly ducked into the recess of the nearest doorway on Race Street, at the nail spa. Sure enough, it was the same SUV we'd seen in the photos.

On my way out, I'd noticed that the archway lock had already been picked, which explained how the four figures had disappeared so quickly from view in the last frame. I heard the SUV stop and the doors open and close, but there were no voices. I half expected the scene to fizzle out, as it had on Regina's computer, so I grabbed the corner of the door recess to steady myself to peek around the corner.

Almost instantly I felt a sharp pain at the end of my right index finger. At the same time, the streetlights flickered. I jerked my finger back to find it bleeding profusely, and it began to throb. I untucked my undershirt and wrapped it around my wound. I figured the explosion had gone off and some shrapnel had hit me. As soon as that thought entered my mind, the explosion did go off. Simultaneously, I heard the sirens of multiple police cars as they came from three different directions toward the SUV.

I peeked again. The explosion appeared to have blown a rear tire off the black SUV, and the vehicle had settled into a cockeyed stance. The four dark figures re-emerged from the archway, as did at least a dozen city police from their cars, guns drawn.

I hadn't seen Regina leave the building, but suddenly she was in the middle of the chaos, dressed in a terrycloth bathrobe. "What's going on? Paul DeVries, what the fuck are you doing here?"

DeVries glared at her, but did not answer. One of the cops spoke up. "Didn't you call us about a break-in?"

"Yes, but these are FBI agents. I think someone broke into the back of my building." She turned back to DeVries. "Why are you here?"

I couldn't make out everything they said, but much of the conversation was loud enough for me to catch from the shadows. The entire troupe, save for one of the city cops who stayed behind to keep watch, soon disappeared into Regina's office to examine the window I had broken about ten minutes earlier. I was looking for a chance to head up the street when another dark SUV, identical to the first one, pulled up. The driver got out, walked over to the first SUV, and examined the damage. He was dressed in typical FBI attire—a dark suit, which seemed out of place this late at night. He spoke briefly to the sentry, then followed the others into the building.

I headed home to nurse my finger after the lone sentry decided to sit in his cruiser. Regina's strategy was finally making sense to me. She wanted to create a reason to bring the city police on site without arousing DeVries's suspicion, so she had me run a reverse pattern through our muddy back lot and simulate a break in. I didn't know why she had me leave an explosive in the gutter, or how she was going to explain it away, or why the tip of my finger was injured, but it looked like she had the situation under control.

I also wondered about her little photographic montage—which was probably the first time an event from the future had actually been photographed. However, a simple calculation explained why the pictures had fizzled out. The amount of energy used, and heat created, was enormous. Typically we ran the machine for less than thirty seconds to obtain a single line of print, in order to avoid overheating. I hoped Regina hadn't had her fun at too great a cost.

Exhausted, I wrapped my finger in a towel but couldn't sleep, so I sat up waiting for morning and Regina's account. I didn't need to wait very long; the phone rang around 4:30 a.m. Regina was deliberate. "Ron, get dressed. Wear the same clothes you did last night, especially your shoes."

"I can't. I bled all over my undershirt." "Why? What happened?"

I explained how my finger had been injured.

"Just put on a different undershirt then, but wear the same shirt and pants and the same shoes. I'll pick you up in five minutes. Oh, yeah, bring an extra pair of shoes."

When she arrived, I climbed into her car and peppered her with questions, but she cut me off. "We've got work to do. Agent Dan Harble, DeVries's boss, showed up last night, and he's coming back this morning." She was speaking rapidly, her eyes straight ahead on the road. "The FBI will want to negotiate a way for me to keep silent about their agents trying to break into my place. I'm sure DeVries never got a warrant, but I also know they don't believe my story about the break-in, at least not entirely. I suspect they might try to find our burglar, maybe with a K-9 patrol, so we—you—need to give them a trail to follow. What happened to your hand again?"

As I explained the weird wound Regina drove across the bridge to the business district, which was just beginning to wake up. She let me off about three blocks from our building. "Walk quickly to our canal wall. Then along the top of it to where you climbed up last night. Turn around and run back over the bridge and directly up Seventh Avenue. I'll pick you up in about twenty minutes."

I did as she'd said, then got back into her car when she pulled up twenty minutes later.

"I'll drive you back to your apartment, but give me your shoes first," she said as I climbed in. "You can't be anywhere near where their K-9 unit might be. In fact, I've got to go scrub our sidewalk with bleach and capsicum. I don't want their mutt tracing our 'burglar' to your apartment." She glanced at my bandaged finger again. "On second thought, I'd better take you to the emergency room first."

"Isn't the building a crime scene?" I asked, thinking about the SUV we'd blown up. "Do you think you should clean it up?"

"The FBI will be conflicted—they don't want a formal investigation into their own activities, but they want to figure out what happened. On one hand, they'll be upset, angry even; on the other, they know I can get a reporter to our building quickly and I'm on good terms with the local cops and a US senator." "That's a conversation I'd like to hear. What's the saying? 'I'd like to be a fly on the wall.'"

"Don't you think we should take care of your finger now? How bad is it?" "I lost the tip, but that ain't coming back and it pretty much quit bleeding."

I held up my hand to show a huge, mostly white gauze bandage. "Does it hurt?"

"Yeah, but I can deal. I'd love to hear you and this Harble agent talk."

Regina flashed me with her trademark wry grin. We'd nearly reached the hospital, but instead of stopping she sped up again and returned to Race Street. "Okay, you look like you'll live. I'll take you to a doctor later."

She installed me in the staircase next to her office. "As long as I keep the dogs outside, you'll be fine here. But don't move. I've got a sidewalk to scrub."

She hid me in the stairway behind the second door leading out of the front office, the one that descended to the hidden entrance to the lab. I sat there on the first step for nearly an hour, contemplating the construction work I was overseeing on the upper floors, when I heard two people coming through the front door.

"...I didn't realize you considered the front sidewalk a crime scene. Does that mean you're admitting DeVries committed a crime?" Regina had a quiet grace even when she was lying.

"We're looking into what happened. It's an ongoing investigation." Dan Harble's voice betrayed a forced patience.

"Maybe the Foxfield police should be arrested for showing up. Or perhaps you could fine me because someone broke into my building. It was your team that made a mess of my sidewalk by detonating that bomb and blowing up your own car. I'm running a business here, and my main business right now is to make sure my tenants can run theirs." Regina was in fine form; I had to stifle a laugh.

"*Someone* blew up an FBI vehicle last night, but it wasn't the FBI." "*Someone* indeed. Maybe this will help you figure out who." I heard a soft clunk on a table.

There was a pause, and then Harble said, "This is plastic explosive. Are you admitting you did it?"

"You've got to be kidding. DeVries blew up my house several years ago and got me fired from the university by lying in his report. That explosive is something he left behind then. My bet is he was going to do the same thing again. I suggest you analyze the explosive that blew up your clown car and see if it's the same stuff he used on my house. And by the way, I've had a piece of that stuff analyzed and documented by my lawyer, I know it's an explosive used by the FBI. If you're going to try to pin this on me, I guess it's time to get some witnesses in here."

"Wait—" Dan started, but was interrupted by a man who had just come through the front door.

"Sir, we picked up the trail but lost it again. We think the intruder got off a bus on Front Street then walked across the Seventh Street Bridge, then along the wall and cut across to break the window where he entered. He evidently left through the same window, ran over to the wall and straight up Seventh Street. We lost him at another bus stop. We could bring Horatio inside to track his route in the building."

"Horatio?" Regina asked.

"Horatio is our K-9," Harble said. "He could show us where this burglar went, maybe help discover whether he took anything."

Regina became livid. I'd never seen her lose her temper before, but I understood she needed to get the FBI to take Horatio away before the dog picked up my scent. "No way! First your men break into my building; then you want to pin your incompetence on me, and now you want to scare the hell out of my tenants. I think I'd better get the newspaper and my lawyer over here now." I heard her pick up the phone.

"Wait, let's discuss this first," Harble said. "Agent Gomes, that's enough.

Write your report, but that's all we need for now."

"I thought you wanted me to search the front of the building too." Gomes seemed genuinely surprised at Harble's dismissal; they'd clearly discussed this previously.

Harble sighed. "No, that won't be possible now. The sidewalk's been scrubbed."

I heard the sound of Gomes leaving, then Harble spoke to Regina again. "I'd like to keep this whole affair quiet if possible, Dr. Russo. Special Agent DeVries might have overstepped his authority this time. Is there anything the FBI can do to assure you that this won't happen again?"

I marveled at the way Regina had manipulated the scene. She paused, as if she were thinking the offer over, but I could have spoken her next sentence. "I never want to see or hear of Paul DeVries again. I don't want him within a thousand miles of here. Reassign him to Pocatello or Abilene or anywhere, so I can get on with what he's left me of my life."

There was another pause, a rather lengthy one. Finally Harble said, "I understand your feelings, but Paul DeVries is one of our best agents. I'll look into this and get back to you."

"I don't mind a little negotiation, but that doesn't mean I'm going to stay silent while you and DeVries screw me." Regina softened her voice to emphasize her meaning.

"I have no intention of screwing you, Dr. Russo."

"Well, *Special* Agent DeVries obviously does, so you'd better control him."

Both Regina and Harble left the office, but I stayed on the landing until she came back. Half an hour passed before she returned to set me free. We'd been so busy

169

trying to cover our tracks that we hadn't had a chance to get down to the lab. As soon as we got to the control room, we discovered the damage was significant. We both knew the flickering lights the night before had indicated some sort of equipment failure, but we didn't know how great the damage was. The control room was intact, but shards of concrete and concrete dust covered the lab. Most of the sarcophagus appeared to be intact, but the explosion had blown off the top door and sprayed debris everywhere.

"I knew I was pushing it last night," Regina said. "I was just hoping the experiment would last a little longer. That's the trouble when you're dealing with uncertainty." She smiled as she said this; it was her idea of a joke, a quantum joke. "We can clean this up later. Harble could return anytime. And I've got to get you to a doctor."

Regina took me to the urgent care unit, but let me go in alone. "Call me when you get out", she said. "Hopefully they won't make you wait forever."

"Yeah, I hope not - it's already been nearly eighteen hours," I said.

"Maybe you shouldn't tell them that," she said, then pulled out of the parking lot.

So much had happened in so little time that I didn't think about what I was going to say until I was finally face to face with a doctor.

"How the hell did that happen?" he asked after he unraveled the towel I had wrapped around my hand and looked at my bloody short finger.

"I was using one of those nail guns that use .22 cartridges, and it misfired," I said. I had no idea if that could happen, and I hoped the doctor didn't either. "You don't look like a construction worker, and your hands sure as hell don't look like construction worker's hands. Maybe you should leave that kind of stuff to the pros."

Clearly I looked dumb enough to make my story plausible.

After I got patched up, we spent the afternoon with busywork—the kind of tidying, filing, and whatnot that always gets put off. We wanted to be available, so it was a good time for a little thoughtless work in the office—especially since I was pretty high on Dilaudid. Regina was certain Harble would be back, and sure enough, he knocked on the front door around four o'clock.

"I'm pretty sure we can work something out, and..." Agent Harble started as Regina led him in, but he trailed off when he saw me. "Who's this?" he asked, snapping his head toward me. I had seen Harble the night before, but only as a dark silhouette. He had the same authoritative posture as DeVries, but he was larger, nearly my size, and older. He had a square face and a flattop haircut that suited his bristle-stiff blond hair. It didn't look like he could comb it if he tried. He was close shaven—he looked like he had shaved that afternoon just before he joined us—and had pale blue eyes that seemed to look carefully at everything. I suspected he was a good agent.

"Agent Harble," Regina began, then turned back to Harble. "Are you a Special Agent, too?"

"Yes, I am," Harble replied without irony.

"Special Agent Harble," Regina continued, "this is Ron Larsen, my business partner. Ron, Special Agent Dan Harble, from the FBI."

Addressing Regina, Harble said, "I'd rather this was just between you and me."

"You can leave," she said. "Ron stays."

Harble took a while to digest this before agreeing that I could stay. "I've talked to everyone, including Agent DeVries. I still don't understand exactly what happened. There are certain discrepancies between your stories." I could tell Regina wanted to say something, but she held back, forcing Harble to continue. "For instance, he admitted he used that type of explosive to enter your country house four years ago, but the department has changed explosives since then, and he didn't need any to enter your property this time anyway."

"Why not?" Regina asked.

"Evidently he, uhh, well he picked the locks ahead of time."

"You're saying he didn't want to blow this building up?" Regina said. "He denies, vehemently, that he blew your house up."

"So who blew up the SUV?"

Harble rubbed his smooth chin, then pinched his nose. He looked a little like a balloon with some of the air let out. "To tell you the truth, he has no answer that satisfies me. It's true that the FBI doesn't use that type anymore, but you had one stick, so maybe you had another."

"DeVries didn't have a warrant to enter my property. For some reason he wants to destroy me. How many people do you think he revealed his plan to? I'll bet even the other agents in that car didn't know what they were doing ahead of time. How the hell do you think I could lay a trap for him? He's lying and he's crazy."

"We're willing to drop all charges and make sure Special Agent DeVries never crosses paths with you again, if you're willing to let this whole incident go. No press, no politicians—it didn't happen."

Regina took a step back and put her hands on her hips. "Drop *what* charges? I'm trying to figure out if you're protecting DeVries or the FBI. Why is he after me? Do you have any idea?"

Harble didn't respond. "Deal?" he said.

"You can guarantee that he'll never bother me again?" "I can, and I do."

"Mr. Harble, I'm going to trust you on this." Regina held out her hand, and Harble shook it.

"I'd like to apologize on behalf of the FBI," he said, then turned and headed out the door without another word.

*

We weren't convinced Harble could keep his promise, but we felt we had at least gotten DeVries out of the way for the time being. Regina turned her attention to repairing the lab and the time machine, which she estimated would take six months to a year. We had to get rid of the debris from the explosion without being noticed, but I had several projects on my plate already: finishing the second floor above Regina's office, including reconstructing a second set of steps and rear door, constructing storage lockers for the tenants in the basement, and landscaping the grounds between the building and the canal.

We increased the building's security, including an upgrade of the exterior locks, and it seemed as if we were back to normal—as normal as repairing a time machine could be. I continued to spend an inordinate amount of time on the lot between the building and the canal. It turned into one of those projects that kept getting bigger the longer I worked on it—an *Alice in Wonderland* scenario where the faster you approach a goal, the further away it appears. The muddy lot had proven useful in creating the illusion of an intruder by allowing me to create obvious footprints, but that was no reason to leave it a mess. Eduardo wanted to use the area for his restaurant. He already was using the covered alley, where he set up tables for diners, but he envisioned a south- facing deck on his portion of the dock if it could be an attractive setting. Regina wanted to accommodate him, but she needed to have parking and delivery capability as well.

"I understand, not everything can happen at once," Eduardo said. I was standing in the middle of the truck lot on a drizzly May morning with Eduardo, Frank Shoupe, the doughnut shop owner, and Emmy Phan, the proprietor of the nail salon. We were discussing everyone's needs. "But I could use it come June," Eduardo said.

"It might not happen until July, but I guarantee it by then," I said.

"Best not guarantee the future," Emmy said. "No one knows the future."

"Haven't you heard, Ron here invented a time machine for the stock market?" Frank joked.

"How come he didn't foresee his wife taking it away from him?" Emmy said. She could be as blunt as her tools were sharp.

"You don't need to guarantee anything, just try for me," Eduardo said. "Construction starts next week," I said.

21

Several months after the incident with the FBI, I was leaning against the canal wall, taking a break after a contentious conversation with my landscape contractor, when a scuba diver emerged from the canal beneath where I was standing. The diver waved at me. I thought I might be hallucinating at first; I had never seen anyone swimming in the canal, as the currents were unpredictable and often dangerous.

"Hi, Ron!" the voice behind the face mask called out. I immediately recognized it as Louise's, and I also noticed that, without the cover of loose clothing, her body was unmistakably female.

"Louise! How are you?" She had removed her mask and was climbing up an iron ladder attached to the wall.

"I'm great. And you?" She was carrying a pair of scuba fins in one hand. "Fine, fine. It's so good to see you. What are you doing here?" "Exploring." She said the word as if it explained everything. It did not. "Exploring?" I repeated.

"Thanks to you, I've expanded my horizon past Northern's utility tunnels. Do you know why there are so many canals in this neighborhood? "They powered factories during the nineteenth century."

Louise nodded excitedly. "And every one of these factories had a turbine beneath it, powered by water flowing through underground sluices. The turbines no longer run, but I've been exploring the tunnels left behind." She smiled. "What are you doing here? I heard you're part of the next big thing."

I gathered she was referring to my stock market project. "I *was* part of the next big thing. Now I'm the construction manager of this building."

I invited Louise over to Frank's doughnut shop for a bagel sandwich and coffee so we could catch up on each other's lives.

"Can you take me to my car first so I can change?" "Of course, pardon me."

She waited while I went out front to get my Lexus. "Wow," she said when I pulled up. "You made some pretty good money somewhere."

"New York was good to me while it lasted. This car is lasting better than the rest of the experience."

She had removed her face mask and pulled off her hood. She climbed into my sedan. "I'm parked about four blocks from here, along Race Street."

I followed her directions and soon pulled up to my old blue Chrysler. "You still have my car!"

"Of course. I even sleep in it sometimes." She crawled into the back of the old sedan, which still didn't have a rear seat, and disappeared under a large blanket covered in Native American designs. She reappeared a few minutes later, dressed in a flowing tie-dye dress and knee-high boots. "I'll follow you, so you don't have to drive me back here."

"Fair enough." We met again inside Frank's, where we both ordered egg and ham bagel sandwiches and coffee.

When they came, Louise took a bite and smiled. "You're eating better sandwiches than you used to."

Louise explained that she'd been traveling across the city via the tunnels left over from the heyday of the canals; she used them to explore the abandoned factories in the area. As this amounted to breaking and entering, she didn't invite me to go with her. Similarly, I couldn't let her know what I was doing with Regina.

Still, we were fond of each other's eccentricities and began spending time together on occasion, especially the occasions when she needed a shower or wanted to cook a meal. She told me she'd been doing part-time janitorial work but hadn't seen a need to rent a place to live, so I gave her a key to my apartment and told her to use it anytime—"Just don't wake me up."

One day a few weeks after our re-acquaintance, Louise approached me in the truck yard with a puzzled look on her face. I was surprised to see her there; this was the first time she'd visited Race Street since the day I'd seen her swimming in the canal. "You're in charge of this building, right?" she asked.

"Yeah, it's not a billion-dollar company, but it's my life right now." "Then there's something I should show you...down there."

She stared down at the water from which she had emerged several weeks prior. "Can you meet me here tomorrow morning—say nine?"

I agreed.

The next morning, Louise drove up in the Chrysler. "Can we change inside?" she asked as she pulled two scuba suits from her trunk.

"Sure," I said, taking the suit she handed me. "I've never used one of these." "We don't need tanks or fins, just the suit, mask, and lamp. You can hold your breath for the short time we'll be underwater." We took the equipment into the basement and changed in the construction room.

"Put your shoes on, you can leave them on the wall," Louise said. "I'll bet your feet are too tender for the stones out there." She pointed to the truck yard, which was being dug up at the time. She left her shoes behind.

We walked across the rear lot, I slipped off my shoes, and we went down the ladder. From there we swam a few yards to a spot along the stone wall.

Louise turned to give me instructions. "The old sluice to your building exits into the canal right here. We need to go down about one and a half feet below the surface to the opening, which is only big enough for one of us at a time. The hole is right below us. Once you reach it, go through, and surface on the other side. Once we're inside, we'll be able to walk the rest of the way. Just take hold of this line and follow it." She handed me a rope I hadn't noticed; one end was attached to the wall, while the other disappeared into the water. Louise adjusted my face mask, flipped my headlamp on, and said, "Take a big breath and go."

I gulped and pulled myself down into the darkness. Fortunately, the rope was secure, because I was disoriented once I was underwater. The rope led down the wall and through the opening. Although I was only underwater for about ten seconds, I panicked a little when my head popped up. I was on my belly in a shallow pool inside an enormous tunnel. I scrambled out of the way to make room for Louise before I looked around.

The sluice was a semi-circular stone tunnel about seven or eight feet high at its peak. The walls were remarkably smooth. The joints between the stones, which weren't mortared, were so tight you couldn't slip a piece of paper into most of them. The hole we used was in one of the newer walled-up sections. Chunks of concrete blocks and mortar were scattered beneath the water on the tunnel floor. I couldn't see them, but after stumbling on a few, I learned to feel where my feet were going. I turned toward the building, but even with my headlamp on, I couldn't see anything but darkness ahead. Louise flopped in next to me.

"It's a good thing you put that rope there. I couldn't see a thing," I told her. "The thing is, this isn't my rope—that's what I wanted to show you." "Someone else has been down here?" I asked.

"Follow me," she said.

The water was a little over two feet deep where we started, but the floor sloped up as we approached the building, so soon we were on a dry surface of smooth, slightly rounded stones. Walking was easy, even with my tender feet. Suddenly a concrete wall loomed ahead, along with some other objects.

"That looks like a portable gas generator," I said.

"I think someone's trying to get through that wall," Louise said. "Look at those bolts sticking out of the wall. Looks like someone was going to attach that drill to it." She pointed to a corer similar to the one Concrete Wizards had used to drill through the slab above the lab. Several other tools lay nearby, some of which I recognized.

"I think they're planning on coming back," Louise said. "What's behind that wall?"

"Nothing. Just dirt," I lied.

"Well, someone thinks something's worth drilling for."

"Paul DeVries."

"Who?" she asked, visibly surprised.

"Never mind. It's a long story." I couldn't explain everything, so I thought it best to say nothing.

She took a step closer to me. "I know that name." "Paul DeVries? How do you know him?"

"I don't know him—I just know the name. Remember when I showed you the rooms Regina allegedly blew up in the physics building?" I nodded. "Well, I heard that story from a woman named Ananda Samien, who said her best friend was the grad student killed in the explosion. The student's name was Manisha Kapoor."

I nodded again. "I remember you telling me that."

"Ananda told me Manisha wanted to go against her family's plans for her. She was in love, she wanted to marry an American, a man named Paul DeVries." I was stunned by this bit of news but said nothing more to Louise. We returned "topside," as she called above-ground. I thanked her for the tour, and she agreed to meet me the next day. I gave her some money for the wet suit rental, but she wouldn't take anything for her time. "You might not have realized it, Ron, but you helped me turn my life around. I'm glad I had the chance to help you in return."

As soon as I saw Louise off, I looked for Regina. Predictably, she was in the lab,

177

working on the time machine. I didn't want to change into my lab clothes, so I pounded on the window to grab her attention. She was so absorbed in her work she didn't notice me at first, but finally she saw me and came out into the computer room. I told her the entire story without interruption.

"Damn," she said. "So that explains DeVries's unnatural interest in me. I remember the sluice, but I never realized there was still an entrance that leads into the canal. My mistake."

"It looks like DeVries might have created that entrance. We should take care of that now."

Regina nodded thoughtfully, then said, "Yes, but it has to look like an accident."

"At least we have more than ten minutes to manufacture a situation this time."

"Maybe not. He could be out there now." I followed her into the shop behind the lab, where she placed her hand on the concrete wall—the wall DeVries apparently was trying to drill through. "No, I don't think he's here yet." She pulled her hand away. "This is about where the sluice left the building. I'll put a monitor on this side; we'll definitely be able to detect vibrations from a corer, even through two feet of concrete." I was again surprised by how quickly Regina could assess a situation and take action.

"But we can't just sit here and listen to him drill through that wall," I said.

Regina laughed softly. "Of course not, this is just a first step." She was already searching through her cupboards for the right equipment. As she taped a small sensor to the wall, she continued to talk, as if she were thinking out loud for my benefit. "This mic will at least warn us if DeVries shows up, but we'll need quite a bit more to stop him."

As soon as she had attached the button microphone to the building's alarm system, she rummaged through a safe at the back of the shop. "As you know, the masonry tunnel is an arch, with all the blocks pushing on one another. If we take one out, part of the arch will fall."

"How do we do that?" I asked.

"Well, we know the sluice runs under our rear parking lot, and the top of the arch is only about four feet below grade at the building. We should target the sluice about a third of the way down, so we're talking about seven or eight feet below ground level." She was mostly talking to herself.

"What are you planning to do?"

"We can attach a small amount of explosive to the outside of the stones, cover it back up, and safely destroy one or two of the stones. The arch will cave in, but it'll look like it failed on its own."

"Is that safe?" The closest I had ever come to explosives were firecrackers, except for the FBI car I destroyed.

"I think so. You'll have to trust me."

That night, using a hand soil corer to create a three-inch-bore hole, we planted a small bomb beneath the truck yard, about a dozen feet from the building. We hit something solid just where the sluice was supposed to be, then inserted the device, and covered it up. The plan was to wait until the truck yard construction was well underway the next day, set off the explosion when it couldn't be heard over the sounds of the machinery and equipment, then act surprised when the sluice caved in.

We were going over the plan early the next morning when the microphone picked up something in the tunnel. DeVries apparently was already drilling, and we had to decide whether to let him continue or possibly kill him.

"I can set off a partial charge," Regina said. "It shouldn't cave the tunnel in, but should shake DeVries up enough to get him out for now. Then we can complete the job after he leaves."

And that's exactly what she did.

From a third-floor window, we watched DeVries pop out of the canal and swim across it. He had a skiff tied to the canal wall on the far side of the Fifth Avenue Bridge. It looked like he was injured, as he was having trouble climbing out of the water. The microphone indicated that the generator was still running, so we knew he had left in a rush.

A couple hours later, Regina completely collapsed the tunnel. The event was anticlimactic. Regina and I were standing ten yards or so from the detonation, to make sure no one else was nearby. We felt rather than heard a thud when it went off, then watched as the ground slowly slid into the cavity, a hole nearly eight feet deep and twelve feet wide at the surface. Paul's equipment was silenced when it was buried in the collapse. We immediately called the city's Department of Public Works, even though we knew there were no utilities nearby.

Tom Jacobs showed up with a civil engineer from the DPW within the hour. They examined the sinkhole in the parking lot, and Tom asked if there was any damage to the building. After they were through, we all stood around the crater, as though we might see something new.

The city engineer, a husky man named Terry Reeves, explained his conclusions. "Fortunately, it doesn't look like any utilities were damaged or threatened. Unfortunately, this is entirely on your property, so you're responsible for the repair."

Of course, that was what we wanted to hear; it meant the city had given up trying to give us a hard time.

That afternoon, I met with our contractor and told him we wanted the hole filled in immediately, but he needed to bring in his engineer to document that there were no potential environmental issues. It would take a few days, he said, but given the danger of having a sinkhole on the property, he assured us it wouldn't be any longer than that.

When I returned to the office, Regina was just sitting there, staring into space. She usually never stopped moving, so I figured this whole incident had hit her pretty hard.

"Do you remember Dan Harble?" she said. I nodded. "DeVries's boss. Why?"

"I just got off the phone with him. I called him to tell him DeVries was seen in town after he'd promised me he would send him away. Harble said that wasn't possible, because DeVries has been rock climbing in the White Mountains. He said DeVries suffered a severe fall and is laid up in a hospital in Hanover, New Hampshire."

"Do you think he's covering for DeVries?" I asked.

"I don't think so. He seemed genuinely concerned for his agent. I guess we must have hit him harder than we planned."

"How bad do you think we hurt him?"

"Obviously, Harble wouldn't give me any details. He's hurt bad enough that he's in the hospital, not so bad that he couldn't drive over two hours to Hanover to cover his tracks."

22

We heard Paul DeVries had been reassigned to Houston after he recovered from his "accident." Regina went back to repairing her equipment, which hadn't run since she had destroyed it with the video that had captured the future arrival of DeVries and his crew. I helped with the heavy work in the lab and also went back to finishing my work on the rest of the building.

On clear evenings, summer or winter, Regina and I would often climb up to the roof after a meal at Eduardo's and watch the stars. Since the upper roof of 58 Race Street was covered with the solar panels, we had dragged a couple of lawn chairs to the lower roof. We often brought a bottle of wine too. Sometimes we even slept there all night.

The wall to the higher roof partially shielded us from Foxfield's urban glow. Of course, the view from the middle of Foxfield didn't compare to the night skies of the Washington Cascades or northern Quebec, but it was still relaxing. Although we lived in the middle of a small city and ran a business that required us to interact with our tenants and contractors, we were also isolated from the world by our need for secrecy. The constant vigilance was wearing, so it was important for us to have an emotional escape. Our time on the roof gave us that respite.

Sometimes we'd discuss our labors of the past day and plan for the next. Sometimes we'd talk about my latest ideas to improve the computer programs Regina's experiments used. For most, night is when Earth grows dark and human activity goes to sleep. For us it was when the sun's blinding glare was removed and the true spectacle of the universe was revealed.

Although at one time I dreaded Regina's physics lectures, I now looked forward to them and would even question her. Sometimes I thought I knew what she'd say, sometimes she obliged me; other times I had no idea what to expect. In every case, however, her approach was subtle, and I knew I'd learn something new.

One warm spring night on the roof, I reminded Regina how I'd originally butchered her concept that awareness creates time. "But I'm still not sure I understand the relationship between awareness on the quantum level and our own awareness," I said.

"I'd love to hear what you have to say when you do understand, because I can't say I do either. But remember, when Newton formulated his theories on force, he had no concept that there were the four forces we now recognize. He worked with gravity of course, and electricity and magnetism were somewhat known, but certainly not as a combined force. The weak and strong forces, which are only felt at a subatomic scale, certainly weren't imagined. And yet Newton was able to observe force at the scale of our existence. Since then, we've surmised that there are only those four forces, we think they are related, and we've discovered the whole world of physics and chemistry, including relativity and quantum physics. Newton knew none of this, but his ideas spawned modern science and they're still relevant—we still say force equals mass times acceleration."

"I'm not sure I'm following you, Regina." It was not the first time I'd had to say that.

"My theory is that awareness creates time at the level of the Planck interval, 10^{-44} seconds. Just as Newton used the known concept of force for a new situation, I suppose I chose a familiar concept of awareness for a new phenomenon because of the similarity between what we've long known and what's newly discovered, despite the difference in scale. Even though Newton didn't know anything about the quantum scale when he created physics, his discoveries were sound. Some people mistakenly claim that relativity and quantum physics have superseded Newtonian physics, but they've only built on it. I think we can expect awareness to act on vastly different scales, just as its inverse twin, force, does. I can't say how. Perhaps someday you'll be able to shed some light on your own question."

I refilled our wine glasses and we stared at the amazing expanse above us, each of us lost in our own contemplations. Cygnus, the great swan constellation, was flying high overhead, as he has for as long as people have viewed the sky. I mused on whether the sky seems more amazing to modern humans, who have a vast and complex understanding of the physical nature of the stars, or to the ancients, to whom the night sky was an ever present and untouchable expanse. Regina spoke up again. "I do think we need to amend Descartes's dictum from 'I think, therefore I am' to 'I perceive, therefore I am; I think, therefore I *know* I am.' It's not as catchy, but it makes more sense."

On another occasion I asked Regina why she thought our equipment had blown up on the night of DeVries's raid.

"At first I thought I'd just let it go on too long," she said. "What were you planning to see?"

"I was going to have us walk down the street, but watch us walking first by viewing those photographs. It's probably a good thing I didn't. I might have blown up the city, and definitely would have killed us."

I cocked my head to the side. "By walking down the street?"

"No, by setting up an endless time feedback loop, kind of like holding a microphone too close to its amplified speaker. But we did it in a small way anyway."

"How? We didn't see us walking."

"So it would seem. But we're missing something," she said. It was dark, and we were both facing the stars above, but she noticed my pause, so she continued. "When we saw the first picture, I thought the initial scene was an empty street, and then the SUV came around the corner. But think about it—what happened just before that?"

"I put your explosive in the gutter. And then I left."

"We can't replay the photos because they were destroyed, but what if we actually caught a bit of you on it?"

I was puzzled. "What if we did?"

"When we watched the scene, you weren't in view—you had already left. In fact, that was what I wanted to test that night, but in a less dramatic setting. I thought we'd just be walking down the street. The only thing I don't understand is why your fingertip didn't blow off at the beginning, when you left the charge. After that you left the area, didn't you?"

184

"Not quite. After I put that bag down, I didn't have time to cross the street before the FBI showed up. I hid in the doorway leading to the nail spa. I must have stuck my hand out just far enough for the camera to catch it. That's when my fingertip blew off—and when the lights went out."

"Aha! Now it makes sense. Before this incident, we'd only been trying to gain information from the future to use for investing. We see a stock whose price appears to have gone up and we buy it, which might help drive the price up further. If anything, our actions reinforce what we expect to happen. Our usual experiment tries to take advantage of the way we've learned the future is going to unfold. We most emphatically don't want to change the course of the future—our success depends on events occurring according to our observation. "But what happens when we interfere with the future, when we change the course of the universe after we've already seen a future event occur? Perhaps when your finger entered the picture, well, that wasn't supposed to happen. You wouldn't have been there if we hadn't known in advance what DeVries was up to. I think the last picture we saw, the one that showed DeVries and his cronies enter our building, originally didn't show your finger sticking out from around the corner. So as soon as your finger entered the picture, it set off the explosion that tore off your fingertip and blew up our equipment, because that finger existed and didn't exist simultaneously. If we'd seen ourselves walking down the street and then didn't move identically during the actual walk, if we'd messed up even a simple gesture, the explosion might have been worse, much worse."

"So not only did we catch DeVries, but he also might have saved us from... whatever."

"Perhaps."
There were a lot of perhapses in our life.

*

The repair was difficult, even tedious, and involved the kind of work that usually would require a dozen or more strong young men like the contractors' crews, recent high school graduates who'd probably been on their schools' football or wrestling teams. Although Regina was incredibly strong for her size, I doubt she

185

weighed 120 pounds. And though I'm a large man, I've never considered myself athletic.

Our first task was to remove the detritus scattered all over the room, and then we tackled the interior shards of the concrete sarcophagus. From the outside the concrete appeared fine, but the interior showed the effects of the explosion. The instruments and controls were shattered, leaving a mangle of conduit, wires, and piping. Wrecked as it was, however, it still needed to be broken down into movable pieces, mostly with a jackhammer. Everything inside the concrete box was slightly radioactive, so we wore protective clothing inside the lab and when handling the debris. These precautions slowed our progress even more.

As we weren't a licensed facility and couldn't bring our discarded material to the nearest low-level nuclear landfill, which was in rural Georgia, we buried it at Regina's old farmstead. I used our other ongoing construction projects to hide the transportation of the remnants of the lab explosion a little at a time. I felt like a prisoner of war in the film *The Great Escape*.

Even though everything we had done was illegal, Regina had been adamant that we break the law safely, or at least as safely as we could. This meant lining our rental truck with lead sheets and burying each load in the old quarry at Regina's farm as soon as we unloaded it. To expedite the work, we bought a small backhoe. I became pretty good at operating it, as well as the front-loader farm tractor Regina already had. It wasn't so much the volume of material we needed to transport as the double care we needed to use—protecting ourselves from any radiation and not bringing attention to our actions—that seemed to tire Regina.

After we'd cleared out the ruined equipment, we began to rebuild the lab. I say "we," but I didn't have the skill or knowledge to do anything but hand her tools, clean up, and lug material from the truck into the elevator, then into the shop and lab. I also mixed a lot of concrete, which was a monumental task in itself. I marveled that Regina had built this entire suite by herself while I'd been in Seattle and New York.

In any case, I loved working with her. The upper floors and yard of Race Street were nearly complete, and it would have been fruitless to try to work on any mathematical approaches to her machine until they could be put to the test. The repair work definitely wasn't as exciting as discovering what our machine could do to explore the future, but we were able to incorporate new features into the equipment because we were essentially starting from scratch. Best of all, we spent most of our time together. Regina possessed a happy combination of traits—being confident and self-effacing at the same time. I was still in love with her, perhaps more than ever, and I'd never stopped wishing our relationship was more than it was. At times I thought I should approach her about my feelings, but then I would decide that she, who knew everything else about me, must know how I felt and simply did not feel the same way. I felt as if our relationship was like a magnificent, intricate crystal palace full of wondrous spaces and delightful surprises, with a single door I had never been invited to open—and if I attempted it the entire immense edifice might crash to the ground in millions of shards of glass. Still, I discovered that one of the most beautiful gifts she could bestow upon me was her smile.

At times she appeared to be more sprite than human—a Peter Pan or an Ariel, as she flitted around the lab—but she was a master mechanic as well. Because we had to cool our photon "bullets" to below absolute zero to make the machine work, substantial plumbing was involved. One time when we fired up the equipment, one of the pipes emitted a loud clanging sound. Regina explained that it was caused by the fluid surge in the pipes hitting a bend at start-up and being forced to suddenly change direction. I began discussing how we could electronically control the valve so we could ease the flow into the lines, but she just smiled at me.

"Our experiment is complicated enough. Let's do something simpler." She proceeded to install a "water hammer" in the line, a dead-end extension at the elbow joint. "Instead of smashing the joint, the refrigerant will compress the air in this dead end, like a spring, which will soften the blow," she explained.

Although I'd seen plumbers construct these devices throughout our building, I'd mistakenly thought they were potential future line extensions. I suppose there are those who can't understand how I'm able to extract new and unforeseen patterns through mathematics—and in some way we all might have unusual talents—but I was continually amazed at the extent of Regina's practical skills. Her workmanship was certainly of a higher level than that of even our most accomplished plumbers and electricians.

By spending more time with her, I was able to make sure she was taking care of herself. The explosion seemed to have taken a toll on her. I thought the endless jousting with Paul DeVries also might have gotten to her, or maybe it was the Sisyphean effort of having to rebuild the lab. I made sure we ate together, and I also tried to get her to sleep more. Our stock trading from the pretemporal information gatherer was non-existent for nearly a year, so I reverted to using my fractal methods to earn income. Since we were pretending to use those methods anyway, we saw no drop in actual revenue. Naturally I had put a great deal of the money I received from my settlement with Sheila into the lab, and the building was two-thirds full of paying tenants, so we could have easily survived without any income from stock trading. Nevertheless, we felt DeVries might be tracking our activities, so we didn't want to show any apparent change in revenue.

Gradually we rebuilt our machine to be stronger and more efficient than ever. One positive from this was that we now could power our building from the solar arrays, instead of just using it to power the machine. This reduced our electric bills immensely, and our documented success cemented our relations with the various politicians who had made the project possible, which we hoped would help ward off nosy officials.

We planned new uses for our equipment, but mindful of our latest catastrophe, we wanted to make sure we'd first survive these explorations.

23

What didn't change were our conversations on the roof. Regina and I didn't have time to discuss physics while running a cement mixer or attaching plumbing hangers to the concrete ceiling, and we couldn't hear each other above the din in any case. We might begin a discussion during dinner at Eduardo's, but even at dinner we wouldn't have enough time to finish an extended line of thought. Besides, we were both night owls so we'd bring a couple of glasses and our wine to the roof to finish the day. I eventually did manage to get Regina to sleep in, but neither of us was ever inclined to go to bed early.

One night on the roof, I asked her what she thought of string theory. String theory states that all matter consists of vibrating "strings" embedded in extra dimensions we can't perceive. In fact, there needs to be at least eleven dimensions, seven of them hidden from us somehow, for the theory to work. For decades it's been the darling of mathematically minded physicists, so naturally it interested me. Unfortunately, the theory doesn't seem to have created anything except some beautiful mathematics, which is understandably unsatisfactory to physicists. It was nearing 1:30 a.m. and quite dark out, and as Regina didn't reply at first and I could barely see her, I thought she might have fallen asleep. Finally her voice crept out of the night.

"Let's go back to visualizing one dimension of space as a sine wave. When we say space looks like a sine wave, we're imagining we can see a significant duration of time—as many Planck Intervals as we see oscillations."

"I'm following you so far."

"So instead, visualize a particle moving in time along the spiral—it would look like a point was just wiggling up and down as it followed the sine pattern, like the end of a waving string. It's this motion in subatomic collisions that inspired string theory."

"So this wave action of space makes particles vibrate, creating the string motion?"

"Not quite. It's the universe itself that's vibrating, not the particle. Think of a movie where the object being filmed looks like it's moving up and down. But then you notice the background also is moving up and down, so you realize it must be the camera that's moving. If the focal length is short enough, you might not be able to discern which one is moving. Similarly, the experiments that appear to reveal these vibrating objects are actually revealing the wave structure of space and time. String theory will lead nowhere until physicists realize what's vibrating."

Several nights later, after we had settled into our roof lawn chairs, discussed the affairs of the day, and observed the spectacle of the universe in silence for a while, I asked Regina about the connection between the increase in entropy, a measure of disorder, and the so-called arrow of time. This issue has been seen as a central question of physics.

"The fact that entropy increases with time in our universe is undeniable," she said, "but in terms of explaining the nature of time, it's a red herring. You know the difference between cause and correlation, right?"

Of course I did. In creating a scientific theory, it's important to make sure you distinguish between these two possibilities. Imagine two phenomena, A and B, are created together by a third phenomenon, C. If we don't know about C, we might assume A causes B (or B causes A), because they're always seen together. In this example, A and B are merely correlated, as both are always caused by C.

"Let's forget about relativity and quantum mechanics and warped space-time and indeterminacy," Regina continued. "Imagine you live in an exploding universe. In such a universe, you'd still notice a continual increase in entropy with time, because the nature of an explosion is that entropy increases as the explosion expands. Some theories posit that at some point our universe will quit expanding and begin to collapse. At that point entropy would begin to decrease with time, because the universe would be becoming more ordered, but time would still go on. I believe awareness creates the arrow of time, which also means the universe can't be truly deterministic."

This surprised me. "Why not?"

"Well, in order for the universe to be deterministic—that is to say, the outcome of an event is entirely predictable given a perfectly defined starting point—all phenomena must be reversible, so that one can perfectly determine the starting point of an event from its outcome as well. We know quantum physics doesn't allow us to make such a prediction precisely. I contend that awareness isn't a reversible phenomenon; rather, it only works in one direction."

"I'm still not sure why you put so much importance on awareness."

"The conventional view is that an event begins with some force, which causes some result. Given this view, the purpose of physics is to predict the result, and the curse of quantum physics is that the result of quantum events can only be predicted with some degree of probability, not with certainty."

"And what's your view?"

"I think the common view is backward. It is awareness that creates existence. Force is the result of existence, of awareness. And so is time. Remember how I explained that we're only aware of the past, and we use our considerable brain power to guess at the future?"

I nodded, again to myself. "Of course. It was one of your first lessons."

"I also remarked that, despite this, we're conditioned to think we're facing the future. This is a natural mistake—even the simple fact of walking compels us to look where we're going, though everything we see has already happened." "At the time, I thought that was a strange concept," I said, "but now it seems obvious."

Our conversation was suddenly interrupted by a terrific din on the street below—a large bang and the sound of glass shattering. We made our way, in semi-darkness, over to the roof parapet at the corner of Race and Fifth, to see the results of an accident in the middle of the intersection. A small sedan had broadsided an oversized pickup just in front of the pickup driver's door. It looked like the front end of the car was scattered all over the street. As the pickup, which was on Fifth Avenue, had the right of way, it seemed pretty clear that the sedan had run the stop sign.

The sedan driver had opened his door, and gotten himself out of the car enough that his feet were on the pavement, but he was making no effort to get up.

Instead he sat there with his head between his hands as the other driver stood over him and screamed.

"There're two people who have just experienced a sudden increase in entropy," Regina observed, referring to the obvious disorder which had ensued from the collision.

"No doubt they wish they could make time go backward, too," I added. A few other people had approached the accident, as well as a police cruiser. We decided we could be of no help and returned to our stations.

"It's this manner of looking at reality backward that has confused us," Regina said as soon as we settled down again. "We are so focused on our plans that when something unforeseen like that collision happens, we call it an accident. Newton talked about a reaction to a force, but in fact awareness creates reality, and thus force as well. It's ironic that some people still wonder about the arrow of time at all. The puzzle first arose because the laws of physics of the nineteenth century seemed reversible, but no matter how you explain quantum physics, its results aren't reversible. Tonight you began by asking me about the arrow of time and entropy. A more interesting relationship is the one between the arrow of time and memory."

"Memory?"

"The record of awareness is memory. Every moment has a memory—well, a partial memory—of the preceding moment. And that previous moment had a memory of its previous moment, and so on. Thus each moment possesses an embedded memory of the entire history of the universe. This is how we know there's an arrow of time in the first place."

"But you say it's only a partial memory?"

"If one moment had a complete memory of the previous moment, it would *be* the previous moment. There's a cost to memory—a substantial cost." "How so?"

"Take an individual living being, for instance, any multicellular species. Have you ever wondered how nature manages to create a new individual that grows and gets more complex and robust for a period of time, then always begins to decay at some point?"

"I've certainly noticed that happening to me." Regina laughed along with me.

"But what does that have to do with memory?"

"Think of what constitutes an individual over a lifetime: every atom changes many times; its body shape is under constant flux," she said. "In fact, an individual is actually a colony of many thousands of species of microbes. What is kept intact, however, is that individual's memory."

"Do plants have memories?"

She nodded. "Their memory is their form. They build structures that they use to nourish and reproduce themselves. The same is true for us, but we think of our memory as only being our conscious memory. Life-forms without memory can just split up; death isn't inevitable. When an amoeba divides, do you say that one died and two are born, or that one is the original and the other is the new one? Neither description makes sense. But an individual with a memory pays a price in that it can't just split up—it can't renew itself wholesale without destroying its memory—so it eventually accumulates enough damage over time that it can't continue. The drive of an individual being to live is really the attempt to save its memory, and yet the restriction on repairs in order to maintain that memory makes the death of any individual inevitable."

As was true on many occasions during my conversations with Regina, I had no response, nothing to say, nothing to ask. I just sat there swimming among the heavens, wondering what I'd gotten myself into. I thought of various friends and acquaintances in my past and present: Cheryl, Tom, Louise, Sheila. They all seemed like they had a driving passion. While they knew what they wanted for their lives, I felt like I'd just drifted into mine, swimming from star to star. In order not to feel totally useless, I refilled our wine glasses.

"Remember our discussion about the two-slit experiment?" Regina asked, finally breaking the silence.

"Yes."

"I explained that the standard explanation for the results of that experiment is that a photon exists as a wave function that includes all its possible outcomes until it's observed, at which point the wave function is said to collapse into a single event. But a wave function is a mathematical formula, it can't be observed— we infer its existence from the result of its collapse. As soon as it's observed, it vanishes, and an event occurs. The event is what's observed— that's what exists; that's reality. Awareness is what creates existence, sequential existence—that is to say, time.

"We humans are so caught up in our individual virtual time machines that we think almost exclusively about purpose and intent, but except for the rather feeble similarities of other complex animals, nothing else in the universe appears to consider the future, whereas everything is aware of the past, specifically previous instances of existence. And even other animals are unlikely to be so involved in their own planning that they confuse it with reality, as I believe people often do."

"How does that have anything to do with the arrow of time?"

"We should never forget that physics is a human endeavor, created to answer human concerns," Regina said.

"How could it be otherwise?"

"It could not and should not, but we need to be aware of how our preconceptions can mislead us. Think of how wrenching the change from Newtonian space and time to relativistic space-time was. And how even more confusing was the further change from simple causality to the universe of the collapsing wave function. To understand all this, we need to grasp that the so-called collapse of the wave function, due to some inexplicable observation, is in actuality the creation of each moment of the universe from the preceding one, due to the phenomenon of awareness."

Not for the first time, Regina's ideas overwhelmed me. "Your understanding of physics is so different from—and evidently so far beyond—standard physics, despite the enormous amount of time and energy people have spent all over the world exploring these issues. Do you think the rest of the world will ever catch up to you?"

"Perhaps. As you know, I originally developed the idea of the universe as a spiral from Stephen Hawking's concept of imaginary time, and the idea of an observant universe has been kicked around for decades. Maybe someday another physicist will figure these connections out." She paused long enough for me to get lost in the stars again, then said, "There's another idea you might be interested in working on."

"What is that?"

"The great logician Kurt Gödel—"

"The guy who proved all consistent logical systems are incomplete?"

"The same. As you might know, he was a good friend of Einstein's, and they spent a great deal of time together. Gödel discovered that one mathematical solution to how space is warped would require that the universe rotates. He evidently looked for empirical evidence of rotation of the heavens."

"Did he find it?"

"No one has found the kind of rotation he was looking for. But you might try to find out if the minute rotation of the four-dimensional helix fits his requirements."

I told her I'd look into it, and I will someday.

24

After Louise took me to the tunnel beneath 58 Race Street, I began to see her on a more regular basis. Although I couldn't tell her how important her discovery had been to Regina and me, I was immensely grateful for her trust and effort. As it turned out, through her underground explorations of Foxfield and its abandoned buildings, she'd collected a number of tools and furniture items, and moved them to rental storerooms. One day she gave me a tour of her collections—a seemingly endless supply of goods, to the extent that I worried someone might accuse her of having stolen the stuff.

When I asked her about this, she wasn't concerned. "Whoever owns any of it probably has no idea it exists. These buildings are for the most part forgotten and abandoned." She looked at me with the same look as when I had asked her how one could obtain one of those empty lockers in Northern University's tunnel. "What does it mean to own something if you don't even know about it?"

"But someone might see you. You surely don't haul this stuff out through the tunnels."

Louise tossed her head back, shaking her long black hair like a mane, and laughed. "How much of my life do you want to know, Ron?"

I wasn't sure, so I didn't answer.

"Listen, I'm pretty sure I don't take anything anyone wants. I explore all over—or, I should say, under—the city. Obviously I can get into occupied buildings as well as abandoned ones, but it's the old abandoned factories that are the most interesting. It's like I have a free ticket to an amazing museum. I can't just let it all sit there and rot, it would be like letting a Van Gogh mold in a basement. I feel like a curator of sorts. Follow me."

The storage room we were in was set up like a single-car garage—with an overhead door at one end and a bare light affixed to the ceiling—and it was filled floor to ceiling with Louise's stuff. It was one of a long row of identical rooms built into yet another abandoned factory, but this was a steel building from the nineteen-sixties instead of a brick building from the eighteen-sixties, constructed on the outskirts of Foxfield. After I followed Louise out, she closed and locked the door, then led me to another room a few doors down. This room was empty save for a small green step van, complete with a logo and phone number painted on the sides: AAPEX DELIVERY — WHAT YOU WANT AND WHERE YOU WANT IT.

"What do you think?" Louise said. I could tell she was pleased with her handiwork.

"You run a delivery company?"

"Looks good, doesn't it? I found this van one day in an abandoned factory garage not far from Race Street. The keys and title were in a little office in a corner of the bay. It started right up. Of course, the paint job is mine."

The logos looked professional. "You could have been an art student." "Almost was, but I couldn't stand class."

I pointed to the van. "Whose phone number is that?"

"Mine. I bought one of those cheap cell phones at a convenience store. Never answer it."

"So this is how you move your stuff." I knew Louise was a genius at being invisible, but still the van surprised me.

"I only take it out every other week or so. I think it has a broken rear spring, and it barely starts in the cold. I put the Chrysler's plates on when I drive it."

It seemed Louise collected her treasures just because they were interesting curiosities, but I was convinced she could sell some of the stuff for decent money. I mentioned this to her.

"I sell a little on the Internet, but I'm not much into the whole computer thing. I've tried selling to dealers, but I got tired of being low-balled, so I gave it up," she muttered, as we rummaged through yet another of her storage rooms. "Some of this stuff is incredible." She handed me an inlayed wooden box filled with an array of unusual blades, each set in an exquisitely felt-lined bed. I had no idea what they were, but everything about the box was beautiful. "I have to work just to pay for all my storage."

"Regina and I could set you up with the empty store next to Frank's doughnut shop, right by the bridge," I suggested. "Maybe you'd like an actual store better than a computer screen."

Louise looked doubtful as she shook her head. "I don't know how to run a store, Ron."

"We won't charge you any rent until you get started. And the other shop owners could help you. You could make your own hours. Of course, the more hours, the more profit. Let me give you a tour."

We had taken her car, so she drove us back to Race Street. Louise was a good driver, careful and smooth. "Did you drive before I gave you this car?" I asked her.

She gave me a sidelong glance. "Why? Am I making you nervous?" "Quite the opposite."

"No, actually, I didn't. I taught myself how to drive in the university parking lot. One of the security guards caught me one night—I think it was pretty obvious I didn't know what I was doing. Instead of busting me, though, he gave me a lesson every night. Sweet guy." She parked behind the doughnut shop, and we headed for the back door of the empty store next door.

"By the way, have you ever been in the other part of our old sluice, where the water once *entered* the building?" I asked as I unlocked the door.

"Sure. It doesn't reach the old turbine room anymore, but it's tied into the city's combined storm-water sewer system. In fact, it must be right under us."

"It is, and here's an entrance to it, where they used to monitor the flow." I opened a trapdoor in the floor, revealing a small musty room walled off from the rest of the basement. We descended a ladder I'd left there. Once we were down I removed a bar that secured a manhole, then lifted it up, revealing a narrow shaft that led down to darkness. Louise was speechless—but only for a second.

"Holy shit. I knew there was an old access here, but I thought it was covered from above. I could go anywhere in the city from here!"

*

Louise reacted the way I had hoped she would and opened her store a week or two later. Not only did Regina and I want to thank her for tipping us off about Paul DeVries, but we also felt her spelunking underground provided us with extra security and we wanted her to stay around at least until we were sure he wasn't coming back.

Louise called her place the Whimsy Shop. On the placard that was supposed to display the store's hours she scribbled owner's whimsy in large block letters. She set up an illegal bedroom in the back of her store and cleaned herself up in the doughnut shop's bathroom. She also used my apartment for anything she wanted, including me.

Louise's store was as successful as she wanted it to be. I knew she was bright and energetic, but she was also surprisingly personable, considering her propensity for spending so much time alone haunting Foxfield's darkest, most hidden corners. Even more amazing was the extensive knowledge she'd acquired about the items she'd collected.

Her stock fell into two main categories: old office equipment and factory tools. Some of the office stuff was still usable: filing cabinets, desks, even chairs. It also was bulky, though, which posed a problem for her small store. The tools were more interesting: seldom usable, sometimes small, sometimes extremely heavy. Most important, some items were quite beautiful and old, and therefore valuable. Complete sets of bits or dies that came in magnificent wooden boxes sold very well. Individual tools sold too, but for a great deal less. Louise took advantage of her office furniture by using the desks and drawers to store and display the smaller items. The flat file drawers used by architects to store their drawings were especially useful for the smaller machining tools, but she also used file cabinets and office desks. She created a cozy environment with a single labyrinthine aisle, and even included a small sitting area with a few comfy upholstered chairs for her customers to relax in while inspecting her wares. As a result, Louise didn't need to buy any display cases; everything in the shop was for sale.

We carried on our occasional affair for nine months. She didn't move into my place, but she did furnish my apartment with a fine variety of antique kitchenware and furniture. When she wanted a homemade meal, she'd show up unannounced with bags full of groceries and even start cooking before I got home. I had always assumed she lived on fast food, probably because of the way we first met, haggling over a used sandwich. In fact, she was a wonderful cook, introducing me to vegetables I never knew existed and reintroducing me to ones I knew, cooked so simply and so fresh I hardly recognized them. I think the only pan she used was a cast iron skillet (one of her finds, of course).

One evening as I was devouring a plate of sautéed spinach with pine nuts and salmon, I said, "I always thought spinach was just a soggy mess. This is delicious. What's your secret?"

"Olive oil. Good olive oil." "That's it?"

"And fresh greens, of course. And garlic."

On the few occasions I didn't make it home, she'd eat alone. When I did come home, we'd have a lovely meal and a lovely night.

Sexual intercourse being, after all, a physical activity, every lover presents a different experience. Cheryl was an athletic woman who purred quietly during sex; she was a plush lover despite her considerable strength. Sheila made no noise at all but bit my neck so hard and so often that I took to wearing turtlenecks even during the summer. Louise clung hard during sex, screamed more like a wildcat than a housecat, and left deep scratches in my back. Because of her yelps, I never attempted to sleep with her in the bedroom at the rear of her store, but I was always delighted when she visited me.

One day when I stopped by the Whimsy Shop she introduced me to a friend who was nearly her physical double: same height, same weight, same black androgynous clothing. "Ron," she said, "I want you to meet Tony."

Tony extended his hand and gave a slight bow as I shook it. "So pleased to meet you. Louise calls you her savior." I don't know which surprised me more— his words or the accent that carried them. His English was clearly practiced but with a pronounced Italian flavor.

Louise broke in, clearly embarrassed by Tony's revelation of her secret. "Tony's taking me to Rome, Ron."

"Rome? That's exciting." It did sound exciting, but it also sounded like I was going to lose Louise. I tried to hide my disappointment.

"Rome, Ron! Do you know what that means?" Her bright-blue eyes grew large, and her voice cracked. Was this the same cool, cynical woman who used to sleep behind the ductwork in the workers' room at Northern? I did not know what Rome meant.

"The Catacombs!" she said, answering her own question. "Tony's going to show me the Catacombs."

It took Louise only a few days to clean out her shop. One afternoon she came by to say good-bye as I was about to leave my office. "I think this place could use a little sprucing up," she said.

I still used the front room for my space. It provided a buffer, a place to meet with contractors and vendors in order to keep Regina's spaces private. Still, I hadn't done anything to it in the two years since I'd moved in, except add more rolls of plans and stacks of paper.

Louise handed me an envelope. "Here are the keys and addresses to my storage rooms. Please feel free to outfit your office, then lose these." As I reached for the package, she put her other arm around my neck and gave me a long kiss. "You've been the best friend I ever had. Thank you so much."

"For what?"

"For taking me seriously."

"I do, and I'm sure you'll enjoy Rome." I didn't want to make her feel bad, so I tried to keep myself from tearing up.

"I hope to. But Ron, if anyone comes looking for Tony or me, you know nothing, okay?"

*

I probably shouldn't have been surprised when a couple of local detectives showed up a few weeks later looking for a Tony Rinaldi. Both were heavyset men with faces you forgot while looking at them. One was nearly as tall as me, but the shorter man did all the talking.

"Who?" I asked, not making the obvious connection. "We think he was hanging out with Louise Jenney."

I put on my best poker face. "Ms. Jenney cleared out her shop a couple weeks ago," I said. "Didn't say where she was going."

"Did she leave you anything? Do you have any copies of her checks?" "She paid me in cash."

The two detectives looked at each other, then at me. I had a feeling they knew about the break-in incident with DeVries, and were happy to assume the worst about me. These weren't the street cops who had befriended Regina; rather, they looked like they might even have FBI ambitions themselves. I wasn't going to give away anything about Louise if I could help it, but I also didn't want these guys hanging around.

"Do you have records for her cash payments?" the shorter man asked.

I was ready for this line of questioning. Opening a drawer from a beautiful oak file cabinet I'd just requisitioned from one of Louise's storage units—and bypassing the file containing the keys and addresses to her storage rooms—I pulled out an old-fashioned ledger. "I have several residential renters who sometimes or always pay cash, though Ms. Jenney was the only commercial one. She was also the only one who paid weekly."

In reality, I hadn't collected any payments from Louise, but from the beginning I felt I should document some. Regina had taught me to keep our collective nose clean. I pointed out the entries to the detectives.

"Whimsy? What the hell is that?" asked the lead detective.

"That was the name of her shop." "Did you know her before this?"

"Yeah, we dated in college a little," I lied. "What happened?"

"Not much. I moved to Seattle, and we lost touch until a few months ago." "And you don't know where she is now?"

It's much easier to tell a lie surrounded by a few truths. "I'm sure she'll show up again someday."

"Let us know if she does, okay? It'll be for her own good."

Oddly, I partially agreed with him. Tony worried me, but I owed it to Louise to let her live her own life. "Sure thing," I said.

I was always aware that I'd given up a fabulous life of fame and wealth in New York for a more interesting but also more obscure and less wealthy life in Foxfield. I never regretted that trade-off, but Louise had made me realize how regulated my life had become. I needed to get up early every morning to meet with the contractors first thing, I needed to have the phone nearby at all times to handle any emergencies that might arise, either from the ongoing construction or the tenants, I needed to be at the beck and call of any of the town inspectors who needed access to the building. There was a time when I'd ridiculed Tom Jacobs for his rigid schedule, and now I was easily his equal. I use to call him "the walking plank." Now that Louise had left, I wondered if I'd turn into a board myself.

25

"I think I'm burning out," Regina told me one night. It was the rare night that we were eating somewhere besides Eduardo's. Regina had suggested a small Tunisian restaurant in West Foxfield, near where I had lived when I attended Northern. The restaurant was new, and in fact the entire town appeared more vibrant than it had the dozen or so years earlier when I'd called it home. I doubted the old me could have afforded an apartment in the new West Foxfield.

"Maybe we should switch gears for a while," she continued.

"Which gear would that be?" I asked. I had been worried about Regina's health, so I was happy to consider slowing down for a while.

"Well, we might have proven that our method has severe limitations in altering the course of future events. We can't even use our pre-knowledge to create more wealth for ourselves than we can by using your investment strategy, for fear of drawing attention to ourselves. Perhaps we can launch a different experiment, one that won't require all this secrecy, one we won't have to be afraid of." Regina's eyes were red and a little swollen, her once smooth skin appeared dry, her cheeks slightly puffy. She looked tired.

"What do you have in mind?"

"Two things. First, if we can prove that using our machine as a weapon would always destroy the person using it, we could relax our secrecy. Second, some early work is being done on creating quantum clocks. If we had a second site prepared when the new clocks are operational, we could prove our ideas on the origin of dark matter."

"Let's go back to thing one."

"I want to set up a satellite lab, smaller and cheaper than this one. If we can switch the control of our machine to a satellite location before interfering with the future, and destroy it instead of the main lab, we'll have created a way to use our invention as a weapon without committing suicide, and we'd still have to keep our work hidden. But if we could show that our pretemporal machine can't be used except as a very expensive suicide weapon, perhaps we could reveal our findings."

I found Regina's scenario of proving our machine unusable as a weapon unconvincing and, in fact, frightening. Just because we couldn't figure out a way to use it as a weapon safely didn't mean someone else couldn't. Also, we might kill ourselves in the process. I felt Regina was making a desperate attempt to become respectable, but I didn't contradict her.

Her second motive was more intriguing. Experiments with quantum clocks were being designed to measure incongruities in Earth's gravitational field, to gain a clearer picture of the planet's composition. Regina wanted to take it a step further and measure incongruities in the universe at large, to prove her theory about dark matter—namely, that it's a vestige of a disturbance in space-time, caused by a collision with another universe in the first fraction of a second after the Big Bang.

For both experiments, she decided to find an abandoned mine far away from Race Street, rather than another building with a secret basement. Even with my reservations, I encouraged her. I, too, thought she needed a change.

Her first trip was to Pennsylvania, but she came back disappointed. "A lot of those old mines are on fire—fires that have lasted decades and left whole towns abandoned."

She made a few trips farther west, to Montana and Wyoming, again without results. Then, one day in late July she e-mailed me a plane ticket to Las Vegas. I knew she was serious, because this would be the first time we'd both be absent from Race Street for an extended period of time.

I hadn't been out west since my grad school days in Seattle, but I knew as soon as I disembarked at the Las Vegas airport that the Southwest definitely wasn't the Northwest. The first gulp of air made me feel like I'd swallowed a lit torch. So did the second.

Regina picked me up in a large white Land Rover; I was hoping for a sporty convertible. We drove to an inauspicious motel on the outskirts of town. I was hoping for Caesar's Palace. On the ride over, she asked about Race Street and I told her she was looking like her travels had done her good, but she didn't talk about why she wanted me to come to Nevada. "Get some sleep," she said, as soon as we were settled in at the motel. Sharing a room was as close I could get to sharing a bed with Regina, but for the moment my thoughts were on this new adventure she was leading me to.

"We have a long day tomorrow," she said. I was expecting that.

The next morning, over hash browns and bacon, Regina began to fill me in. "I think I've found just the place to set up our satellite lab."

"In Las Vegas?"

"No, it's a little over five hours from here."

It turned out that five hours was practically next door in Nevada; there was almost no one in between. Nevada occupies the Great Basin, the area between the Rocky Mountains and the Sierra Nevada. Topographically, the Great Basin is laid out like a crumpled towel, with a seemingly endless number of smaller north-south ridges and valleys between the two massive mountain ranges that define the American West.

That morning, Regina and I took a highway along one of these valleys north of the city and traveled through a sparseness like nothing I'd ever experienced. New England has a way of covering its past so that one needs to look closely, as Cheryl often pointed out, to uncover the histories of past generations. The Great Basin Desert doesn't cover up anything. The slightest road remains tattooed on the landscape—if not forever, at least for centuries. I've heard that the ruts left by the pioneers' wagon trains are still visible in places.

We had passed a few ranches, mostly far off the road, and a fleeting town or two, when Regina turned onto one of the tattooed roads. From the highway it appeared that the road shot through a distant saddle between two peaks on the ridge east of our highway, but the road was longer and rougher to actually traverse. Now I understood why Regina hadn't rented a sporty convertible.

Once over the ridge, we dropped down into the next valley. This valley was truncated at the southern end, where the adjacent mountain range merged into the one we'd just crossed. In this crotch sat a ranch house, a barn, and several corrals—none very fancy to begin with and none particularly well cared for. In New

England's humid weather these structures would have decayed into the ground long ago, but in desiccated Nevada they persevered just fine.

The road we had traveled on split in front of the ranch. One fork continued over the next range, the other headed left, up the valley to the north. The north fork appeared to have been the most used. The one straight ahead appeared less traveled but had a line of electric poles following it into the distance. There were no other buildings in sight.

Regina turned into the driveway and stopped next to an old red Ford pickup in front of the house.

The house was rather small, with plank walls, a low roofline, and a front porch with no floor but the earth. The barn was barely taller and was covered with boards that had shrunk so much in the unrelenting sun that I could see light all the way through. The corral fences were rusted barbed wire with a combination of wood and metal posts. A handful of horses stood in the barnyard, and a few head of cattle were grazing in the distance.

An elderly man ambled out of the barn. He looked like I imagined a rancher should: weathered, lean, faded blue jeans, faded chambray shirt, and a beat-up straw cowboy hat.

"Howdy, Regina. You came back," he said. Regina extended her hand. "I told you I would."

The man smiled as he shook her hand. "People say a lot of things." He turned to me and examined me like he might a horse.

"This is my associate, Ron Larsen," she said. "Ron, Ed Choate." We shook hands; his hand felt like bones covered with sandpaper—strong bones, coarse sandpaper. I'm sure he noticed my soft, fleshy grip.

"You want a tour too?" he asked me.

Regina answered for me. "We could look around the yard a bit. Is your daughter here?" On the drive up, she had told me that the owners wouldn't complete the sale of the property without their daughter, a store manager in Reno, present. Regina, Ed, and Marilyn, Ed's wife, had reached an agreement the week before, but Ed and Marilyn wanted Jeanne to approve the deal before they sold the ranch. Regina thought it would be nice if I saw the place too, but I don't think she felt she needed my approval.

"Not yet," Ed said. "She's coming from the city. She'll be here soon." Apparently the city meant Reno, not Las Vegas, here. "Care for some iced tea?"

We turned toward the house to see a short, round woman, dressed much like Ed, carrying a tray with a pitcher and glasses.

"This is my wife, Marilyn," Ed told me. "Honey, Ron Larsen."

The woman smiled and nodded to me, then turned to a picnic table under the porch roof to set down the tray. "You folks don't look like ranchers," Marilyn said after we all sat down. "What are you planning to do with the place?"

"Take up mining," I joked. Regina kicked me under the table.

Our hosts both laughed. "You look even less like miners," Marilyn said, then turned to me. "I gather your partner here told you about the mines." She hadn't, but I gathered I should shut up and let Regina talk.

"It might sound strange to you," Regina said, "but we're looking into making a kind of...how can I explain this? A sort of boutique dude ranch."

Ed looked at Regina as if she had switched languages. "Boutique what?" "There are a lot of rich people," Regina explained, "who'd be willing to pay good money to spend time here in God's country by themselves...well, with a little help."

Regina told them about her idea to create a horse-riding ranch for wealthy patrons. She planned to build a second house for the guests, with air conditioning, and put the staff in the existing one. I half expected Ed and Marilyn to be insulted at the thought of prostituting their homestead, but they were business people trying to make a living in a barren land.

"Damn, we should have thought of that, honey," Ed said.

Marilyn nodded. "If we were younger, we could run the place ourselves."

As they were digesting the idea of making their ranch more financially viable, a late-model BMW sedan pulled up behind our SUV. "That's Jeanne, our daughter," Marilyn said.

Jeanne popped out of her car and walked over to join us at the table. She was dressed in a tan business suit, quite a contrast to her parents. Her cowboy hat was felt and new. She appeared robust, but had none of the weathered look of her parents. Her skin was even rosy, with a natural sheen unavailable from a cosmetic jar. "Hi, everyone," she said as she poured herself an iced tea, then turned to Regina. "You must be Regina Russo."

"I am," Regina said, "and this is my associate, Ron Larsen."

Jeanne and I shook hands. "Good to meet you," we said simultaneously. Jeanne took a sip of her tea. "I've been trying to get my folks to move to

Reno for years. We just needed to wait for the right situation." Of course she meant finding someone to overpay for the ranch, but the price still seemed absurdly low to us.

Ed and Marilyn showed us—meaning me—around the barn and corrals and explained that they owned several thousand acres and grazing rights to the whole valley. However, they only had about twenty head of cattle and half a dozen horses left.

"Really ain't no money in cattle with a spread this small," Ed said. "You might have the right idea for the place."

I'd expected some sort of laconic western conversation, but our hosts were proud of their place, and also happy to get out from under it.

After the tour, though, Ed turned to us with a serious look. "Regina, I know I showed you them mines, and I don't mind showing Ron, but I gotta warn you that the state is trying to close down all these abandoned silver mines, make 'em safe. They say there's arsenic and lead and whatnot in them. We don't say nothing to anybody about ours 'cause we don't want the government poking its nose into our business. If you make the mines part of your ranch for your guests, you won't have them long."

Regina took this all in, but she looked puzzled. "Ed, you only showed me one mine. Are there more?"

Ed, Marilyn, and Jeanne exchanged smiles. "Hop in the truck," Ed said. "Let's all go take a look."

By "hop in the truck," he meant that Jeanne, Regina, and I would sit in the bed while he and his wife sat up front. Ed headed north on the left branch of the road for a mile or so, then turned back southwest up a large draw, as the dry, steep gulches of desert are called.

During the fifteen-minute ride over a horse path much worse than the dirt road we'd just left, Jeanne told us the story about the property. "The Carreford brothers staked their claim to these mines in 1866, but my parents and I think they were here for several years before that. We have more local tales than written evidence about what happened, but when you see the mines, you might give them some credence." Jeanne had to shout to be heard above the clatter of the bouncing truck, but even in her suit and new hat, she sat like she belonged in the back of that truck.

"Sam and Hank Carreford worked together for twenty years on the first mine, a tunnel into the ridge," she went on. "At one point they might even have hired some help, which means they must've found some silver to afford the expansion, but we don't think that lasted long. Anyway, Hank supposedly got discouraged and started to argue that they need to dig straight down. Sam wanted to continue into the hillside. So Hank started a hole about a quarter of a mile out on the flats. One story says they worked like that for twenty more years, living in the same cabin but never speaking to each other. It sounds crazy, but you have to be a bit crazy to be a miner."

Finally we reached one of the mines, but it looked more like a small factory destroyed by a bomb than anything I'd expected. There were troughs and sluices, piles of tailings and empty cans and bottles, the skeleton of a corral and animal shed, a wooden trolley cart on its sides with no wheels, and a couple of pieces of light-gauge rail leading into a low hole in the side of the hill. The mine entrance was maybe five feet high and three feet wide.

"I sold a truckload of scrap steel to a scrapper a few years ago. He left quite a bit behind, but I guess it wasn't enough for him to come back for," Ed said as we looked at the debris.

"That was nearly thirty years ago," said Marilyn. "We sold it 'cause I was pregnant with Jeanne, and we wanted to remodel the bathroom and her bedroom."

Ed grinned. "Like I said, I don't think he's coming back." We crawled into the tunnel for a ways.

"I once got nearly a quarter a mile back there before I got scared I'd get lost in the byways," Ed said. "I unrolled a string as I went, but I was afraid it would break and

I'd never get out."

Back in the sunlight, Ed walked us over to the other mine. It was a circular shaft about seven feet in diameter that went straight down, a hole in solid quartzite. There was no way anyone could get lost in that mine.

"Hank Carreford got about sixty feet into the planet before he died," Ed said. "When he passed on, they say his brother lowered him into this pit and covered him with six feet of his own tailings. He's probably still down there."

I peered inside, but sixty feet is a long way down, farther than my keychain flashlight could illuminate.

We all hopped in the truck and headed back to the ranch house, where they exchanged the deed for a cashier's check Regina had brought. The deal was consummated around a campfire in front of the ranch house. Regina and I had become used to watching the miracle of the night-time universe from our rooftop in Foxfield, and I'd witnessed three weeks of spectacular night skies with Sheila on Lac Perroche, but neither matched the star show we witnessed that night. Not only did there appear to be more stars than I had ever seen, the colors were more varied and vibrant than any night sky I had experienced. The coloring gave the sky a texture that made it seem like you could reach out and grab part of it. I decided I was going to like Nevada.

Ed and Marilyn invited us to stay until morning, but Regina wanted to register the deed at the recorder's office in the county seat, Ely, as early as

possible the next day in order to catch the red-eye out of Las Vegas, so we set out in the middle of the night.

As we drove away from the ranch Regina was as excited as I'd seen her in years. It reminded me of our first conversations in the truck-stop diner, because she could barely finish one idea before another came tumbling out.

"That second mine is perfect," she said. "We can create a miniature machine to lower into the pit and just cover it up if we ruin it and put another one on top of it. It'll be a lot easier than rebuilding the sarcophagus. But before we get started, we should inform the state of the tunnel mine, so they'll think they've cleaned up the entire site and leave us alone. Also, we should find an architect to design the dude ranch. Maybe Jeanne knows one in Reno."

I tried to listen to her, and probably caught most of her gist, but as we sped along the highway I was still transfixed by the huge Nevada night sky. Eventually Regina leaned against me, resting her head against my shoulder, and grew silent. She fell asleep, and I was left by myself to wonder at the Nevada heavens. I felt like I was in outer space hurtling toward the stars. (Scientifically speaking, I realized that we *are* always in outer space hurtling toward the stars.) I looked forward to spending time in our second home.

26

Once we returned to Foxfield, Regina lost no time making plans to have the ranch remodeled. "We can use an RV to set ourselves up in the draw by the mine and take our time setting up the satellite machine, but we need to start making the ranch viable right away. We'll certainly lose the ranch to vandals if we leave it abandoned, which would mean inviting unwanted guests to our mine as well."

By "we," she meant me, because she had immediately began designing and building her satellite lab module at Race Street. I'd become pretty good at construction management from my work on Race Street, but working on a remote site in the Great Basin Desert is quite different than it is in a New England city. My first real decision was to hire an architect.

I didn't want to work out of Las Vegas. My antipathy might seem ironic, given that it was once the destination of my dreams. I couldn't say whether I'd changed or whether Las Vegas was different than I'd imagined. Probably a bit of both.

I started by looking for an architect in Reno. I hoped Jeanne Choate could help me, but then I met Roger Stennet at the Reno airport while I was waiting for a flight home. We struck up a conversation, and he told me he was an architect based in Salt Lake City. He specialized in setting up huge ranch factories across the West. When I told him about our plan to build our little vacation ranch, he said, "I'm just the man for the job. No one knows what a ranch should be and could be better than I do."

Roger and I arranged to sit next to each other on the flight. He was as tall as me, but as thin as Ed Choate. His eyes were dark, thoughtful, intense. His chocolate-colored skin was littered with small bumps where he'd shaved. His fingers were long and expressive; when he talked he used them like he was playing a piano. By the time we reached Salt Lake City, he had convinced me he was right.

We decided to let him take care of designing the ranch while Regina and I turned our attention to setting up our experiment. We quickly divided the land into two parcels, to separate the hundred acres or so that contained the mines from the rest of the ranch. Regina's idea was to park a trailer over Hank's mine to hide it, and to access it from inside by means of a hole in the trailer floor. We moved the overburden and tailings from the vertical shaft excavation to the tunnel mine and positioned our trailer over the hole before asking the state to help us close the tunnel mine.

I invited Roger to make use of the trailer to stay in during his site visits. We hadn't yet opened the floor over the mine shaft, so it was a good way to provide an extra presence in the area. A couple of times he and I stayed there together to go over the progress of the dude ranch. Part of the cover was to show our interest in our project. As a result, Roger and I spent a few evenings together among the heavens, watching our campfire crackle. Campfires seemed as much a part of Nevada culture as lobster rolls are of New England's. Because the Choate ranch was over a mile high and even summer nights could be chilly, the fire often served as more than just scenery.

One evening in October we sat around our little heat source, sitting near each other on the windward side trying to protect the fragile flames. Roger had convinced me to buy an oilskin duster, so we sat like two cowboys, gazing at the flickering tongues of light in front of us.

"Do you find it unusual being an African-American architect in Utah?" I asked him one evening. After the words left my mouth, I realized how rude my question sounded, but Roger took it in stride.

"The facetious answer would be that being African-American anywhere in America is unusual...and likely in Africa as well." He chuckled. "More seriously, being alive is unusual. Why do you think Utah would be more or less unusual than anywhere else?"

"I don't know much about Utah—just that it's very Mormon, and Mormonism seems to have some overtly racist attitudes." The wind gusted for a second, as if in agreement, and swirled dust, smoke, and ashes into our faces, which we momentarily protected with our dusters' large lapels.

Roger wasn't fazed by the wind or my questions. "The operative word being 'overtly.' We're kind of a project for the Mormons—blacks, that is. Honestly, there might be less hatred here, if as much condescension."

"So how did you end up here?"

"Ah, that's an entirely different story, I'm a son of the West. My great grandfathers and great-great-grandfathers were mostly cowboys—some black, some white."

"Black Cowboys?"

He smiled. "A great many cowboys were black. It was a perfect fit." "A perfect fit?"

"Well, after the Civil War a lot of ex-slaves wanted to leave the South. And they had the skill set necessary for the West."

"How's that?"

"They were pretty tough, for one. And who do you think took care of the plantation animals of the antebellum South?"

I learned a lot from Roger aside from architecture, but most of all I learned I could trust his judgment. Not only did he finish the project in less than eight months, but he also introduced me to a young couple who could manage the ranch.

Sally and Gerald Sanchez had both grown up in the high desert, and unlike Jeanne Choate, they wanted to work and live outdoors. I gathered Sally's folks had owned a ranch somewhat larger and more prosperous than the Choates' in Montana, but the one ranch couldn't support four adult kids, so their folks sold it to send them all to college. Gerald's folks worked as hands on a large ranch in Wyoming. Sally and Gerald met at the University of Wyoming, got married, and were searching for a work opportunity when Roger mentioned our enterprise to them. They considered it a perfect situation, and they seemed like the perfect couple to me—energetic, enthusiastic, and smart. Hiring them allowed me to focus more on my work with Regina.

My trips from Massachusetts to Nevada were frequent. I'd learned to work long hours as an undergraduate, and I'd been very busy ever since. The pace of life in New York City was nonstop—frenetic, really. But the word "grueling" more aptly describes my life while setting up the Nevada site. Ed and Marilyn had political— or, perhaps more aptly, ideological—reasons to avoid government intrusion on their land. Regina and I had more immediate reasons to minimize government meddling in our affairs.

Instead of hiding the mine, we wanted to satisfy the state so there would be no reason for them to come around. We agreed that we should legally close the tunnel mine as quickly as possible while building the new ranch house. Roger recommended a Reno engineering firm to do the survey and permitting for the mine closure. Because the mine had been abandoned and the tailings were determined to not be environmentally dangerous, the process was pretty straightforward. Still, I didn't want any engineers poking around the site by themselves. This meant I had to shuttle between Hartford and Reno on a weekly basis, with more to do on either end than two of me could accomplish at one. I quickly grew to resent air travel.

Regina spent the first several months after our trip to Nevada designing a small mobile unit we could build in Foxfield, then disassemble and ship to a warehouse we'd rented in Reno. We could drive it to the mine ourselves. Meanwhile, I wrote a lot of the software instructions for both machines and oversaw the architects and engineers out west.

I didn't see much of Regina during that period. We had learned to work so seamlessly that we hardly needed to talk. I was heartened that she seemed to have renewed her enthusiasm for our work, even though I wasn't entirely certain of the wisdom of her goal. In a way, I was more interested in my friend's enthusiasm than the project itself. The best way to help her seemed to simply do my part.

Many of the threads we were working on came together at once. The tunnel mine was closed to the state's satisfaction. The dude ranch, which we named the Double C, after the Carreford brothers, began taking guests. We started our lab up again—but although the machine worked more efficiently than before, it seemed we had reached the limit of how much information and how far into the future we could manage.

We hadn't tempted fate by replicating our experiment in photography— that could wait for the mobile units—but we knew we could actually see as far as six hours ahead of time. And though we still did most of our stock trading from five to fifteen seconds ahead, we could process an entire transaction in just under a second, nearly triple our earlier speed. And all this took a fraction of the energy of the earlier machine.

It took Regina over a year and a half to complete her first mobile unit, which I received in Reno, assembled in our trailer, and lowered into the abyss below, to share the depths of the Earth with Hank Carreford. I've seen pictures of mines in South Africa that archeologists say could be four thousand years old, possibly older, that look pretty much like Hank's nineteenth century shaft. As I placed the mobile time machine in the bottom of his pit I mused about how much has happened in the last hundred and fifty years.

And now Regina and I were ready to begin an exciting new phase in our adventures.

27

One morning when I arrived at my office at 58 Race Street, I found a note from Regina asking me to come down to the lab. I could enter the lab anytime I wanted, but at that point I sometimes went weeks without going down there. I finished a few errands, then headed to the basement to change into my Tyvek suit.

I walked through the control room without seeing Regina. We had added a lot of electronic equipment to the machine, so it was harder to see from the control room into the lab. It was also harder to see from the lab back into the control room, which suited me fine.

Regina was alert and engaging when around people—she seemed to possess a glow that brightened those around her. By herself, however, she was different. Instead of the light, sure, dancelike movements she made in the company of others, she appeared pensive and serious when alone. Sometimes she even seemed to have an almost tragic bearing. I had long ago realized that she often saw things no one else did, and eventually I came to wonder if she saw too much. Occasionally I'd quietly enter the control room on the pretense of some business just so I could watch her in her element. I don't think she was insincere around people; there were simply two of her, and although I was in love with both, I could only observe the solitary Regina from afar.

This time, however, I didn't tarry. When I entered the lab I saw her standing, naked, on top of the concrete bunker. I'd never seen her other than fully dressed, and I admit my first reaction was to note how lovely she was. I'd known Regina for nearly fifteen years, which put her in her early fifties, but she looked more youthful than that unclothed, like a dancer or a gymnast in her prime. She stood quietly, as if waiting for the music to begin.

"What are you doing?" I asked as I approached her. Then I noticed the lesions and open sores covering the front of her torso. "Regina—oh, my God.

218

What happened?"

She smiled sadly. "Nothing recent, just foolish relics à la Cu[...] talking about?"

"Curie, as in Marie Curie, the great Madame Curie. She too dieu .. radiation poisoning, so I'm in good company. My dear Ron, it's time for me to remove the obstacle."

I had no idea what she was talking about and told her so.

"I've always cautioned you against conflating the awareness each moment the universe has of the previous moment with the awareness we have as conscious beings, but I believe there is a connection. The universe can be understood as a torrent of awareness, as I hope you understand by now. I view our consciousness as an eddy in this flow, a whirlpool where the universal stream separates, swirls, and collides again. Our mind is the obstacle that creates this eddy, like a rock jutting from a riverbed. What we call consciousness is created when these two divided streams of awareness—one that travels through us, organized by our nervous system; the other that is our environment—meet again through our perceptions. Instead of only being aware of the previous moment, a part of the universe becomes aware of itself, aware of awareness. When this obstacle is worn down, consciousness disappears; the flow of universal awareness smooths out and continues unobstructed."

She looked down at me from her concrete perch like a bird about to fly away. She stared at me with the same golden eyes she had the day she seemed to have descended from the clouds onto my chess set. "Life is beautiful, too precious to squander, but being a ripple of something vastly larger is also beautiful. We always want more; we want to live forever. We get much more, but it might not be what we thought it would be."

"Are you telling me you intend to die?" She nodded, almost imperceptibly. "I am." "Can't your sores be healed?" I heard my voice pleading for her to be wrong. "The sores you see are the least of it. I've explained to you that one of the dangers of my work is the possibility of instantaneous collisions as particles move out of time, causing the kind of radioactive explosion that killed Manisha.

I'm afraid my early body protection wasn't up to its task." "But why just your knew the danger and tried to protect myself," she said. "I guess my gloves and visor, as well as the lead table I worked on, were sufficient to block the radiation, but not my body shield."

"So you have radiation poisoning?"

She nodded. "My kidneys and liver are shot. Now the cancer is spreading." "And what? You're going to commit suicide?"

"It's more complicated than that, Ron. Do you recall Hawking radiation?" "A particle and antiparticle momentarily appear out of the vacuum flux of the universe near the event horizon of a black hole," I said automatically. "Before they can annihilate each other, the antiparticle is swallowed by the black hole and the particle takes off, which, by virtue of conservation of energy, means the black hole is diminished by one particle."

She smiled, a soft, wistful smile. "Good. Hawking called his initial statement that nothing could escape a black hole his greatest mistake, and Hawking radiation was his solution. He came by it because he was sure information couldn't be lost, so he needed a way to obtain information from a black hole."

"So you're going to create a black hole to disappear into?"

Regina looked at me with eyes that seemed to be looking for something new in my countenance, or a deeper comprehension than I had shown before—then her eyes softened again. "I'm not sure, Ron, but I was thinking that launching something into the future is usually a one-way trip, somewhat like entering a black hole. Maybe something will escape, like Hawking radiation, maybe a part of my existence, my memory, will outrun my death and survive."

Regina was standing on the concrete structure in the middle of the lab, the structure I often called the sarcophagus, but now the irony of the term horrified me. Of course I couldn't reach her from the lab floor.

Looking up at Regina, I saw the top door hanging above her head, so I knew she was standing over the top opening. I climbed from the floor up to the three foot high bench next to the taller structure. I knew how fearless and determined she could be, and I was afraid of what it looked like she was about to do. I wanted to keep her attention while I positioned myself to grab her ankles, which were just beyond my reach. "So, why no clothes?"

"This isn't a repeatable experiment, you know. I'm trying to be as careful as possible, and I think the clothes could confuse the issue."

"So, you're just making this all up," I said. "You don't know what will happen to you."

"I know enough. But that's not what I wanted to talk to you about. I transferred my ownership of this building to you last year."

"How did that happen?"

She sighed. "You know, Ron, you need to read everything you sign. I could have just as easily taken it all away."

"I always considered this *your* project."

"Well, consider it yours now. Call me in as a missing person. The police will find my car down by the river. When my medical records are examined, it'll be pretty apparent I committed suicide, just not here."

"This isn't right. Are you sure there isn't some other way?" "I'm sorry, Ron. There's none I want to live through."

"I'm going to miss you." I was almost ready to jump at her.

"You will, and you won't. I'll be gone, so of course you'll miss me. But you and I are entangled beings, and like entangled particles, we can't be separated."

"I don't understand."

She smiled wistfully again. "Sometimes there is no understanding; sometimes there's only love."

As she spoke I leaped forward onto the top of the bunker and sprawled out to grab her. Simultaneously she dropped through the opening. My outstretched hands brushed her legs, pubic hair, and buttocks as she fell, then her back and breasts. At the same time, she screamed, "No, Ron!" and I instinctively pulled my arms back.

Regina disappeared through the opening, the heavy concrete lid above her head slammed the opening shut. She clearly had arranged for the top to drop into place and the machine to turn on. If I hadn't retracted my arms, they would've been crushed, possibly severed. She also had disabled the pulley and rail systems, so it took me several hours to gain access to the interior. I suspect she did that so I couldn't rescue her if things didn't go as planned.

There was no trace of her inside the sarcophagus.

28

I was numb. I don't remember shutting down the equipment and turning off the power, though I must have before I entered the bunker. It was months before I returned to the lab after that day.

Meeting Regina was what gave my life order; losing her nearly took it all away. Thinking about her theory that awareness creates time, I tried to personalize it, to make sense of my own situation. Regina might have disapproved of my analogy, but as my life became confused, my sense of time did suffer.

I managed to take care of the minimum of necessary business, but not much more. I'd show up at my office every morning, as usual, then sit there for hours without doing anything. Day after day my routine was the same. It was more than not being able to do anything—I couldn't think of anything that needed to be done. The construction of the building was complete, we had hired a realtor to rent all the spaces, except our office, the battery room, and, of course, the secret lab. I asked the realtor to take on the building's maintenance as well. Sally and Gerald had been managing the Double C without much input from us. I considered visiting them—it was April and the desert is spectacular in the spring—but I couldn't summon the will to buy tickets.

I was on friendly terms with my tenants, especially Eduardo, Frank, and Ina. They also missed Regina and knew how close we were. They were careful not to dwell on her around me and they comforted me as best they could. Sometimes I chatted with the cops who dropped in at the doughnut shop at night, but my social life mainly consisted of beers with Tom Jacobs once a month.

Our friendship had started out as meetings a couple times a year to discuss his investment fund, and that was only because I wanted to be sure I was in his good graces so he wouldn't let DeVries or his cohorts use his office to harass us again. At first I maintained the slight condescension and disdain I'd had when I was a freewheeling gambler and considered him a semi-robotic engineering student. But time is strange, and as I became more and more like Tom in my habits, we began to meet more often. Tom hadn't married and we didn't discuss our personal lives very much. I think our mutual aversion to discussing anything close to home was what allowed us to be comfortable with each other. Nevertheless, he did give some advice, which probably rescued my sanity.

"You look terrible," Tom said, one evening a few months after Regina died. "Are you drinking a lot?" We met in a neighborhood bar named O'Brien's Warren, a few blocks from the town offices, usually on a Tuesday or Wednesday evening when we knew it would be quiet. They often had homemade soup and bread to go along with the brews, and they didn't care how long we stayed. It was handy for Tom, as he often worked late, and anything was handy for me because I hardly worked at all.

"No," I said. "Just when you and I get together." "Are you doing anything?"

"Trying to keep my building together." "In other words, nothing."

I danced my fingers up and down my mug, as if I were playing my beer like a saxophone. "Yeah, I'm not doing much of anything."

"Not good." We both sat there in silence, warming our glasses of beer for a while. "You know what I think?" Tom finally said. "You need to get involved with new people."

"Got anyone in mind?" I thought he was joking.

He leaned in toward me and with an emphatic whisper said, "Have you ever coached kids?"

"Tom, I've never played any sports, much less coached one." I leaned away from him. I didn't want to just dismiss him, but I didn't want to be cajoled into an activity I wouldn't enjoy either.

"I thought you were some sort of chess wiz in school. I'll bet every middle school and high school in the state has a few kids who would love to have a little help. I help with the baseball leagues every summer. It's a lot of fun."

I raised an eyebrow. "You played baseball?" This was a side of him I'd never known.

Tom nodded. "I was set to go to Northern on a baseball scholarship, but I broke my wrist the summer before I started. They still let me in, but I couldn't throw. No baseball and no scholarship."

"Bummer."

"I'm getting over it."

"But that was over fifteen years ago."

"Some dreams take a while to get over. The point is that coaching helps. You ought to try it."

"I'll think about it." I felt he meant well, but the idea didn't interest me much. Still, his revelation of his early disappointment, which had occurred the year before I'd met him, and his manner of dealing with it, opened my eyes to another facet of his personality. I had to start taking him more seriously.

Tom pushed a book across the table. "I thought you might be interested in this."

The cover consisted of four pictures of what appeared to be the same type of plant. I recognized the plant—they're called "doll's eyes" because their berries are round white globes with small black dots, which look uncannily like doll's eyes—and the title, *The Colors of Sex*.

"Where did you get this?" I asked.

"A bookstore. I recognized Cheryl's picture immediately. She's Professor Cheryl Wilkie now. She's married."

The back dust-jacket flap had a picture of Cheryl with two young children, along with a few biographical notes. In her photograph she looked like a typical mother cum university professor, but I recognized her large, inviting eyes as the same ones that had introduced me to our planet. She was a biology professor at a small liberal arts college in rural Vermont.

I gathered her life had balanced out again, and she was able to spend time tromping through her beloved woods. The picture didn't include her husband, but evidently she was happily married to a stonemason. I pushed the book back toward Tom, but he refused it.

"I bought it for you. I'm sure it's interesting, but I can't quite understand her thesis. I'm not much of a botanist. You might get more out of it than I did."

The book was a culmination of the theory she was working on when I used to accompany her on her hikes, namely that isolated varieties of flowering plants populated the natural landscape, ready under the right conditions to evolve into separate species. It was gratifying to realize I had named the book, but I decided against trying to look her up again. There would be nothing of our old relationship to re-create, and I didn't want to embarrass her now that she was married.

A few weeks later, Tom called me and said he was moving. "I need to roll up my account with you, Ron. I'm taking a job in Florida...Jacksonville."

"Another building inspector job?"

"Nah, I'm going to be a code consultant for an architectural firm. The money's much better—and so is the weather—and hopefully the grief will be a lot less in the private sector than it is in the public."

I agreed to settle his accounts and to get together with him sometime, maybe winter in the Sunshine State. It was funny: there was a time when I did everything I could to avoid Tom Jacobs, and now he was the one person I wished would stick around.

Over time, I began to realize that I needed to change along with the universe. I followed Tom's advice and started mentoring kids at some local student chess clubs. I also made my way back down to the lab. Although I wasn't in Regina's league as a mechanic, I knew enough of her machine to operate it, if I wanted to. As soon as I entered the lab, though, I knew I'd never start it again. I left the lab not knowing if I'd ever return.

One day, as I was puttering around my office, I got a call from my ex, Sheila. "Hi, Ron. I just wanted to tell you how sorry I was to hear about Regina."

"Thanks."

"And I also wanted to invite you to a convention of financial traders." "Thanks, but I don't think so." I didn't want to be reminded of the life I'd left behind.

"It's in Boston next Friday. I don't want you to take this the wrong way, but I think you'd enjoy it."

"Why?"

"Because I'd like to see you."

"I mean why would I enjoy it?" I knew she'd misunderstood my question on purpose, but I was in no mood for light banter.

"Because you probably need to get out of your rut."

It occurred to me that she might try to induce me to return to the trading world. Although she'd been extremely successful with her business, I knew from tracking its returns that it hadn't made a significant improvement over my original approach. I wasn't interested, but decided to play along. "Okay, where is it?"

"Boston Harbor Hotel. Just give them your name; I'll register you. And Ron, dear, you can wear anything you like, but I think you might want to spruce up a little."

Talking to Sheila brought up a torrent of memories. I'd resented the way she had cut off our relationship, but looking back, I realized it was only because she saw what I was doing more clearly than I had. The big difference between us was simply that she'd always known what she wanted to do with her life, while I had no particular objective at the time. Which was the road less taken?

*

Boston is the capital of New England, but I'd spent very little time there. From its name, I deduced that the Boston Harbor Hotel was on the harbor, but I had no idea what a dazzling edifice it was until I reached the lobby. I'd taken Sheila's advice and worn a nice suit and tie for the first time in years. My first impulse had been to just dress as I always did—casual, to say the least—but as I entered the hotel, I realized that would have made me stand out. My thousand- dollar suit allowed me to disappear into the opulence. I expected to find a sign indicating how to get to the conference, but instead a very dignified-acting man in a tuxedo approached me as I entered the lobby.

"Mr. Larsen, I presume?" he said, with a confidence showing there was no presumption. I recognized Sheila's handiwork. He guided me through the elaborate hotel to a large room overlooking Boston Harbor. I recalled Sheila's father's office and concluded a taste for grand scenery ran in the family.

The room was set for a large dinner gathering and accompanying speeches, and for the most part it was already full when I arrived. This surprised me somewhat, as I thought I was on time, even a little early.

I felt, more than heard, a slight buzz follow me as I was escorted to my table. Sheila was there, as was Mark, one of her brothers, and a few people I didn't recognize. We were all introduced, and I sat down. A lovely gin Gibson was awaiting me, which I didn't hesitate to quaff before ordering another. I was beginning to wish I hadn't come. I hadn't been around this many people in ages—probably since I left Victoria Sound. And though I thought Sheila would behave herself, I was not so sure about Mark.

"We're so glad you came," Sheila said, as if in counterpoint to my unspoken thoughts. She stood up to greet me and offered her hand, not as in a handshake but just to hold hands. When I took it she gave me a light kiss on my cheek. "You're looking good, Ron," she whispered.

"You're looking pretty damn good yourself, Sheila." She was the same gorgeous Venus I had once witnessed emerge from the cold waters of Lac Perroche.

After a few minutes of pleasantries and other small talk, a second drink, and part of a third, a dignified-looking man from one of the other tables, with a shaved head and goatee, headed to the podium.

"Ladies and gentlemen," he began, "I'm Nelson Rogers, president of the American Traders' Association. Welcome to our yearly conference. Tonight we have an impressive roster of speakers who'll engage your interest with a variety of viewpoints concerning our profession. We'll hear about near- and far- term prognoses on the domestic economy, world trade trends, and legislative issues, all of which take on particular importance since the onset of the Great Recession we are in. Finally I'll hand the gavel to next year's president, Ms. Amanda Childress. And of course we'll dine and converse. But before any of this, I wish to introduce a legend—some may have thought he was a myth— who has graced us with his presence this evening. Ladies and gentlemen, welcome Mr. Ron Larsen!"

During this announcement, I was finishing my third Gibson and admiring my ex-wife, intoxicating myself on her good looks. She hadn't seemed to have aged at all in the years since we separated: she had let her full head of red hair down so it flowed around her halo fashion, her green eyes still lit up the room, she was still every bit a Celtic princess. No wonder I had fallen in love with her.

I hardly heard the speaker, and it was only when Sheila grabbed my elbow to indicate I should stand that it dawned on me that I was being introduced. As I stood, I felt the same buzz I'd noticed when I first traversed the room, only much louder. Then the room erupted into stunning applause. I looked at Sheila, as if to ask her what I should do next.

"It's okay, Ron. Just smile and sit down."

I made it through the evening in a haze of gin and disbelief. Obviously Sheila had given me substantial credit for her methods, so much so that many in the industry thought she had made me up to hide the true source of her success. I barely listened to any of the speakers, nor did anyone else, as far as I could tell. It's an honor, I'm sure, to be asked to give a speech at an association's annual convention, but there's the likely corollary that no one will listen to it.

Sheila took care of me after the ceremony by asking my guide to take me to a room at the hotel. I had expected to drive home but was in no condition to do so. I passed out and woke up on top of the bedspread still in my suit.

In the morning I found a new change of clothes on the dresser, along with a cell phone wrapped in a note with an unusual request from Sheila...

Dear Ron,

Please use the cab waiting for you on the fourth floor of the hotel's parking garage. When you get in the taxi, call me using this phone to receive your destination instructions.

Love, Sheila

I knew her competition was ruthless, and extreme secrecy was required, so I was careful to do just as she had asked. Once I was in the taxi, I called her and she directed me to an address in Brookline. When we arrived, I paid the cabby and entered a small, busy deli. It was unobtrusive, one of several storefronts on the block. I couldn't help thinking it would fit in well on Race Street. In the back, at one of a handful of tables, I spotted Sheila sitting alone. I handed her the cell phone as I took a seat. "You must have some pretty tough competition to need this degree of cover."

"The cover is for *you*. Or possibly the memory of Regina." "Me? Who's following me?"

She leaned in over the table in a manner I was used to. "Do you know Paul DeVries?" she whispered.

"Damn, how do you know DeVries? What's he up to now?"

"I don't know what he's doing now—I'm just being careful." Sheila paused for a few long moments. "I have an apology to make," she finally said. "Two apologies, in fact."

"For what?"

"This is difficult for me—I'm usually the one demanding apologies from people. First, about Paul DeVries...he hired me to track your investments." Sheila watched me to see my reaction.

"And you did?" I hissed. I had never considered that Sheila would betray me, even after our split.

"Yes." She stared down at her clasped hands, almost like she was giving a confession.

It made sense, at least on DeVries's part. Sheila might be the only person in the world who could possibly understand what I was doing. "Why?" I asked.

"I think he thought you were helping Regina launder money." "I mean why did you agree to help him?"

She perked up and shrugged. "Curiosity. Anyway, I'm really sorry, Ron." She paused again. "Okay, I need to make my other apology. I was jealous of your relationship with Regina, to be sure, but by that time I'd already decided it was a mistake for me to get married. A marriage is a relationship of equals, and I just don't like being accountable to anyone. I acted like it was all you, but it wasn't. I treated you poorly. That's why I decided it would be good for you to come to the conference, so I could show you what your reputation is in the financial community. Also, it was a place where you and I could get together without arousing suspicion."

"Regina and I were not lovers. We never lived together," I said.

"Why not? You were in love with her, and I'm sure she felt the same way." I didn't want to talk about Regina with my ex-wife; I didn't want to tell her I had no explanation. I changed the subject. "So DeVries is still watching me? That's why you had me take the cab here?"

"I don't know if he is, but I don't trust him. I told him last year that you appeared to be using the same fractal analysis that we pioneered. Nothing unusual. Then a month after Regina died, he showed up again and asked me to look at your trades. I told him they looked the same and said I didn't want to spy on you anymore."

"Thanks," I said sarcastically.

She narrowed her eyes. "You should mean that, you know."

"Why should I be thankful that you spied on me? What did you tell him?" I was surprised to feel anger at her.

"It's what I didn't tell him, Ron. It's pretty clear to me that you tailored the results to make your earnings average what you'd be making if you *were* using the fractal method. Honestly, it looked like you had insider information but were trying to hide it, so you covered up your profits." She looked at me for an explanation, but I didn't oblige.

"Do you want another bagel?" I asked her as I got up, but she shook her head. The early crowd had dissipated, so I figured I'd take a few pastries home. I also wanted a distraction to give me time to digest her story. I gathered my bagels and returned to the table.

"You're right, Sheila, I do need to thank you. You believed in me when I was unsure of myself; you gave me an opportunity to succeed on the big stage; and you always treated me fairly, as an equal. I felt terrible that you felt I betrayed you. I want to thank you for how you treated me, for the reception last night, and most important, for your apologies. I never meant to hurt you. I never considered leaving you for Regina."

"You might not have considered it, but you would have eventually."

I ignored her remark again; I knew she might be right. "And I also want to thank you for not feeding DeVries's paranoia."

"Was it just paranoia?"

"Maybe 'psychotic paranoia' is more accurate." "I think you were up to something."

Sheila was a brilliant woman who knew me as well as one person could know another, but I was determined not to give her any more grounds to believe I was hiding something from her. "You know, I didn't go braindead just because you decided to ditch me. I've been trying to refine my original methods, and Regina had some original ideas as well."

"Was she a fractal mathematician too?"

"Her specialty was quantum physics." I didn't want to lie to Sheila, especially after her recent magnanimity and honesty, but it was the only course I had. I figured that since no one really understood quantum physics, implying it was involved in our investment calculations would slow Sheila down, if not intimidate her. I didn't want to give her a reason to spy on me for DeVries again, and I also didn't want to give her any useful information in case she did.

We finished breakfast talking about her family and a few people at the company whom I knew. Her father, Jake, had retired but still advised her on running the business. Her brothers ran their dad's old firm, but the two family firms were closely allied. Sheila had stayed single and clearly preferred life that way. As I had no family, I didn't have much to add to the conversation. We parted as friends and promised to stay in touch, which we have...kind of. A small part of me was glad to know Sheila had purposely created our breakup. I'd married her in good faith, and I knew by the time of our separation that Regina and I would never become sexually involved. But that was in the past. A bigger part of me wondered what it meant that DeVries had tried to get Sheila to spy on me. Had she convinced him that Regina and I weren't doing anything unusual? Would he continue to hound me even though Regina was gone? I knew if I made any inquiries, I'd probably make things worse. Sheila's caution reinforced my fear that DeVries was still dangerous.

29

My visit with Sheila had yanked me out of my doldrums. I decided to dismantle our offices at 58 Race Street and move all of Regina's research notes downstairs. My initial motives were to protect her papers and to rearrange the building to make room for another storefront.

Regina had used the room we'd called the back office, and I used the reception lobby for the old factory, which we'd called the front office. The arrangement had worked well because initially we didn't want tenants in our wing of the building, and we could keep an eye on each other's space. But now I thought I'd feel safer if I used a corner of the battery room, which was below our offices and, of course, above the lab. Also, I felt I owed it to the merchants to fix up the whole block, and our un-refurbished office entrance was an eyesore in an otherwise attractive and modern facade.

Moving Regina's papers wasn't as difficult as it could have been, as much of her early work had been lost in her house fire. Still, the effort kept me out of my torpor and gave me the energy to read through what was left. She'd never talked much about her past, so I was eager to see if anything might shed light on her early career. Reading her papers was a little like being with her again; I hoped they would also help me say good bye.

Her papers were divided into roughly three groups. The oldest were remnants of documents rescued from the explosion. Much of it was from her journals of her early experiments, but only the center pages of any particular journal had been saved. They came from the period before I met her, when she'd first landed her tenure-track position at Northern, much of it before the explosion that had killed Manisha Kapoor. Closely related was the second group, which consisted of a single red leather-bound diary that promised to unveil her personal life; unfortunately, she quit writing in it after less than a dozen pages.

The third group consisted of documentation of the experiments we carried out at Race Street. They were thorough, voluminous, and I was familiar with almost everything in them. I moved all her papers to my office so I could go through them at my leisure.

I read the red book first, all ten pages, then fumbled through the damaged documents. I knew Regina's mentor, Ralph Hasted, was a professor at a state college down south. Dr. Hasted had been a protégé of Fred Hoyle, a British physicist noted for his iconoclastic brilliance. Hoyle had been called "the greatest physicist never to win a Nobel Prize." He was instrumental in developing the theory of nucleosynthesis, which describes the creation of the chemical elements in stars. Later in his career, though, he was outspoken in his rejection of the Big Bang Theory, and his reputation suffered from his having opposed scientific orthodoxy.

From the scraps of Regina's notes that had survived the explosion, I gathered that Hasted was affected by Hoyle's fall from grace. Rather than face public humiliation for proposing even more unusual theories, he worked out much of the basis of Regina's theories privately. Evidently Hasted had explored various concepts arising out of the possibility that the direction of the three spatial dimensions and the time dimension are local rather than universal. He created the model in which two four-dimensional universes intersect. When Alan Guth proposed his theory of rapid inflation of the early universe back in the seventies, Hasted had a mechanism explaining how it could happen and, almost more important, how it could have ended. Around this time, Regina joined him, her proficiency in the lab giving them an opportunity to devise methods to test Hasted's ideas.

Unfortunately, many of their ideas required budgets only nations— wealthy nations—could afford, and Hasted was determined not to publicize a theory until he could prove it. One of his ideas, for instance, was based on the fact that when the two universes cross paths, their gravitational fields would only act upon each other's spatial dimensions, not upon their respective time dimensions. This means our universe wouldn't inflate along the direction of the time dimension of the other universe, so our universe should be slightly lopsided. Regina had explained this to me, but Hasted also pointed out that it should be possible to determine what that direction was (or is). He died an obscure professor, shortly before Regina took her position at Northern University.

Reading about Hasted made it clear why Regina had started her career with such a bent toward secrecy, but it was a cruel irony that made her continue in that vein. At some point she realized she had invented a device that could cause terrible harm, as well as advance our understanding of the universe. She faced the same dilemma as the physicists who had created the science behind nuclear weapons, but without a Hitler to goad her into revealing her findings, she tried to find a way out on her own. And now her terrible secret had become mine.

Several weeks into the transfer of Regina's notes, I thumbed through her most recent journals, hoping they might shed some light on her illness. Instead, I found detailed notes for her new experiments. She had continued thinking about using quantum clocks to prove her theory about dark matter. Her plan was to build three mobile labs connected by a quantum clock. By moving them around, she hoped to discover slight differences in the gravitational pull between the labs and ferret out the shape of local non-terrestrial gravity. It appeared she also hoped to obtain funding for her work on dark matter and to be able to publish some results, while also using satellite locations to continue to develop strategies to determine whether our time machine could ever be used as an effective weapon without destroying the user.

My heart sank when I first read her proposals. I knew I didn't have the skills necessary to construct these kind of facilities. Upon further consideration, however, I was relieved. I'd decided I couldn't continue to use the time machine, and reading Regina's notes gave me the freedom to dismantle it. I wasn't sure what she'd meant when she said we were entangled beings, but this seemed like a good way for me to disentangle myself.

As I'm more of a theoretician than a technician, it was ironic that the first major job I had to do entirely on my own was dismantle Regina's life's work. Thanks to Sheila, I'd inherited her paranoid fear of Paul DeVries. I'd also inherited several storage rooms from Louise, the ones I hadn't disclosed to the authorities. I thought that would be a great way to get rid of the contents of our lab. I could mix the stuff Louise left behind and our stuff, and just pay the rent on the units until I felt it was safe to abandon them. The question was how to get the stuff there. When Regina and I repaired the lab, there was a lot of construction going on, so we just used a truck that looked like all the other contractors' vehicles. This task was much larger, and there was no major ongoing construction work. I couldn't fit much of it in my car, and I couldn't hire anyone else to do it.

One day, as I was crossing the rear courtyard to get a cup of coffee at Frank's, I was struck by a line of delivery trucks lined up to use our dock and elevator. I recalled Louise's phony delivery company and decided to copy her method. I'd gotten rid of her old van, but it wouldn't have been useful for the task at hand in any case. I was able to purchase a larger van from my old friend Davey Dickie, who always kept a few on his lot.

Louise had explained that she'd chosen the name Aapex because it was such an obvious ploy to be first in line alphabetically in the phone book that she felt it was an inherently untrustworthy name and would deter people from calling. I did her one better and named mine Aacme Delivery, but without the catchy motto. I had the truck painted with a nice logo and listed the phone number of a cheap prepaid phone I'd paid for in cash on the side. I never answered the phone, but I did listen to the voice-mail recordings, just to see if someone might be suspicious of my company.

My plan wasn't fool proof. If DeVries, or one of his associates, looked into who owned the truck, they'd eventually find my name. If they looked into the company, they would discover it didn't exist. But I hoped that if I was inconspicuous enough, no one would investigate.

I threw away the electronic equipment from the lab, as most of it was already obsolete, given the incredible advances being made in computer technology. But I saved the shop equipment: the drills, lathes, saws, and other tools. Even though they also were older, Regina's machines were very high quality, and beautiful to boot; perhaps some of Louise's aesthetics had rubbed off on me.

I also saved two nearly complete mobile prototype pretemporal information collectors, Regina's last project. I had no use for them, but I had no reason to destroy them either, and they had their own beauty.

After a few weeks, everything but a single computer hard drive containing all the work we'd ever done was gone. The hard drive and the sarcophagus and the second basement that shouldn't exist. Removing our equipment was incredibly hard work, but the effort had given me more energy.

After I'd finished emptying the lab, I had to figure out a way to fill in the room. It would be an easy job for Leo Casillo, the original contractor, but I didn't want outside help. During our meeting Leo had intimated to me that he thought she might have been hiding something, and besides, he'd been her friend, not mine.

I now owned Regina's old country house as well—or rather, the old farm it used to inhabit. Regina had let the fields begin to take over. She could barely bring herself to visit it after the fire, which was why I'd been the one to bury the radioactive materials there. I, on the other hand, had found it a good place to visit after her death.

The land still had an old barn, and there were several acres of woods behind the fields. As I wandered around, I thought of the months I'd spent with Cheryl exploring the forests of Massachusetts. Although we had passed many farms and even had traversed a few to get to her research sites, we hadn't spent much time looking at farmlands. "Too many invasive species, not my thing," she'd said, but she still enjoyed musing about the generations who had taken the time to plant the trees and flowers around the houses and along the stone walls.

After Regina was gone, I would often sit in a spot in the woods near her field and listen to a hermit thrush warble its beautiful, lonely cry for hours. At times I imagined it was Regina singing to me, at times I imagined it was my whole life calling out to me, at times it was both.

One day I asked a neighbor to mow the hayfields before they could not be recovered.

"Too bad the fields are so far gone," he said. "I won't be able to give you anything for the hay." He seemed genuinely disappointed.

"What would it take to get them back?"

He looked out across the low scrub, then down at the ground. "Tell you what. I'll charge you two hundred for the first mowing, and I'll take care of them after that. Should be able to get some hay by next year."

I suspected he was getting a good deal, but it was just one more thing I didn't have to worry about.

In one corner of the farm was the quarry where Regina and I had buried the radioactive detritus from the first sarcophagus. We had buried the waste beneath the excavated flat area in front of the quarry cliffs. I realized there was enough sand left in the quarry itself to fill our lab, and I could use the farm tractor to load it into my truck.

I couldn't imagine wheelbarrowing that amount of dirt into the Race Street subbasement, so I worked up a plan to drain it in. I hid a large tank inside the rear of my delivery truck and, at the farm, filled it with a mixture of sand and water to create a slurry, using a gas generator to work the well pump. At Race Street, I parked at the elevator and let the slurry flow down into the lab at night. Pumping would have been faster, but I didn't want to make any noise, so I chose times when no one else needed the dock. I completed the work DeVries had begun in creating a hole in the bottom of the wall but drilled from the inside. I hoped the slurry fluid would drain out through the remnants of the tunnel we had destroyed, leaving the sand behind. After some trial and error, my plan began to work. It was slow going, but I wasn't in a hurry.

At one point I considered destroying the remaining mine in Nevada as well, but it didn't hold the same emotional charge or present the same danger as the Race Street lab. The Double C was doing well as it was and it seemed better to just leave it alone. I figured someday I might move back there for a while, and I could do what I wanted with the mine then.

30

Although my basement office was more efficient than the ramshackle rooms Regina and I had used, it never felt right. The new space, which I'd designed to be hidden and secure, was *too* hidden. Regina was gone; Tom was in Florida; and Louise was evidently haunting the Roman Catacombs. I'd taken Tom's advice and was helping some of the local schools' chess clubs, but I still didn't have a meaningful social life.

To compensate, I did much of the paperwork for the building at Frank's doughnut shop. Being around people—even people I didn't know and who didn't notice me—soothed me. I spent most of my time when I was not destroying the lab drinking too much coffee, sitting in one of Frank's plywood booths.

One day, as I was examining a new tenant contract my realtor had proposed using, I looked out the window to see Paul DeVries crossing the street, limping toward me, dressed in cotton slacks and permanent-press dress shirt, but no jacket, no tie. His countenance was taut, but his commando elegance gone and his cheeks had begun to sag. He looked like an older man, certainly much older than his fifty-some years.

I placed my papers in a folder and waited. I didn't know if he was going to arrest me, shoot me, or just say hello, but he knew where I was, and I couldn't get away.

"Hello, Ron," he began. I could tell he didn't just want a friendly chat but guessed he wasn't going to kill me either, as I was still breathing.

"Hi Paul. It's been a while."

"Seems like a lifetime." I searched his face for a sign of sardonic satisfaction that, in fact, Regina's life was over. I didn't see it.

"A lot has happened," I said. I felt like I was back playing poker. I didn't want to give DeVries a comfortable opening for a conversation.

He gestured toward my booth. "Mind if I join you?"

I intentionally hesitated to show I did mind, but he sat down anyway. "Still with the agency?" I asked.

"No, I went private, specializing in white-collar crimes—you know, embezzlement, insider trading, fraud, that kind of thing." He looked across at me to see if his words had any effect on me, then continued, "I'm going to get a coffee—want a refill?"

"No thanks, I'm good."

He walked over to the counter and returned with a large coffee and two donuts. I could see why he didn't look like a commando anymore.

"It's funny, the FBI was once my entire life, but I don't miss it a bit. I make more money, my cases are more interesting." He looked at his meal. "I can eat donuts at work," he laughed quietly.

"You look sore. Get shot?"

He gave me a quick look. In poker we call that a tell, but I already knew his cards. I was the one who had collapsed the tunnel on him. He shook his head. "Just an old climbing accident."

The lie seemed particularly pathetic because I knew more about what happened to him than he did. I didn't reply, as if I expected him to say more.

"I heard Regina died," he said, "drowned herself."

"They found her car but never found her." I didn't know if this was news to him, but the implication that Regina could still be alive seemed to unsettle him.

He leaned back into the booth and wriggled around a little to find a comfortable position. He crossed one leg over another and clasped his hands behind his head in almost exaggerated nonchalance. He might have been a lousy poker player, but he knew how to project power and authority. "I've been to Manhattan a few times these last few years. You're quite a legend there in certain circles."

"It's a pretty small circle, Paul."

He nodded. "But a powerful one. I've often wondered why you gave up that life for this one." He motioned at the air around us.

"I was disinvited from those circles," I said matter-of-factly. "I heard you chose to leave."

"Not true, but I've never regretted the move."

He laughed—a loud, rueful laugh that reverberated through me. "Managing an apartment building instead of ruling the financial world? I don't think so."

"It's a great building and more than just apartments. I'd show you around, but you've probably seen everything already."

DeVries ignored my humor. "You're a very smart man, Mr. Larsen. You could be very rich."

"My ex-wife, Sheila Park, used to say, 'You don't have to be smart to be rich; you just have to hire smart.' I guess I was her hire."

"She hired you by marrying you?"

I shrugged. "We got along pretty well. For a while." "And you didn't choose Regina over Sheila?"

"My relationship with Regina was not the same as with Sheila. Sheila chose not to see that."

"But you were close to Regina Russo. You were with her for years."

"We never lived together. Sheila introduced me to wealth and power. Regina introduced me to myself."

"So you won't tell me what she was up to?"

"Regina was a great physicist and a better teacher. You pretty much ruined that, so she tried her hand at urban renewal." I pointed across the street to a remodeled factory that housed a medical center, and diagonally, to a block of refurbished apartments. "Those buildings would still be rotting if she hadn't fixed this block up."

"She pretty much ruined my life, too, you know." This time his voice was lower.

"Manisha Kapoor?" I asked. Paul DeVries didn't surprise easily, and he covered it well this time, but I could see he didn't expect me to know about Manisha. "Regina felt terrible about that. She never understood what happened, never knew why Ms. Kapoor was in the lab that night. Do you?"

"No, but given Regina's track record, it's pretty clear it was her lab that exploded."

"Her track record?"

"She had had at least one explosion before. Do you know what she was working on?"

"No," I said, "but she never denied it could have been her fault—she just didn't know." DeVries was still fishing for answers I was unwilling to give him, so I fed him an assortment of lies and evasions wrapped in things he knew.

"I think Regina knew. I think she was up to something, and I believe you know what it is."

"Here's the truth: she tried to apply quantum physics to my fractal model of stock fluctuations, but we never improved on the original methods I pioneered with Sheila. It was pretty abstract—no bombs. The only explosives I saw were the ones you and your fellow agents dropped when you broke into this building."

"There was something off about that too. We didn't have any explosives, and the agency had stopped using that type of C-4. And it was weird how the cops seemed to know we were there."

"Do you think someone ratted on you?"

He shook his head. "No one knew what we were going to do. Not even my crew."

"So Regina could read your mind?"

DeVries glared at me, and almost spoke, but his position was untenable. He couldn't seriously claim that Regina knew what he was going to do (though she did); he couldn't discuss the tunnel; he couldn't discuss our finances; he couldn't ask me any of the questions he wanted to. Instead he reached over the table to shake my hand, which I accepted. I might have convinced him I was pretty clueless and very loyal, a dead end, but I knew I hadn't convinced him Regina hadn't been up to something.

He left looking even older than when he had arrived, an irrelevant Ahab with a lousy pension—not a happy end for the agent who once had thought he'd end up at the top of the FBI. I felt sorry for him until I realized I was in a similar situation, and I refuse to feel sorry for myself.

I knew DeVries hadn't given up and realized I'd made the right move in getting rid of our time machine and the lab. He no longer had the resources he'd had when he was with the agency, but he didn't have the restrictions he'd once had either.

31

I didn't want to favor one school's chess team over another, so I began to sponsor, and get other groups to sponsor, tournaments not unlike the one I'd found so much solace in when I was in high school. I guess I have a romantic streak, but I wanted to teach kids that, in agreeing to compete against one another at a game, they also were cooperating with one another. I had never forgotten Mr. Staling's pleasure at outwitting me from time to time and finally had realized that he had enjoyed seeing me create a beautiful win as much as if he'd done it himself. It's strange that one can look back on an event in one's life twenty years past and still find something new in it.

I succeeded in starting small tournaments all over New England, New York, and beyond. I can't say whether it was more satisfying to return to a recurring event—one that had sunk its roots deep enough into the local turf that it could sustain itself, and that provided a venue for young players to improve and mature over time—or to come across a young prodigy for the first time. Fortunately, I didn't have to choose; I could enjoy both, sometimes at the same time. It was as if I'd discovered the personal history Mrs. Gretchen, my lovely grandmotherly friend on the casino bus all those years ago, had wished for me.

One clear summer day, I visited a group of players in Danbury, a small city in western Connecticut, a little more than an hour from Foxfield, when the local chess factotum directed my attention to a young woman not yet in high school. "She has a very interesting, even intimidating style, Ron. You should play her. Her name is Diana, Diana Fletcher."

Of course I wasn't nearly the player I'd once been, but I could usually hold my own in a match. It was always nice to test oneself against a talented strategist, so I sought the youngster out. When I found her, she was playing an older student. They played several games, all of which she won. I was too far away to be able to understand their game in full, but both clearly were strong players.

I was also mesmerized by the set the girl used. Every piece was different: a different style, a different material, a different color. There were several brass pieces, for instance, some cast, some brazed. There was stainless steel, ceramic, jade, wood, and more. There were even two cheap plastic pieces of the same impoverished style I once used. And yet it was easy to tell one side from the other, and just as easy to tell what each piece was.

When the older boy stood up, I sauntered over to her table. "Those are interesting pieces," I said. "Where did you get them?"

"I made them. Except the plastic ones, of course."

Her face was more round than oval, with cheekbones from Central Asia, and perhaps the eyes, too. She barely looked at me as she arranged her men for a new game.

"Why the plastic ones at all? They seem out of place."

"The games go on just fine, I'm learning how to form glass." Her tone was straightforward and confident.

"You're making glass pieces to replace the plastic ones?" "Eventually."

"That should make the set perfect."

"Maybe," she said, "but I rather feel trying for perfection shows a lack of imagination and a misunderstanding of reality. I just want the game to be interesting and beautiful."

It was one thing to be a prodigal player and craftsman, quite another to echo Regina Russo's personal philosophy back to me. "My name is Ron. Would you play a game with me?"

"Of course. I'm Diana."

I played several games with her, but it was obvious halfway through the first game, which I drew, that I was no match for her. When I began to pepper her with questions, she showed the same disdain in answering them that I'd shown Regina so many years before.

Predictably, she questioned me as well. "So what do you do, besides play chess?"

"I'm a mathematician—I hope a better mathematician than chess player." My new friend smiled, but only briefly. "Mathematics? So what can you prove?"

I finally began to understand entanglement. "I can prove awareness creates time."

□

About The Author

Robert Leet is a structural engineer who has designed hundreds of buildings, but this is his first novel. He lives with his wife in western Massachusetts surrounded by a wildlife sanctuary, where they attempt to keep their dog, cats, and chickens safe.

To learn more about Robert, please visit:

roberleet.com

□

Made in the USA
Middletown, DE
10 January 2021